Four Weddings and an Alien

Alienn, Arkansas 5

FIONA ROARKE

Four Weddings and an Alien
Alienn, Arkansas 5
Copyright © 2020 Fiona Roarke

ISBN: 978-1-944312-30-5

Want to know when Fiona's next book will be available?
Sign up for her Newsletter: http://eepurl.com/bONukX

To the fans of this series, thank you so much for loving my aliens hiding in plain sight in Arkansas!

Exiled society princess Francine Hayward Duvall has learned to stand on her own two feet in the Alpha colony hiding in plain sight in Alienn, Arkansas. It helps that the residents don't give a hoot about who she used to be, only who she is. She's a hard-working supermarket clerk who takes pride in earning her way. There's really only one thing missing from her new life.

Ichor-Delta bounty hunter Luther Raphael Boudreaux left his family and all the royal trappings behind long ago and is fully aware that there's no place for a woman in the nomadic lifestyle of his chosen career. He never expected his heart to be captured by a certain sweet redhead with nothing more than a look.

When Raphael offers to help Francine attend her sister's wedding on Ichor-Delta, by posing as her fiancé, she jumps at the chance. In return, she'll give the charming bounty hunter the cover he needs to help a friend in trouble. And if she can indulge in a little romance—or more—so much the better.

Francine might think he's doing her a favor, but as far as Raphael is concerned, she is *the one* for him. He'll go to any lengths to convince her that their adventure doesn't have to end.

It's only the beginning.

Prologue

Francine Hayward Duvall left Valene and Wyatt Campbell's party after only an hour. It had been a very nice get-together, but she wasn't in the right frame of mind for a celebration. She didn't want the reason for her bad mood to be misconstrued.

She was elated for Valene and her unexpected happily-ever-after with her mostly human sheriff. Their subsequent reunion after being separated by fate and circumstance was thanks to a technicality, but whatever worked. Valene deserved to be happy.

Plus, the news of a little one on the way for the youngest and only girl of the Grey clan—while initially getting her six very protective older brothers riled—inflated the joy of the party. It was too much happiness for Francine's *woe is me* attitude. Not to mention the fact she'd decided to attend the party for one reason only. She couldn't get Luther Boudreaux out of her mind.

The mysterious bounty hunter captured her attention when he arrived on Earth to help round up the escapees from a gulag-bound ship. She'd seen him twice in the underground facility hidden from the human world by the Big Bang Truck Stop, first with a cadre of Grey brothers and others on their way to hunt the escaped prisoners, then, later, engaged in a hushed, serious discussion with the Big Bang's Fearless Leader, Diesel Grey, and his brother and chief of security, Cam.

She hadn't spoken to Luther either time, so this was her chance.

Wyatt introduced them almost the moment she stepped inside the door. "Francine, this is Luther Boudreaux. He's a bounty hunter from Ichor-Delta. Boudreaux, this is Lucy's sister, Francine Duvall." She offered her hand in human greeting, her skin tingling in anticipation of his touch.

"Pleasure to meet you," he said and reached for her hand, his gaze so intense she almost faltered.

"Nice to meet you, as well," she managed to say in a rush as she came to her senses. Barely. Their fingers connected and slipped into a full-fledged grip as his gaze drilled deeply into her soul. She was embarrassed to feel heat rising in her face from chin to roots at his mere regard. He didn't say anything else, but one side of his luscious mouth, which fascinated her, lifted in a sexy half smile that made the warmth in her cheeks intensify.

If he noticed her reaction, he didn't call her on it, earning her eternal gratitude.

A large man she didn't know clamped a paw on Luther's shoulder and unceremoniously started to hustle him through the foyer, jerking Luther's hand from hers. "Come on, Boudreaux. We gotta go."

She had no idea who the big man was, and frankly didn't care. He'd pulled Luther from her personal space, and that made him a nameless enemy she would never forgive.

Luther resisted the man's hold long enough to meet her eyes. "Sorry, I have to leave. Hope to see you again, Francine," he said before his companion shoved him right out the front door. She waved, but knew he hadn't seen her. Pity.

Francine couldn't wait for their next meeting. Would they really meet again? Or was he on his way across the galaxy to catch his next bounty and she'd never see him again? Perhaps he was simply being polite.

If she put a bounty out on herself, would he accept the contract and take her down? She used to have the means to make it lucrative for him, but no longer. She mentally sighed. Besides, how sad was that? Paying a man to take an interest in her.

Francine shook her head at her own foolishness. Yes, the idea of being *taken down* by the very attractive bounty hunter from Ichor-Delta was more than appealing. And foolish. Too foolish to give another thought.

Chapter 1

Francine Hayward Duvall, formerly of the Designer-class Duvall family, *the* Duvalls of Alpha-Prime, experienced the abrupt panic of an uncontrolled fall as her face headed for the concrete walkway. One moment, she walked the path without giving her destination much thought, mind on other things. The next, a little black kitten landed in her path from seemingly nowhere.

The acrobatics that ensued as she attempted not to squash the small, sweet creature underfoot led directly to the disaster. As she went down, a recently read detail flitted through her mind concerning some Earther superstition about crossing the path of a black cat or some such thing leading to a curse for seven years, maybe even longer. Or was that if she stepped on a crack? Either way, she didn't want to hurt the tiny animal with her clumsiness.

Mere inches from the ground, Francine felt strong

arms wrap around her body, pulling her up and away from a pain-filled tumble. *What?*

"Got you," said a familiar masculine voice. Her body, tense as it braced for impact, went limp in a rush of relief and surprise. *Where did you come from? And, boy, do you smell good.*

Those arms effortlessly maneuvered her upright and stayed around her as he steadied her on her feet. Her eyes focused on the most handsome man she'd ever seen in her life on any planet, but definitely here on Earth. Dark hair, dark eyes, sunglasses propped on his head despite the late hour. His complexion was light, nearly pale, but it didn't take away from his looks in the least. Or his muscles. Or his height. Or how amazing he smelled. She resisted the urge to lean closer and sniff his chest. She hadn't seen Luther Boudreaux around town lately and assumed the beefcake bounty hunter from Ichor-Delta left the planet to go, well, hunt bounties.

Francine's memory of their first official meeting rose to the front of her mind, bringing with it a hot blush she felt to the roots of her hair. He'd been on her mind often since that all-too-brief handclasp and introduction at Valene and Wyatt's party.

If she noticed then how great he smelled, she might have done a bit of her own hunting to indulge in a longer introduction. *Who are you kidding, Francine?* She would never be so bold, even in her wildest dreams. That wasn't her style—though it would be fun if it was. She wasn't interested in seeking any sort of romantic relationship with a man, no matter how much he made her think less-than-pure thoughts. Was she?

She was too busy building her simple new life, away from her controlling, social-climbing parents who were always on the lookout for opportunities to make more money, gain more status, even at the expense of their daughters' happiness. So what if life had been lonely of late, her general mood rather blue. Maybe it *was* time to seek someone to share a little uncomplicated romance with. Maybe this man wouldn't crush her heart and soul.

Wrapped in his arms and pressed close to the extremely well-defined muscles she could feel under the fabric of his shirt, she couldn't seem to think clearly. Giddily, she inhaled deeply and felt her eyelids grow heavy in sensual delight. A voice inside her scolded that she had more brain cells than this, more self-possession, but a louder internal voice said, "Take another sniff, Francine. You know you want to."

The man—she couldn't for the life of her bring his name to mind with her scattered brain cells—shifted his hold on her.

Luther, that was it. Luther Boudreaux. Even his name was sexy. There was no way to say it without a throaty purr.

His face had lived in her memories, since she hadn't managed to get his picture. Yet.

She thought fleetingly of the cell phone in her

pocket, wondered if there was a discreet way to pull it out and snap some frames, maybe a few dozen. With just the two of them in a mostly empty parking lot at midnight, that could be a challenge. Still, she was up for it. Once she released him—if she ever did—she'd snag her phone and get a quick selfie with him.

"Thank you," she managed, forcing her eyes from his face. There was a very real risk she'd just keep staring until drool escaped her lips. She didn't move her hands—they gripped his upper arms like her life depended on it—because he felt so good. Solid. Muscular. Nice.

The scolding voice inside her amped up the volume, demanding that she get a grip on her hormones. Francine Hayward Duvall had some pride. She'd learned her lesson about good-looking men and their machinations.

A disastrous breakup had made her much more practical about love and relationships, to the point she'd agreed to the arranged marriage demanded by her parents. She'd narrowly averted disaster in that case, too. Was it any wonder she didn't date much? Okay, at all.

Her mind flashed to the first time she saw Luther Boudreaux. She and her sister, Lucy, were shopping at some of the intriguing extraterrestrial shops under the Big Bang Truck Stop. Luther stood out in the group of Grey brothers and other men because he was the only one wearing sunglasses indoors.

More, they seemed so natural on him that it didn't look like an affectation. Seeing them propped on his dark-haired head now made her recall that the people of Ichor-Delta were used to dimmer natural light than Earth's sun. The dark of midnight must be a welcome relief to him.

Although Ichor-Delta was in the same solar system as Alpha-Prime and a similar orbit, relatively speaking, its atmosphere heavily diffused the sunlight that reached the planet's surface.

It seemed her brain cells had started firing again, because Francine abruptly realized that the "attractive alien from Ichor-Delta" Lucy mentioned earlier tonight in passing was, in fact, her own Mr. Gorgeous with the hip sunglasses.

And their sister, Prudence, was about to marry someone from Ichor-Delta in the final arranged marriage their parents had contracted for their daughters, the famous Duvall Five. There had been five, but no longer. Francine's wedding—if she ever married—would never be celebrated by their parents. Even if they were invited to some mythical future wedding, they wouldn't condescend to attend it.

She'd been banished. Erased from her family's official record. No one was allowed to even speak her name in her parents' presence. She didn't exist in their world anymore.

So be it.

But that didn't mean she'd erased her family from her life, or stopped caring for them. Francine wished she could attend Prudence's wedding. That wasn't going to happen, not after the mortification of her attendance at Drucilla's nuptials.

Her parents—rather, her former parents, as they insisted on being called—had rained down holy hell on anyone who would listen when she showed up at her sister's nuptials with Lucy and Axel, Francine's brother-in-law and former betrothed. She'd hoped to escape notice by sitting at the servants' table, eating quietly, watching intently.

She'd restyled her hair to a much shorter shoulder length and changed it from her signature blond to a stunningly different red hue called rusted cinnamon. Even so, her parents spotted her.

At least they hadn't realized she'd attended the wedding and subsequent reception of her eldest sister, Ardelia. The extravagance of that event had lent itself to anonymity. She dressed down in simple clothing, sat with the servants and no one, not even Ardelia, noticed her.

That successful endeavor led her to try it again for Drucilla's wedding. She didn't see why her disgrace and what the family considered an unforgivable mistake should prevent her from seeing her siblings start their new lives. They *were* her sisters, after all.

However, the scene at Drucilla's wedding had been humiliating. Lucy had tried to shield Francine as best she could, but their mother was relentless. Francine had been thrown out of the reception—

well, escorted forcefully by the Guardsmen who'd been called—and placed on the next available interstellar ship headed for the Earth colony. A week later, she'd received a bill from her parents for the cost of that expensive flight home.

If she wanted to crash Prudence's wedding, she'd have to wear a better disguise—like turn into a completely different person. Maybe she could schedule a visit to Nocturne Falls, Georgia, where a friendly supernatural being could help change her into someone else.

She battled back a resurgence of sadness at the thought of missing Prudence's celebration. At least she had Lucy and Axel and the friends she'd made here. The Alphas who lived in Alienn didn't care who she used to be, only who she was. Who she was becoming.

As much as she'd learned to take pride in her growing self-reliance, Francine thought it might be nice to have someone to lean on sometimes.

Francine stared into her savior's eyes and wondered if he did other jobs beyond bounty hunting. For example, could she hire him to be her bodyguard at Prudence's wedding? Would he do it? Would he throw himself in front of her to thwart her parents if they tried to kick her out? Would she have the nerve to even ask him? Maybe. Likely not.

Once the escaped criminals were back in custody and on their way to the gulag, perhaps he'd decided to stay on Earth, make it his base. She hadn't seen him since the party, yet he'd just saved her from a painful tumble.

The kitten, unaware or unconcerned about its near-death experience, just sat there, looking cute. "Mew. Mew. Mew."

The little cries drew Luther's eyes to their feet. "What is that?"

She didn't feel the need to point out how he continued to hold her. "A kitten."

"Kitten, huh? It's very tiny. Kinda cute, though."

"Definitely cute and very lucky, too. I almost smushed him. Or her." She squeezed his arms. As if just realizing he still held her, he let go. Reluctantly, she stepped back a few steps.

He held out one hand. "I'm Luther Boudreaux. We met at Wyatt's home, I believe. You're Lucy Grey's sister?"

She nodded and quickly grasped his outstretched hand. "Yes. I remember. I'm Francine Duvall." An odd thought circled her mind. *Boudreaux is a royal name in some circles, isn't it? Is he Ichor-Delta royalty? As a bounty hunter? Probably just lucky to have an important name.*

"Right, of the famous five Duvall sisters of Alpha-Prime," he responded, shaking her hand slowly, as if he didn't intend to let go anytime soon. His steady gaze seeped inside her soul with flattering intensity. "I like the new hair color, by the way. Goes great with your green eyes. Red's my favorite color."

Ooh, you're so nice.

She smoothed a palm down her straight, shoulder-length bob. The shorter length continued to surprise her. "Thank you. But I'm not one of the Duvall sisters, famous or otherwise. Well, not anymore." She couldn't seem to take her gaze from his face.

"Oh? How does that work? Not being a Duvall sister anymore, I mean."

Francine paused, trying to get her brain to work, then explained. "When I didn't end up marrying the man my parents selected for an arranged marriage, I was summarily kicked out of the family."

"Huh. Was he awful?"

"Oh no, Axel is completely wonderful. He's also just as madly in love with my sister, Lucy, as she is with him. I switched places from bride to bridesmaid so Lucy could marry him instead."

"Axel Grey's a good guy."

"Yes, he is. Anyway, before the ink was dry on their marriage license, my parents disowned me when I refused to let them get an annulment and they named Lucinda as their new second daughter."

"New second daughter?" His genuinely quizzical expression soothed something in her. She liked it very much.

"Yeah, like Lucy used to be third born, but with me out of the family she became the second daughter."

"Wow. That's harsh."

She shrugged. "It is, but I don't have any regrets."

"I see. You're a troublemaker, then. I like that."

"Why? Are you a troublemaker, too?"

He nodded. "I am. I was kicked out of my family a long time ago for not conforming and I have equally zero regrets."

Francine grinned. He was fun. "Well, I do have one small regret."

"Only one?" His answering smile was nearly irresistible. She leaned forward, but caught herself and attempted to shake off her lust.

"Okay. One big regret." She used air quotes around the word big.

"What's your big regret?" he asked, mimicking her air quotes.

"I'm going to miss my little sister's wedding. Lucy and I are the closest in our family, but Prudence is a sweet soul. She's second youngest, and nothing like our eldest sister, Ardelia the Bossy, and our youngest sister, Drucilla the Spoiled Brat, both of whom can be rather horrid. I would love to attend Pru's wedding."

"Another arranged marriage?"

"Of course. That's the only kind of marriage my parents believe in. Lucy and Axel have invited me to go with them to Ichor-Delta, where Pru's groom-to-be is from, but the last family wedding I went to was a total disaster. I'm not sure it's a good idea to try to sneak into this one, as much as I want to."

"What happened at the last wedding?" His dark eyes remained fixed on hers like he couldn't turn away, couldn't resist her. She liked it.

"Well, I crashed it with Lucy and Axel's help. I sat

with the servants at the reception afterward, but the ceremony was smaller than the one held for my elder sister and my sharp-eyed mother found me out."

"They were unhappy you were there?" He sounded surprised her presence had generated so much ferocity. She'd expected they'd be angry. Lucy hoped they wouldn't make a public scene, perhaps only speak harshly to her. They'd both miscalculated on that score.

"Oh no. They were furious."

His regard grew even more intense. *Is it getting hot out here?* "What did they do?"

Francine closed her eyes briefly before answering. "They got two Royal Guardsmen at the festivities to rush me quickly out of the reception—even though I didn't put up a fight—and drop me onto a hastily arranged flight back to Earth without my bags. I didn't even have time to say goodbye to anyone."

"Wow. That *is* harsh."

"Yes. I underestimated their willingness to punish me in front of all the wedding guests." She shrugged. "Even though it was embarrassing, I would still love to see Pru get married, if I could be assured I wouldn't be kicked out and humiliated again." Luther kept staring. She paused a beat and added, "Aren't you from Ichor-Delta?"

He nodded. "I am."

"I can't go." The little kitten wove around her ankles, meowing in earnest, as if trying to entice her into taking a tiny new pet home.

He looked down at the black ball of fluff. "You can't go because you have to take care of your kitten or you can't go because you're afraid of being caught again?"

"This isn't my kitten. Besides, my parents would do the exact same thing if they found me on Ichor-Delta for Pru's wedding. I'm certain they will be extra diligent this time to ensure I don't dare show up. They disowned me after Lucy and Axel's wedding, they have held fast and hard to their decision and will likely hold a grudge forever."

He shrugged. "Maybe they will soften after more time goes by."

Francine shook her head. "Oh no. They are committed to this rancor, as they proved with the last wedding I attended."

"Maybe they were simply surprised and regret sending you back to Earth so expediently."

Francine let out a grim little laugh. "They didn't have any regrets."

"Why do you say that?"

"Right after they kicked me out of Drucilla's wedding and sent me packing on a speedy transport straight back to the Earth colony, they billed me for the exorbitant cost of the flight. It'll take me a year to pay it off." She pointed a thumb over her shoulder at the Supernova Supermarket. "I went from part-time employment to a full-time position, plus I take any and all overtime offered so I can pay off my debt as fast as possible."

"Wow. That *is* hardcore. I guess they meant it when they disowned you. I'm sorry." He looked down at the kitten, which now leapt up against her leg, trying to get attention or begging to be picked up. "Are you certain that isn't your kitten?"

"Yes. I'm sure." The kitten stopped jumping and went back to weaving around her ankles, meowing its little heart out.

"Looks like your kitten."

Francine picked the fluffball up. A quick check proved it was a girl kitten. She started purring like a motorboat roaring across a lake. The comparison came to mind because Francine had seen that very thing while visiting an old friend, Ria, who lived with her new husband, Cam Grey, in a cabin right next to a beautiful lake.

"Sounds like your kitten."

"How do you know what kittens sound like, but didn't know this was a kitten until I told you?"

A slow, sexy smile appeared on his luscious mouth. "I guess you've got me there. But that noise it's making sounds very happy." He studied the fluffy creature in her hands. "See? Its little eyes are closed, and it looks like it's smiling."

Francine watched him as he examined what was likely to become her new pet and felt a touch of awe.

"Well, since you think I should keep this kitten, what name would you give her?"

He stroked the tiny head with one finger and said, "Troublemaker."

"That's certainly appropriate, but quite a mouthful for such a little bit of soft fur."

"Speed Bump could be an option, or maybe Pancake, which she almost was until I scooped you up." For some reason, his expression turned sensual.

Francine eyed Luther Boudreaux. He didn't look like a Luther to her. He looked more like a dark knight or perhaps a raven-haired Norse god from human mythology, although the names Batman and Thor were taken. It didn't matter that Thor was blond, there was something electric about being in Luther's presence. The god of lightning seemed apt, in his case. Perhaps she'd give Luther a nickname.

"Do you go by Luther?" she asked. "Or do you have a nickname?"

He looked surprised. "I typically introduce myself as Luther, but I used to have a nickname. How did you know? Are you one of those mind-reading types?"

"No. I don't read minds." Francine shrugged. "You just don't look like a Luther to me, that's all."

"I see. What *do* I look like?" he asked in that low, sexy voice he had, with the slight Ichor-Delta accent. They all sounded a bit like Earther British Royalty.

You look like perfection.

"I don't know. What's your nickname? Or should I think one up for you?"

"My younger brother couldn't pronounce Luther, so he called me Rafe, short for Raphael, my second name."

"On Earth, Raphael is an archangel from one of their religions. He is associated with healing."

Francine had been studying up on Earther culture and history since before she'd been kicked out of her family. It fascinated her.

"Yeah? Well, I'm a bounty hunter, not a healer." He looked like a dark, sexy hunter.

Francine glanced at the kitten and rubbed her nose against the sweet little feline's pink nose. "I am going to call you Angel." To Luther, she said, "And I'm going to call you by your second name, Raphael, regardless of your healing skills."

"Are you?"

"Problem with that?"

He stared at her so intently, she almost took it back. "No," he finally responded in that low, sexy as sin voice. "I like it."

"Excellent. I have a question for you, Raphael."

"Only one?"

"Probably not, but I would really like to know where you came from."

"Ichor-Delta. You already know that."

"That's not what I meant. How did you get to my side so fast when I fell to keep from crushing little Angel here? The parking lot was completely empty when I walked out."

His eyes darkened, if that was even possible for his obsidian-rimmed gaze. "Perhaps I run exceedingly fast."

"Speed-of-light fast?"

He shrugged. "No. Just Ichor-Delta fast."

"Vampirically fast."

He laughed. The low rumble made her a little woozy with joy. "You think I'm a vampire?"

"Maybe."

"Are you afraid?"

"Of you? No. Not even a little."

"Maybe you should be."

"Why? What are you going to do?" Francine took half a step closer, hoping he was about to kiss her senseless. That was what she wanted. His kiss. Even before shaking his hand in Wyatt and Valene's foyer.

What I wanted to do the moment we met at Valene and Wyatt's place.

Francine stared into his dark eyes, willing him to read her mind, move closer, take her in his arms once more and kiss her like he wanted to turn her into his vampire bride and spend eternity loving her. An odd wish to have, since she hadn't wanted anyone in a very long time. Not since someone she once loved broke her young heart into a thousand pieces. His cruel betrayal had seen to that.

The intensity of Raphael's gaze didn't subside. Time stood still as their gazes became all-consuming.

Kiss me. Kiss me like you want me.

Seconds later, Francine got her wish.

Luther Raphael Boudreaux pulled her loosely into his arms, taking care not to squish the kitten, cupped a hand to her face, lowered his mouth to hers and kissed her hard, deep. Her eyes wanted to roll back in her head at the delicious joy his lips sent through her. Francine engaged. She kissed him back, harder.

She could have been more intense, but she still held Angel in her fingers.

He seemed surprised by her explicit acceptance, but the growl low in his throat told her he liked it. He promptly kissed her harder, twisting his lips over hers in some sort of sensual thrall meant to capture her heart and etch his essence onto her soul forever. She was unquestionably captured and etched. They might have kissed forevermore if not for the intrusion of a sound.

"Mew. Mew. Mew."

Angel squirmed in her hold. The kitten's tiny claws sank into one of Francine's fingers and she felt—barely—the bite of kitten teeth. Their passionate kiss slowed to a stop, their lips barely parted from each other, the intense gaze returned. She wanted him.

A long-lost feeling low in her belly made her remember why she'd fallen so hard for the last man who'd seduced her. And betrayed her.

Raphael wouldn't do that, would he? He wasn't the type to lead her to near ruin and then marry someone wealthier, with more political stature. Was he? She hoped not. Francine was about to throw caution to the wind and explore a relationship with this enticing man.

"Well, well, well. What do we have here?"

Chapter 2

Luther Raphael Boudreaux kissed Francine Duvall like his life depended on it. Maybe it did. He certainly understood her lot in life. He knew what it was like to be let down by the people you should be able to trust the most. He'd been kicked out of his family by his unhappy sire and remembered the feeling of loss well. Harsh words had been spoken, and even harsher feelings had left wounds on both sides. In his humble opinion, Francine's family took the word vendetta to a whole new level.

She wanted to call him Raphael, and he liked that more than he could say. His father had called him Luther, and the disdain in his sire's tone echoed in his memory. He was going to start introducing himself as Raphael Boudreaux and let the chips fall where they may, to borrow an Earther phrase. He'd studied an Earther book of common sayings before coming to the colony planet and he had a very good memory. He never forgot anything he read.

Holding Francine, Raphael wondered how he'd existed before discovering her. He'd seen her the day he landed in Alienn, Arkansas, in the basement of the colony's secret hidey-hole beneath the Big Bang Truck Stop.

If he hadn't been introduced to her at Wyatt's house, shaken her hand as she blushed and been completely intrigued by the Alpha woman, he'd already be gone, on to the next bounty, on to the next hunt. But in the short time he'd been on Earth, he couldn't get her out of his mind. She looked dramatically different with red hair versus blond. He loved her new hair color.

He wished he hadn't been pulled away from Francine to go on what turned out to be a fool's errand with fellow bounty hunter Charlie Adler. Their too-brief encounter served to make him even more intrigued.

Intrigued enough after capturing the notorious Indigo Smith to accept short-term employment as a bodyguard working for Diesel Grey, the Fearless Leader of the Big Bang Truck Stop.

For the past few months, he'd been in and out of Alienn, Arkansas, clandestinely escorting members of the Grey family due north to a recently discovered community with Alpha-Prime ties in the state of Minnesota, aptly named Suspicion. He hadn't concerned himself with why they were up in the very cold northern area, but heard enough to put together what must have happened.

An Alpha had been stranded or abandoned after a crash landing a very long time ago. The Alpha made his way to Suspicion, but lost his memory and thought he was human. The Alpha and the human he married had a dozen children—common for the time period, apparently. His offspring went on to have a plethora of their own children. After a couple of generations, the town was filled with descendants who had the ability to read minds.

The leadership in Alienn was carefully exploring a relationship between the two communities with the leadership in Suspicion. It was all he knew about the situation and all he wanted to know. His role was simply to ensure the conversations between Alienn folks and Suspicion folks remained civil.

Once he wrapped up his bodyguard duty, Raphael opted to take a short vacation on Earth to pursue a private mission: Francine Duvall. That was why he was on the spot to see her almost fall on the kitten tonight.

He'd been waiting for her to get off work, hoping for an opportunity to "accidentally" run into her, speak to her, then woo her.

Racing to her rescue had played perfectly into his plans. At least he hoped so. Their passionate kiss made him glad he'd changed his loose plans to take on a new mission and remained on the Alpha-Prime colony planet a little longer. The luscious kiss was a worthy reward for his patience in seeking her out.

He'd led a somewhat solitary life as a bounty hunter in the decade since his departure from his family's home on Ichor-Delta. Tracking down criminals across the galaxies didn't lend itself to long-term relationships or any sort of family life. At least at the beginning of his career. Now that he had a reputation as a skilled and reliable bounty hunter, his options were more family friendly than when he'd started out and had to take every job that came along to build a name for himself.

His heart warmed in his chest at the thought of exploring a romance with Francine. Was she interested in more than just a single blistering kiss in the parking lot of the Supernova Supermarket? Perhaps he was getting ahead of himself with the idea of any sort of permanent arrangement between them. But he didn't want to end the kiss to ask about her intentions.

Their first kiss would be emblazoned on his soul. Did she feel the same way about any kind of future with him? Maybe he would offer to be her escort to Ichor-Delta so she could see her sister married. Would that make her happy? Would it endear him to her? Didn't matter—he'd do it.

Given the reputation of the Duvall family in their part of interstellar space, his prestigious former family might even have an invite to the festivities. By taking Francine to Ichor-Delta, he'd risk running into a family member of his own, even if none of the Boudreauxes attended the wedding. It was always a possibility when he went to Ichor-Delta. Besides, so what if he did see a member of his family there? It's not like they would have Guardsmen wrestle him onto a flight bound for an Alpha-Prime colony planet and promptly bill him for the expense.

The worst thing, from his point of view, would be if the remaining members of his family pretended not to know him. Ostracized and ignored by his father and possibly every other family member.

He felt sorry for Francine's situation, though he'd learned to live with the exact same thing in the years since he'd left home. Her parents were incredibly vindictive to go to such extremes. Maybe he'd send a missive to Ichor-Delta and have a friend discover if his family would be at the Duvall wedding. If not, he could safely take Francine there, keep a low profile otherwise, and be her hero without instigating a fresh quarrel with his father.

Raphael wanted to be Francine's hero.

He'd been back to Ichor-Delta several times without crossing paths with his family. It was both a boon and a disappointment, truth be told. There were some relatives and household retainers he wouldn't mind seeing again.

He missed his younger brother, Alexander, who'd once called him Rafe. Alex was likely being taught all the things Raphael would have taken on regarding the family businesses and positions. He didn't miss any of that. Their elder brother, William, would eventually take over the family businesses and patriarchy, if he hadn't already. No one had informed Raphael of his father's demise, but it was possible his sire had relinquished his position as head of the household to Will and retired.

Would Will carry on the crusade their father had started and treat Raphael with unconcealed disdain? Raphael didn't know how his elder brother felt and for a long time wasn't ready to learn the truth of it. As time passed, he wondered, but hadn't taken the opportunity to discover his eldest brother's feelings about his exit from the family. In this case, no news *was* good news. He'd be lying if he said he didn't think about his family.

That decided him.

Raphael would go to Ichor-Delta and discover the truth of his status with his own family. It should make it easier if he used the Boudreaux name at an extravagant public wedding. He'd do it for Francine. Guarding her gave him the perfect reason to consider a trip back home. Two for the price of one was another apt Earther expression.

As their kiss ended, he prepared himself for a second sensual foray.

"Well, well, well. What do we have here?"

At the sound of the unwelcome, if familiar, male voice, he reluctantly turned his attention from Francine. The sight of the kitten chewing on Francine's finger brought a smile to his soul, but he shaped his expression to an impassive one when he looked over his shoulder.

"What do you want, Edgar?"

His unfortunate acquaintance from the bounty hunter world had landed on Earth the day before and practically attached himself to Raphael's hip, as the Earther expression went.

"I came to tell you about a bounty."

Randel Edgar stood tall, but his narrow shoulders remained perpetually hunched, as if he'd spent his early life only looking at the ground. The excess flab he carried over his belt had grown into a full-fledged potbelly from excesses in drink and rich food on paydays. When he wasn't talking, he looked like he was perpetually trying to hold his breath, thereby holding in his stomach, which didn't work to slim him.

He looked older than his actual age. Though not unattractive, Edgar's excesses had been hard on his body. Bounty hunting could do that to a person, but Raphael decided long ago not to let it happen to him.

Raphael pushed out a silent lungful of air. He'd been dodging the man since his arrival, hoping Edgar would take the hint and leave him alone. Now that he'd finally hunted him down, Raphael suspected Edgar would continue to be a noisy nuisance.

"No, thanks. I'm not looking for a bounty right now. I'm on vacation."

"I see that."

Raphael cut his eyes to Francine. She looked sweetly dazed, and didn't seem to notice the kitten's nips on her fingertips. Had he done that with his kiss? Made her mindless? He hoped so.

"Aren't you going to introduce me to your new girlfriend, Boudreaux?"

"Nope." *She's not my girlfriend. Yet. But maybe soon.*

"Why not? Afraid I'll steal her away from you when she finds out the truth about you?"

He wasn't certain what truth Edgar wanted to share, but suspected it was unflattering. Edgar was considered jaded by most everyone he knew, and what Earthers called a big jerk.

Raphael typically worked alone. On occasion, he teamed up with another bounty hunter if it suited his purposes. Edgar would never suit his purpose.

"Again. No, thanks." Raphael kept his gaze on Francine, not looking at his fellow bounty hunter. Edgar knew the truth about his history, but Raphael didn't want him to spill it. Not now. Not yet. She'd find out soon enough, but he wanted to tell her in his own time.

"So polite and yet still from the gutters of Ichor-Delta," Edgar taunted. Mentally, Raphael rolled his eyes.

"Better to be from the gutter than to be an annoying tattletale," Francine said under her breath, loud enough for Raphael to hear. He grinned and winked at her, garnering a lovely smile.

"What was that?" Edgar asked, leaning closer, his expression squinty, tone demanding.

"Nothing. Go away."

"Don't you want to discuss the bounty hunter job?"

"No. Like I said, I'm on vacation."

Edgar huffed. "More likely you're just a lazy bodyguard with benefits."

That's it! You've stepped on my last nerve.

Raphael released Francine and marched over to stand toe to toe with Edgar. In a low, growling tone, he said, "Shut your filthy mouth. Here is the candid truth. Whether or not I'm looking for a bounty, I'm most assuredly not interested in working with you, ever. Whatever your purpose here, give it up. I'm not listening to you. I'm not helping you. I'm not going to work with you. Ever. Have I made myself clear?"

"Indeed, you have." Edgar's swagger was back as his eyes narrowed. "But hear this, Boudreaux. You're making a big a mistake. This bounty might change your circumstances."

Raphael cracked a mirthless smile. "I'm not making a mistake. I don't want to change my circumstances. I do not want to work with you. I repeat—go away."

He returned to Francine and took her gently back into his arms. He hoped Edgar would leave, but the odious man had to speak his mind.

"The bounty is for Victor Campion. So be forewarned, I'm going to bring him in and collect the vast bounty, with or without you."

Raphael froze.

Victor. What's happened?

Francine heard the man Raphael called Edgar say Victor Campion and immediately recognized the name. The Campions were royalty on Ichor-Delta and noted as such throughout their galaxy.

The name Boudreaux was most assuredly a royal name, however, there were others in the lower echelons of that society named Boudreaux. Possibly like the names Smith or Jones in Earther terms. However, *all* Campions were royal.

"Victor Campion?" Francine said the name out loud without realizing she intended to speak. "I know that name."

Raphael had straightened abruptly when Edgar said the name. He gazed at Francine with a certain amount of pain in his expression when she repeated it.

With Angel in one hand, still chewing on her finger, she put her free palm on Raphael's chest. "I'm sorry. Are you okay?" she whispered.

His expression relaxed slightly. He inhaled a deep breath, winked at her and turned toward Edgar. "I will *definitely* not help you hunt down Victor."

Edgar shrugged. "Then I'll just take the entire bounty and the credit when I catch him. I was trying to do you a favor."

"No, you weren't. You need me along to have even a snowball's chance in hell of finding Victor."

Edgar's eyes narrowed in confusion. Perhaps he didn't understand the Earther reference. "You won't catch him, Edgar," Raphael said in a dangerously low tone. "You're wasting your time even attempting it."

The other man's expression soured, as if he knew Raphael spoke the truth, then slid into a smirk. "We'll just see about that, won't we?"

"No. You'll see how ludicrous this job is once you've spent a month—or however long you last—without so much as a sighting. I pity you."

"You're making a mistake, Boudreaux."

"No. You are. Leave Earth, Edgar. Don't come back. And do not bother trying to track down Victor Campion. You'll just embarrass yourself."

Edgar grabbed hold of the lapels of Raphael's jacket and leaned forward. Francine bit her lip, and held Angel closer, worried about what might happen. When Raphael did nothing more than give him a cold stare, the portly bounty hunter spit on the pavement, let go of the lapels and walked away, whistling as if he didn't have a care in the world.

"Foolish man," Raphael said into the air, and turned to fix his gaze on her. Her tension eased, despite the intensity of his stare.

"What are you going to do?" Francine asked.

"About him?" Raphael pointed a thumb over his shoulder at Edgar, exiting the parking lot. "Nothing. Like I said, I'm on vacation."

He gifted her with another spontaneous and beautiful smile. "Okay. Will you hold my kitten while I run back inside the store to get a few new pet owner supplies?" She held Angel out to him. He smiled and cupped his large hands beneath hers.

"Sure." The kitten released her finger, jumped into Raphael's hands as if she understood what they'd said and attacked one of his fingers, putting all four paws and her tiny teeth into the effort.

Francine noted the interesting ring on his right middle finger. It was a silver and black infinity band with purple baguette stones set in a channel around the center of the metal. It looked expensive and, if the stones were the heliotrope gems or violet diamonds she suspected, it was an *extremely* rich piece of jewelry.

No doubt Raphael was every inch the dangerous bounty hunter he looked like outwardly, but she also saw a different side. A wounded side from being kicked out of his royal family over some long-ago indiscretion, or simple rebellion. Or maybe he was another of the many illegitimate children thrown into the gutters of Ichor-Delta without any care, someone who was, if Mr. Edgar were to be believed, not worth very much.

Francine didn't believe him, though. A man who kissed her like he wanted to devour her and make her his sensual focus was a treasure no matter where he started his life. Francine wanted to be his entire focus, if for only a short time. The length of his vacation. Perhaps she would hire him to be her bodyguard and take that trip to Ichor-Delta to attend Pru's nuptials. She wouldn't even mind having a bodyguard with benefits, as Mr. Edgar had so crudely insinuated. In fact, even a temporary arrangement would be just fine with her.

Once her parents learned a Boudreaux from Ichor-Delta was attending Pru's wedding and reception on Francine's uninvited and unwanted arm, they'd never embarrass *him* by having her shuttled back to Earth. They would grit their teeth, bear up and never make a scene in front of their peers, at least in this instance. It was likely her only chance to see Pru's wedding. Not to mention, being on Raphael's arm for any reason would be a boon.

Her parents would surely find a way to punish her, but Francine's desire would be fulfilled in the short term. Besides, showing up at a big event without having to worry about being kicked out would be worth any later punitive action, especially if she attended on the arm of Raphael Boudreaux, darkly sensual bounty hunter, fellow soul wounded by his family and blazingly incredible kisser.

Francine hurried back into the store, nodding at the night manager and a stock boy on her way to the pet aisle to get one of the kitten starter supply kits she'd shelved only a few nights ago. It had everything a pet owner needed for a new kitten. There was kitty litter, a litter box, a rug to place the litter box on, litter box liners, a cozy cat bed, a food bowl, a water bowl, a mat to put the bowls on and three kitten toys. She also got a bag of kitty food and some kitty treats.

The new cashier, Roberta—Francine hadn't

spoken to her yet—rang up her purchases. She grinned and asked, "Did you just buy a cat?"

"No," Francine said with a straight face. "Why do you ask?"

With a quizzical expression, Roberta pointed to the items still waiting to be bagged. "Because you're getting a bunch of cat things." Apparently, Roberta didn't get the joke.

Francine smiled. "I was just kidding. I found a kitten on my way home. I'm going to see how it goes."

"Well, good luck. I have three cats and I love them to pieces. Just wait and see, one won't be enough when you find out how fun they are."

"Thank you. I know who to talk to if things don't work out."

Roberta shook her head. "Nope. My husband says three is the limit. I had to do some groveling for the second one and some outright, on my knees begging for the third, but I have no regrets. You won't either."

Francine grabbed her purchases in one arm, winked at Roberta and hurried back out to the parking lot.

Raphael had placed Angel on his chest, where she purred so loudly Francine could hear her from several paces away. "I think that kitten is in love with you. Maybe you should be the one to take her home."

His gaze lifted and he gave her such an intense

look filled with smoldering passion she nearly dropped her purchases and leapt into his arms to purr on his muscular chest alongside Angel. She stood staring at the big bad bounty hunter who could likely kill someone with his bare hands, holding a kitten like it was the most important thing he'd ever guarded, and fell in lust with him all over again.

She didn't know how long she stood staring at him holding her kitten until he finally spoke. "What?"

The single husky word was enough to make her shiver. *Maybe I'm in love with you instead of simply in lust. Will you take* me *home? Make me purr?*

Francine snapped her lips closed, shook off her lust or love or whatever it was, passed by him to keep him from seeing how impacted she was by his mere presence and moved toward her prized vehicle.

Raphael didn't say anything. He fell into step behind her, letting Angel purr on his chest as he held the kitten cupped in one strong hand. She had purchased the SUV with lots of help from her former fiancé, now brother-in-law, Axel. He said it was an older model Ford Escape with low miles, had been regularly serviced and was in perfect shape. It was the vehicle's name that sold her on it. Escape. How fitting. She loved it.

Francine had escaped from the near disaster of an arranged marriage to the man her sister loved. Axel was a good man, but she didn't have the same feelings for him Lucy did. He was like the brother she'd never had. No lust. Not even a little. And most certainly not what she felt for Raphael. A single blistering gaze from him made her weak in the knees.

"Is your vehicle nearby?" Francine asked, inserting the key in the rear door and lifting it up to load her new kitten supply purchases.

"I don't have one. I walk."

"Really?"

"Yes. Why?"

She shrugged. "No reason." She slammed the back hatch and gestured toward the passenger side. "You'll hold the kitten on the way to my home, right?"

"Of course."

They walked around to their respective sides, him careful to shield the kitten from any harm, her watching intently every move Raphael made. He was the very definition of poetry in motion. He was tall and very muscular, but moved in a way that wasted no movement, even as he exuded swagger and a "don't even think about messing with me" aura. He was lithe. Predator-like. She was smitten. About to drool.

The drive to her house—something called a duplex, with two living spaces separated by a wall— was silent. The actual abode didn't share a wall, only the laundry rooms and the garages connected the homes in two places.

Her landlady, Mrs. Greenstone, lived in the other half and was a very sweet older woman. She treated Francine like a daughter, in a good way. Her parents hadn't treated her nearly as well, especially recently, so it was a treat to have someone who was nice to her on a regular basis.

Francine pulled into her oversized one-car garage, which had plenty of room all around to open the doors, even the back hatch when the garage door was closed.

Angel hadn't moved, purring the whole way against Raphael's firm chest and cradled in his capable hands. Francine already knew Mrs. Greenstone would allow her to have a pet. Her landlady had two cats and a small dog and had encouraged Francine to get a pet if she wanted, so she wouldn't be lonely. She'd recommended a cat, since Francine had a job and was away from her house for several hours every day.

Mrs. Greenstone was what was known as a "talker," but Francine didn't mind.

She retrieved the supplies from the back of her SUV, rounded the vehicle and headed to the inside door with the sack slung in the crook of one arm, letting Raphael follow. She realized he'd see her place in seconds. Would he like it? Think it was too spartan? Too Earther-like? Well, it was too late.

Little bundle purring against his chest, he stepped inside the hallway that led to the kitchen, trailing her slowly, quietly, intensely, like the dark angel he was named for.

Her small dining area, with its table and two chairs, was visible from the kitchen. Around the corner was her living space with a hand-me-down sofa in front of a battered coffee table. It folded out into an uncomfortable bed. The two bedrooms, each with a full-sized bathroom, featured only a donated bedframe with her new mattress set in one and the boxes from her move in the spare bedroom. She loved her place. While she didn't have much stuff yet—and what she did have had been contributed by various and generous members of the Grey family— she was very happy here.

Even without all the extravagant things her parents had provided until she'd defied them, she was happier to be on her own.

Francine put her sack on the dining table, opened the kitten starter kit and retrieved the cozy kitten bed. She placed the red-and-black plaid oval on the far edge of the dining room, leading into the living room area. She then got the kitty litter box ready.

Grabbing the rug to place beneath it, she said, "Follow me."

"Delighted to," he said. *Oh my.* His sexy voice registered low in her belly with every single word he spoke.

Francine carried the litter box to the half bath off the hallway with the garage door, at the end furthest from the kitchen. It was the perfect place for the litter box.

She usually left that bathroom door open anyway. She placed the litter box and the litter mat down on the far side of the pedestal sink, in the corner.

"Put her down inside the litter box, please," she said, stepping back to give him room.

Raphael used two hands to scoop Angel off his chest and place the black ball of fluff in the kitty litter box. Angel walked around in a circle twice, sniffing here and there, squatted, peed and covered it up quickly and efficiently with her tiny paws. She hopped out of the litter box, sat on her haunches and said, "Mew."

"Good little Angel." Francine bent over and patted the kitten on the head, then scratched under her chin. She picked her up and carried her to the bed next to the living room, placing her in the center of the cushion. Angel walked around, sniffing the space.

"She won't pee in there, will she?"

"Nope. You show them the litter box and then that's where they go."

"Oh? That seems too good to be true."

Francine shrugged. "My landlady has two cats. She said I should get one and told me all about the care and feeding of cats, in quite a bit of detail." She smiled at the memory. "I thought it was useless information, as I hadn't intended on getting a pet, but now I'm grateful."

She went back into the kitchen to put out bowls of water and food. Angel abandoned the bed to sniff out the water, taking a few laps, sniffing the food and taking a bite or two before heading back to the bed.

Raphael put a hand on her shoulder, sliding it along her back to the other shoulder, pulling her into his warm frame. "I'm glad you have a new kitten."

"Why?"

"Because I witnessed the very beginning, when you two first met." He hugged her against his side as they watched Angel prance around the bed before settling at one side, curling in a ball and closing her eyes. She'd never heard of such a well-behaved kitten. Not that she was an expert or anything.

Francine put her hands on Raphael's solid chest and looked into his eyes. "What are you going to do next?"

"I don't know. What do you *want* me to do?"

Kiss me. I want you to kiss me like you did before we got interrupted.

"I liked the kiss earlier," she said candidly, gazing into his darkly sensual expression.

His eyes narrowed. Smoldered with passion. "As did I."

He didn't make a move toward her, which was surprising. She expected him to make a move. Perhaps he wanted *her* to make the next move. *Fine with me.*

Francine wanted him with a hunger she'd never felt before. She wanted another toe-curling kiss. She lifted on her tiptoes and kissed *him* this time.

He made the low, growling sound in his throat and his hands slid around her middle. Encouraged, she stepped things up a notch and licked his bottom lip.

Chapter 3

Raphael wanted to kiss Francine more than he wanted his next breath of air, but didn't want to presume. He was in her private domain, therefore, he decided not to instigate anything. If she wanted a repeat, she could kiss him, and he'd oblige.

He was so glad she did. Her luscious body pressed into his, her lips slid sensually over his mouth, parting to engage him in an even deeper kiss than they'd shared in the parking lot. His arms encircled her waist before he even realized he'd touched her. It was much easier to hold Francine without the kitten between them.

Francine's arms slid around his neck, locking into place as they kissed and kissed and kissed. He was lost in seconds, tightening his arms around her middle, lifting her to make the passionate kiss easier to negotiate, pressing her perfect body even closer. He couldn't seem to get close enough. Raphael heard her moan. Or had he made the noise? Either way, he tightened his grasp on her, tilting his head to kiss her harder, deeper. The best kiss ever.

One of her legs, now dangling a few inches off the ground, lifted to wrap her ankle around the back of his leg. They were molded together from lips to knees and he never wanted this heavenly experience to end. He could die happy right here and now.

Buzz. Buzz. Buzz.

What is that? The pressure of her lips on his intensified. *Don't care.*

Buzz. Buzz. Buzz.

Francine broke the kiss to glance down at where they were connected at the waist. "Is that your phone or mine?"

"Phone?" he asked, unsure of the term and puzzled as to why they weren't kissing.

Buzz. Buzz. Buzz.

"That's yours. Mine plays music."

"Music?" He was reeling from the kiss. Then it hit him like a meteor. His communication device was making noise. Not very many people had the ability to contact him. Those who knew how only did so if it was important.

Raphael pulled one arm from her back to put his hand on the vibrating device. He pushed a button to open it, put it to his ear and said fairly wrathfully, "What!"

"Something unexpected has happened. We need to have a conversation."

He recognized the voice instantly. Victor. Raphael had hoped Edgar was lying about the bounty. Did Victor know about it?

"Where are you?" Raphael asked.

There was a long pause. "Do you remember where I told you I'd never be caught dead?"

The Ossuary Valerian Space Station. The name translated loosely to dead room sleep space station. Halfway from Ichor-Delta to the next populated planet in another galaxy on the far side of Alpha-Prime. It wasn't truly a space station in the traditional sense, but rather an ancient asteroid complete with ginormous engines and an imitation atmosphere, parading itself as a small planet.

"Yes, I remember. However, I'm not on Ichor-Delta."

"Where are you?"

"Too far away. Also, a bounty has been issued. Had you heard?"

"Yes. That's why we need to have a conversation."

"I'm not certain I can help you."

"You're the only one who can. The only one who will maybe disregard the bounty out there in the short term and help me prove my innocence before I'm swept up."

Any bounty on Victor Campion would be, literally, a king's ransom. He was heir to his family's throne on Ichor-Delta. Well, perhaps not anymore.

Raphael had been the second son and his family had easily cast away long ago. And that still wasn't as toxic as having a bounty put out across the galaxy.

"How long will you be at your current location?"

"Only as long as I remain safely hidden here. Which is likely not very long with a rich bounty on my head."

Raphael didn't dare book a flight directly to the Ossuary Valerian Space Station. Edgar was not the best bounty hunter, but even his limited skills would lead him to follow any unexpected trip on Raphael's part. A sudden plan to help Victor dropped into his brain. He'd been thinking about offering to help Francine go to her sister's wedding by posing as her fiancé. Perhaps they could continue that ploy after the wedding.

"Hold on for a moment," Raphael said, and turned his gaze to Francine. Her lips were moist and swollen from their kiss. "When is your sister's wedding on Ichor-Delta?"

"It's a week from today. Why?"

Raphael kept his gaze on Francine, but said into his communication device, "I'll be headed to Ichor-Delta in one week for a wedding. If you can meet me there in our usual spot, fine. If not, I'll head to the place you wouldn't ever be caught dead directly afterward. Will that suit?"

"Yes. Thank you."

"Don't thank me yet. I don't know if I can help you."

"Just knowing you aren't gunning for me earns my eternal gratitude."

"Stay safe, my friend."

The line went dead and Raphael stared at

Francine with the knowledge he could kill two birds with one stone. He'd help her attend her sister's wedding, she'd give him cover for being in the area. She could be his reason for heading to an unusual place he'd typically never go, as a couple scouting a possible wedding venue or honeymoon spot.

The Ossuary Valerian Space Station wasn't the first destination couples thought of to celebrate nuptials or a honeymoon, but it wasn't without precedent. Those seeking the unusual or something different often set weddings there. He could make it work, if Francine would go with him as his pretend fiancée. The stop on Alpha-Prime would be business related. He could get better information on the bounty for Victor, such as who or what entity had drawn it up and why.

"I have a proposition for you."

Francine's eyes widened. "What do you mean?"

"I can help you attend your sister's wedding in a week. In return, you can help me out on our way back."

Her lovely eyes narrowed. "How would I do that?"

"What if we go to your sister's wedding and I pretend to be your escort slash fiancé? My family name would certainly keep you from getting kicked out and sent home on an expensive flight that they'd only bill you for. They wouldn't take a chance on that with the Boudreaux name involved, would they?"

"I doubt it, but you never know."

"I can certainly make them believe I'm a member of the royal Boudreaux family." *Because I once was.*

"Really? You would do that for me?"

"Of course. Besides, I doubt anyone would call me out on it."

Francine shook her head. "Even as vengeful as my parents are with me, I can't imagine anyone in my family's household would dare risk embarrassing someone with the last name Boudreaux. And if they do bother to check, it will be several days later when they try to elicit a business meeting or some other connection with the royal Boudreaux family. By then we'll be long gone."

"Perfect. I'll ensure you have a gigantic jewel-encrusted engagement bracelet, necklace or maybe even a finger ring, whichever you prefer."

"Ring, I think."

He nodded. "A ring it is. We'll arrive close to the start of the ceremony to avoid any possibility of someone contacting a member of the Boudreaux family to check on my non-existent status." *At least not anymore.* "We'll also attend the reception, but leave early, just in case someone does manage to get hold of a royal Boudreaux family member on the wedding day."

"Do you really think it will work?"

He leaned close, inhaling her uniquely seductive scent. "Would you be offended if I told you that I've used this ploy before with a female bounty hunter in order to catch a particularly lucrative bounty?"

Francine giggled. "No, not offended." If he wasn't in love with her before, her sweet laugh pushed him over the edge and into uncharted territory. He'd never been so intrigued by anyone. So enticed. So out of his depth with the promise of possibility.

Francine sobered. "You weren't truly engaged or in love with the female bounty hunter, were you?"

He made a huffing sound of denial. "No. Not even close. She was merely a means to an end, just like I was for her. We split a very nice bounty after spiriting our quarry away during the reception without ever sharing a single kiss or even holding hands."

Francine's smile resurfaced. "Okay. Good. I'll call tomorrow and schedule the time off from work."

"I'll make a few arrangements so that when we arrive, no one will suspect that you aren't the intended bride of an Ichor-Delta royal Boudreaux family member."

"Excellent. Thank you so much, Raphael. This means a lot to me."

"My pleasure."

"What do you want me to do for you in return?" she asked.

So many things.

Raphael cleared his throat. "After the reception, I need to meet someone at one of two possible locations, where no one will suspect what I'm doing. I thought we'd pretend to check out a couple of places for our fake future nuptials and honeymoon. What do you think?"

Francine stared at him intensely for a few seconds before saying, "That's perfect. I'm happy to help you out with anything you need, but how long do you think it will take? I want to ensure I take enough time off from work."

His mind spun with possibilities at the mere idea of spending several days pretending to be her fiancé. "A day or two after the wedding, three at the most."

She nodded. "Good. Okay. That will work. A week off should be enough time, I think."

"Excellent. We'll leave Earth on Friday."

Raphael stepped away from her, though he didn't want to. "I'll go and get started on our plans." He grabbed Francine's hand and placed a soft kiss on the back of her knuckles, just like he'd seen someone at the Big Bang Truck Stop do. Wyatt Campbell. The sheriff had stared lovingly at his bride, Valene, like she was the only other person in the world and kissed the back of her hand. Valene had looked like Wyatt handed her the world on a platter.

Raphael thought the gesture had been romantic. Francine's cheeks flushed with color when his lips met her skin. Her small hands were soft, and their gazes locked before, during and after his gentle kiss.

"When will I see you again?" she asked in a whisper.

"Tomorrow. We should make our new engagement known around town. It wouldn't hurt for that rumor to spread and pave the way on our trip."

"Good idea. I agree. Can't wait."

Raphael planted a short, swift kiss on her lips. "I can't wait, either."

Francine looked across her small living room. "I'll let you out through the front door instead of the garage. It's not like we want to hide our connection from anyone." She moved to the door. "Do you have a place to go?"

"What?"

"Do you have a place to go, like a motel or something?" she asked, her gaze seeming to convey some kind of unspoken message he wasn't picking up. Was she asking him to stay over?

Raphael wanted to say he was homeless and ask her to take him in. Reluctantly, he said, "I do have a place to stay, belowstairs at the truck stop. Thanks for asking."

Her obvious disappointment gratified him when she said, "Okay. Until tomorrow."

He exited her place before she could ask him outright to stay, because he'd deny her nothing. Using his speedy ability, Raphael fast-walked to the Big Bang Truck Stop's aliens-only entry point and was in his room before anyone could stop him to chat.

Francine stayed on his mind as he fell asleep. He thought about the way she looked when he kissed her. Extraordinary. Her sweet expression when he kissed her hand. The way she moved and talked and simply existed. Was he infatuated? Perhaps. Would she ever consider a life as the bride of a bounty hunter? Did he want a wife? Maybe, but only if Francine was his intended.

And wasn't that a crazy thought. It had been a long, long time since he'd considered a future for himself that involved a woman at his side.

This journey might be equal parts agony and ecstasy if she wasn't interested in any sort of a future with him after their adventure ended.

Francine slept fitfully after Raphael departed. She'd been about to ask him to stay the night, which would have been impulsive. Although he'd caught her eye a couple of months ago, she hadn't really talked to him in any significant way until tonight. It was hasty to invite a guy to spend the night right after talking to him for the first time, wasn't it? Yes. It most definitely was. She hadn't been that rash since...well, since just before her former love betrayed her.

She watched through the narrow slit in her drawn living room curtains as Raphael crossed the street. Suddenly, he was gone in a blur. Ichor-Delta fast, he'd said. Vampirically fast, she'd insisted, and smiled at the memory.

She dreamed about him, of course. How could she not? In her dreams, her mind rewrote the embarrassment of the last wedding debacle, changing it to include Raphael, standing in front of her swinging an ancient battle axe menacingly in one hand and cradling her kitten, Angel, in the other.

In this new version, no one threw her out of the reception. No guards dragged her out and put her on a shuttle bound straight for Earth. Instead, Raphael handed her the kitten, grabbed her up in a one-armed clench and together they left the reception as he spouted threats of a royally commanded social demise for her parents.

The dream was far better than the facts of that debacle, but so farfetched as to make her laugh when she woke and thought about it. Before her eyes opened, she felt something soft, warm and furry cuddled against her cheek. Angel had managed to climb up the blanket and find a spot next to her face on the pillow. Francine opened one eye and looked at the clock on her nightstand. It was early. She didn't have to get up yet. Her shift didn't start until late tonight. She burrowed further beneath the covers to conjure more dreams about her bounty hunter.

An hour later, she woke to hear the phone on her nightstand playing a distinctive clip of music, signaling a call from her sister. Francine smiled sleepily. She sure had a lot to share after her interesting evening.

"Hi, Lucy."

"Fancy, are you alone?" her sister whispered, using her favored nickname as if some clandestine plan were underway.

"What? Of course I'm alone." *Wait. Why would she ask that?*

"I just came from the Supernova Supermarket where a new cashier gave me an earful about you, an orphaned black kitten and a certain delicious-looking bounty hunter with whom you apparently went home. She heavily implied there were some sort of carnal activities on the menu for you last night."

Francine gulped. "What?! She did not!" She never would have suspected Roberta of dropping a dime on her.

"Oh, yes, she did. Carnal activities were mentioned more than once during her summation. And all the people in the grocery line behind me got an earful, too. I suspect I wasn't the first to hear the story, either. So, I'll ask again—are you alone?"

"Yes, I'm alone." *Well, unless you count the kitten.*

"Did you drive home with a delicious bounty hunter in your SUV?" Lucy asked, sounding rather breathless, clearly caught up in the titillating intrigue. "Were there any *carnal activities*?"

Francine sucked in a deep breath, balking at confirming Roberta's gossip-filled dialogue with strangers at the local supermarket.

"I take it by your silence the answer to my questions would be a resounding yes."

"Okay. I drove home with him. So what? I'm of age. I have been dismissed from my family by our parents. It's not like I have a reputation to sully. What does it matter what I do, or who I do it with?"

"I just want you to be happy, Francine. Tell me all. Is he wonderful? Did you kiss him? Was it amazing? Does he make your toes curl?"

Francine loved Lucy so much. She sighed dreamily. "He *is* wonderful. I did kiss him. It was amazing and, yes, my toes curled a couple of times last night."

"Ooh. I'm so happy for you, Fancy. When do I get to meet him? Maybe we could double date."

"I'm not sure, but I do have some good news."

"What is it?"

"He agreed to take me to Pru's wedding on Ichor-Delta."

"Really? How? I mean, how can he take you there without our parents reacting badly again?"

"Raphael's last name is Boudreaux. He said he'd pretend a royal connection so Mother and Father won't kick me out like last time. By the time they find out he's not really a royal Boudreaux, we'll be long gone."

"Wow. That's awesome. I can't wait to go. I was dreading the idea of leaving you behind. Now we can go together, and I can look forward to the trip."

"Me, too. We'll arrive right as the ceremony starts and probably leave midway through the reception, just in case Mother and Father do feel inclined to cause trouble, but I don't care. I'll get to see the wedding and part of the reception. That's all I wanted anyway."

"I'm so glad, Francine. I'm super happy you found someone."

"Well, don't get too attached to the idea. We've only known each other one day. I do like him and, as I mentioned, his kisses make my toes curl."

"Mew. Mew."

Lucy asked, "What's that noise?"

"My new kitten, Angel." Francine scratched under the kitten's chin and she started purring.

"Huh. I'm glad you told me about the bounty hunter before the cat. I might have thought you were on the wrong path in life."

"Wrong path?"

"You know, where you become the crazy cat lady of Alienn, Arkansas."

"Very funny."

Her sister hung up with a joyful and giggly goodbye. Francine fell back against the pillow, smiling at her goofy sister. Angel snuggled up to her, purring sweetly. Francine drifted into a light sleep, wondering if she should do anything about Roberta and her gossipy ways. What *could* she do?

Francine didn't dream about Raphael.

An hour later, she'd risen, showered, dressed and started looking for something to eat when there was a knock on her door.

Peeking out the front window, she saw Raphael on the porch, a paper sack in one hand.

She pulled open the door with a bright smile. "Hi."

He grinned back. "Hello. Have you eaten lunch yet?"

"Nope. Come on in."

Francine held the door wider. As Raphael crossed the threshold, she noted again how good he smelled. It was all she could do not to grab him, bury her face in his chest and breathe his scent in.

"I was at the Cosmos Café and decided I didn't want to eat alone."

"How thoughtful. What did you bring?"

Raphael lifted the bag. "The waitress there told me you like their triple-decker grilled club sandwich."

"Was her name Dixie?"

He brightened. "Yes."

"That's what I always order. It's delicious."

"Good. I got one for each of us. And something called chips."

"Of course. Chips are the best."

Raphael put the sack on the dining room table and pulled out the boxed lunches. Francine got napkins and plates and they devoured their lunch.

"You're right, delicious food. And I love the chips."

Francine smiled. He seemed so extraordinarily pleased by a simple diner lunch.

"Thank you for bringing me lunch."

"Certainly."

"Are we still on for the wedding?" she asked.

"Absolutely." He paused, as if bracing to impart bad news. "I wondered if it would be possible to leave two days earlier. I'd like to take a couple of days to acclimate on Ichor-Delta before we go to the wedding."

Francine nodded. "Sure. I was going to add my approved vacation time on the schedule tonight anyway. I can take a couple more days."

"Good. We'll leave Wednesday and return the following week, on Friday. That should give us enough time to search for wedding venues after your sister's ceremony."

"Perfect." Ten days of vacation delight with a delicious bad boy bounty hunter turned heroic bodyguard especially for her. And best of all, everyone would think she was engaged to him. She refused to ponder *not* being with him when this was all over. That was too depressing.

He helped her clean up the remains of their lunch. They stood together in front of the sink. She tipped her face up at him. He leaned closer. Closer. Just when she thought he might kiss her, he stepped back and patted his front pocket. "Oh. I almost forgot. I have something for you."

Francine felt a rush of excitement blaze a path from head to toes. *Something for me?*

Raphael dug a hand into his front pocket and pulled something out. "I figured the sooner we start, the better our story will be once we get to Ichor-Delta." He opened his closed fist and held out a ginormous violet diamond ring in his palm. It was in what was termed a vintage setting with fancy carvings and other stones in a design around a single large oval center stone.

She squealed in surprise. "For me?"

"Yes. We are going to be engaged for this trip, right?"

Francine looked up into his face. He seemed a bit shy about giving her a ring for their engagement. "It's so beautiful. And big," she said, reaching out to touch the violet stone.

"Nothing but the best for my royal bride-to-be."

She nodded. "That's right. We must be royal, or I'll be sent home and billed for the ride."

"Put it on." He moved his hand closer, urging her to take the ring. "Or do you need me to fall to one knee and propose?"

Before she could respond, Raphael did just that. He dropped to one knee on her tiled kitchen floor. "Francine Hayward Duvall, will you be my fake fiancée for our trip to Ichor-Delta and beyond?"

Francine giggled. "Yes, Luther Raphael Boudreaux. I will be your fake fiancée for as long as you want."

He stood up, his massive frame towering over her, and helped her put the ring on her left hand. It fit like it had been made especially for her.

"Thank you," she said, meeting his intense stare. She may be helping him out as part of this trip, but he truly was a hero to be going out of his way to help her see Pru's wedding.

"You're welcome."

Francine put a palm on his cheek and leaned closer. He met her halfway and their lips touched. She sighed into his mouth. It was like magic had been released into the room all around them.

His hands slid around her waist to her lower back, pressing her tighter into his body. She slipped an arm around his neck to get even closer. Like the last time their lips met, the world fell away until it was just the two of them and the toe-curling kiss.

She swayed in his arms, barely staying on her feet. She danced him backward toward her sofa as they kissed and kissed and kissed like only the two of them existed in the world. Just when she was about to push him down onto the sofa, ready to straddle his lap and really kiss him, the doorbell rang. Loudly. Twice. Then a third time.

Francine broke away from Raphael's mystical lip lock and shouted, "Just a minute!" She bit her lip as she tried to get her ragged breaths under control.

He leaned his forehead against hers. His breathing seemed as unsteady as hers. "Do you think we'll ever be able to kiss as long as we want to?"

"No. I'm afraid erratic interruption is our new normal."

"Well, that just sucks."

She laughed. "Sucks? Where did you hear that?"

"I read an Earther expression book."

Ding-dong. Ding-dong.

Francine pushed out a breath, disengaged from Raphael's arms and stomped to her front door. She wrenched open the door, ready to give the visitor what for, but surprise stopped the words in her throat as a large, imposing figure filled the entrance.

"Diesel. What are you doing here?" The Fearless

Leader of the Big Bang Truck Stop wasn't a typical guest for Francine.

"Sorry to drop by unexpectedly, Francine. Actually, I was looking for Luther Boudreaux. Is he here, by chance?" As if pulled by an unseen force, Diesel's gaze dropped to the huge diamond ring on her third finger. His eyes widened, but he didn't say a word about it.

Francine felt rather than saw Raphael move in quickly right behind her.

"Diesel," Raphael said. "What's up?"

"Trouble."

"Of course. Why else would you be looking for me?"

"Sorry to interrupt, but we just got a missive from Alpha-Prime. A couple of days ago, an extensive team comprised of the worst scum in three galaxies broke a recently incarcerated master criminal out of the XkR-9 gulag."

"No," Raphael said flatly. "Not possible."

"Yes. Indigo Smith has been liberated. One likely destination he'll consider will be this Earth colony."

Chapter 4

Raphael shook his head in disbelief. "Indigo Smith is on the loose? Again? I find I'm almost at a loss for words."

"Yep. Me, too." Diesel looked not only annoyed, but like the weight of a planet rested on his shoulders. As the Fearless Leader of the Alpha colony on Earth, Raphael supposed it did. "We caught him and apparently sent him to a sissy gulag. They only managed to keep him confined for a few months before he danced on out of there like the security was nothing more than a paper ribbon tied across the gate."

"Why does anyone think he'll come here?"

"The gold ingots."

"Ah, yes. His booty. I thought it had already been returned to some financial institution on Alpha-Prime."

Diesel grinned. "No. We confiscated the treasure and hid it away here on Earth. We don't actually know where he got the gold from, so no way to know who to return it to. It's possible he stole it from different places over a period of time, had it melted down and reformed into the ingots we found.

"We just spread it around that it had been sent back to the homeworld. If Indigo Smith goes to Alpha-Prime, he'll figure out soon enough that it's a lie, if he hasn't already. It's possible the scum-filled gang that helped spring him has already figured out where the treasure must be and shared that information."

Raphael nodded. "So, logically, he'll come here."

"That is the going theory, which makes me glad you stuck around." Diesel's gaze flicked to Francine, his gaze dropping to her ring finger before returning to Raphael's face. Raphael wondered how far Francine would want to take their fake engagement. Should they try to fool all the Alphas here on Earth?

"When will Indigo Smith make his way here, do you think?"

"There's no way to know for certain, but I'd say two to three weeks. It will depend on the criminal contacts still willing to support his antics and Indigo's ability to fund them. My understanding is that he pays those who help him very well, but he's got to lay low for a while. There are Guardsmen scattered across several galaxies between here and the gulag, all of them hunting for him. Unfortunately, Indigo has lots of help and certainly more than one plan to stay free."

Raphael nodded. "I'm headed to Ichor-Delta for a wedding in a few days, but I should be back in time to help keep a lookout for him."

Diesel nodded. He looked meaningfully at Francine's ring finger. "Is it *your* wedding?"

"No. Not our wedding. Not quite yet." Raphael slung his arm around Francine and hugged her to his side. "Don't worry, Diesel. I'll ensure Indigo is put back in a gulag before I leave Earth permanently. Hopefully, he won't be placed in the same sissy gulag as last time."

"We can dream. Thanks, Boudreaux. I appreciate it." Then he grinned and looked from Raphael to Francine and back. "Also, congratulations."

"Thanks." Raphael nodded once and squeezed Francine's shoulders. He pondered the new information on Indigo Smith as Francine closed the door. After a few silent minutes, he caught her watching him with a small frown.

"What's wrong?" he asked. "Should I not have told Diesel about our new *relationship*?"

"No. It's fine. Besides, Diesel probably won't gossip."

"Then what?"

"Nothing really."

"Something."

"Okay. I really hate the thought of you leaving Earth permanently." She shrugged and gave him a sad smile.

"I see. Well, I hate that thought, too." He moved closer, so near he was able to press her into the door. She didn't stop him. "Let's think of something else. Where were we before that bothersome interruption?"

Francine touched a finger to her bottom lip. "You were kissing me like you wanted a real fiancée."

He pinned her with an ardent gaze. "I've never had a fiancée before." He paused and added, "Well, except for the fake one with the bounty hunter I told you about, but it wasn't even for a full day."

"Why do you think that is?"

He lifted one shoulder in half a shrug. "I'm a bounty hunter. I go where the jobs are, and while my permanent residence can be anywhere, I've never really settled down in one place. But I could."

"Could your permanent residence even be on Earth?"

"Indeed. Even on Earth." *Even though it's hell and gone from everywhere I usually work.*

"Okay." With that, she draped her arms around his neck and pressed her lips to his, resuming the incredible kiss. Raphael would worry about Indigo Smith later. Much, much later.

The kiss intensified, if that was possible. Francine started urging him toward the sofa in her living room, like she had before Diesel showed up. What would she do to him if they made it all the way over there?

The doorbell rang again. Francine ignored it, continuing the kiss and the subtle herding toward the sofa. A knock came next. Outside, a female voice shouted, "Yoo-hoo, Francine! I heard a very interesting rumor at the Supernova Supermarket this morning and I came over to see for myself."

Francine broke the kiss and her eyes widened. "That's my landlady, Mrs. Greenstone."

"Should I hide?"

"No." Francine brushed her soft fingertips over his mouth. "Just wipe the satisfaction off your face."

"Nope. I can't do it. I won't do it."

"Aw, come on. We don't need any more rumors about us floating around out there."

Raphael paused. "Maybe we do. I mean, we are officially fake engaged now. Why shouldn't the world know it?"

She pondered what he said before nodding. "That's a really good point. Fine. Keep the satisfied look, then."

"I will. I hope you do, as well."

Francine gave him a saucy smile with a quick wink before she returned to the front door and opened it. A beautiful blush came up in her cheeks as the elderly Mrs. Greenstone came in without waiting for an invitation.

As she did, Angel scampered into the room, little body leaping, front paws batting as she seemed to play only with the air around her as a toy.

The older Alpha woman laughed at the kitten's antics. "Well, now, I guess both rumors I heard were true."

"Both?"

"A new kitten *and* a new gentleman friend." Mrs. Greenstone looked pretty joyful at her discovery.

Raphael stepped forward, offering his hand.

"Hello, Mrs. Greenstone. I'm Raphael, Francine's fiancé."

"Fiancé?" Her eyes widened and zeroed in on Francine's hand with the violet diamond ring.

"Wow! What an unusual engagement ring. Is that amethyst?"

"Violet diamond," Raphael said. "A rare and perfect gem for a rare and perfect woman."

"Well, aren't you just the most romantic breeze to sweep through Alienn in a long while."

"Thank you."

"Have you two known each other long or is this an arranged marriage sort of thing?"

Raphael settled his arm around Francine's shoulders, hugging her close. He loved having her pinned to his side. "Oh, no. This is a love match, not arranged."

"Well, good. That's the best kind. I just haven't seen you around here before."

"I came from out of town in conjunction with my employment. I saw Francine the day I arrived and couldn't keep myself from her. She is exceptional."

"That's so romantic." Mrs. Greenstone looked enchanted.

"I hate to ask," Francine said, "but we planned to go to my sister's wedding in a couple days for about a week. It's out of town. Would you be willing to look in on Angel while we're gone? I hadn't planned to get a kitten, but I stumbled over her on my way home from work last night and now I'm attached."

"Of course, dear. I'd be delighted to."

Mrs. Greenstone met Angel, cooed over her and then left as quickly as she'd come. She gave Raphael several side-glances of seeming approval in the short time she was there.

Once they were alone, Francine took her gaze from Angel and stared at her new fake fiancé. He stared back.

"Dare we try again?" he asked.

"What?"

"Kissing."

She grinned. "Yes. We should definitely kiss again. I just can't promise who will promptly knock at the door next."

"When do you have to leave for work?"

"Not for hours."

"Excellent." He let his eyes roam over her and guessed he looked rather possessive. "Want to go around town and let everyone know we are together?"

She shrugged. "Or we could stay here and kiss until the next townsperson shows up and knocks on the front door. Shouldn't be too long. And then more will show up. Perhaps they can just form a line down my street."

"Maybe that's a good thing."

"How do you figure that?"

"Perhaps the universe is telling us something."

"What?"

"Don't let things go too far too fast."

Francine made a face. "Like I'm worried about that."

"Aren't you?"

"Nope. I didn't have an untarnished reputation to live up to even before the arranged marriage. But I was banished from my family for doing the right thing. These days, I do exactly what I want, when I want, how I want. And I don't let anyone else decide what's good for me—or not."

"I don't blame you. I do the same."

"So, kissing or walking around town?" She crossed her arms as if daring him to not choose kissing.

He shrugged. "Both. Why don't we walk around town and kiss as we go? It would show our intentions far more…visually than just telling people we're a couple, don't you think?"

"Yes. You're right. Both it is." She took his hand and ushered him toward her garage and vehicle.

"Where shall we start?"

"The Big Bang Truck Stop belowstairs and then we'll head to a few choice places in Alienn to show off our kissing superpower."

Raphael couldn't wait to squire Francine all around Alienn, Arkansas, showing her off as his fiancée, kissing her at will. Even if this ended up being temporary, he would relish their time together.

There was something very satisfying about taking Francine out and about, kissing her as she wore a family engagement ring not many people on Earth would know the history of.

The violet diamond center stone was unique. If anyone in his family ever discovered he'd given it to Francine, they would lose their minds, as the Earther phrase went.

Raphael didn't care. Francine was the only person he'd ever considered giving the ring to, and he hoped she might want to keep it, and him. He'd never felt this way before and took it as a sign that she was the one for him. Perhaps he'd convince her to make things permanent as they traveled the galaxies together on this coming trip.

Francine drove them to the Big Bang Truck Stop and parked her SUV. Together, she and Raphael slipped into the Alphas-only door and went down to the underground facility. They held hands, lingered in various stores, browsing as if they didn't have a care in the world. Truthfully, she didn't.

They stopped to get a sweet iced tea at the Celestial Barbeque Shack, which touted the best BBQ on the planet, and do some canoodling in a centrally located booth. Best of all, they kissed, a lot, everywhere they went. Lots of folks took notice, just as they wanted.

As they exited the Celestial Barbeque Shack, they spotted Cam Grey and his wife, Ria.

"Boudreaux," Cam said, giving Francine a quizzical look, but not making a big deal about it.

"Cam," he responded.

Ria, meanwhile, grinned at Francine. Then her expression turned to shocked delight. "Oh my gosh! Are you two engaged?" She pointed to the ginormous violet diamond ring and Francine held her hand up.

"Yes. We are." Francine wiggled her fingers and the gemstone sparkled obligingly.

"When did *that* happen?" Cam asked. The surprise in his tone was hard to miss.

"Today," they both said at the same time and laughed.

"Wow. Congratulations." Ria's eyes remained fixed on the engagement ring. Francine felt a spurt of possessive delight. It *was* stunning.

Cam gave Raphael another questioning look. Francine knew he was rather quiet at the best of times. She hoped he didn't disapprove of their engagement, though he'd have no idea it was fake.

"Does that mean you'll be staying on Earth?" Hope seemed to color Cam's tone.

"Possibly," Raphael hedged. "I'm considering Earth as my new home base, at least."

"Excellent. I'd love to put you on my security staff even part-time, if you're looking for permanent work."

"Thanks. I'll keep that in mind."

Cam nodded and tugged on Ria's hand to get her moving.

"Again, congratulations," Ria said with a grin, briefly resisting Cam's urging. "I love your ring."

"Thank you."

"It looks like a family treasure passed down for generations." Ria eyed Raphael as if seeking verification.

"Something like that," he said, neither confirming nor denying the legacy of the piece as the couple moved away.

Francine didn't know where he'd gotten it. Stunning as it appeared, she was certain it wasn't a true violet diamond. It must be a reproduction. Violet diamonds were more common on Ichor-Delta than any other planet she knew of, but the giant center diamond and luxurious design had to be fake, right? Otherwise, the ring would be worth a king's ransom.

As they walked through the Big Bang Truck Stop's underground retail concourse, he paused at a kiosk with sunglasses and gave her a shuttered look. "You aren't going to ask me if it's real, are you?"

"Are you reading my mind again?"

"Maybe."

Francine glanced down at her hand, letting the facets of the violet diamond catch the light and sparkle. "Are you going to tell me about it? If it was real, it would be priceless."

"I'd be what Earthers call a big jerk if I gave my fiancée a fake ring."

"I prefer the word reproduction and I would never call you a jerk."

"You're adorable."

"So it *is* a real violet diamond in an antique setting?"

He nodded. She paled. "It's not stolen or anything, is it?"

"Of course not." Quickly, he added, "What if I told you I acquired it as payment for a job?"

Francine looked at the ring. She'd have to give it back, but planned to enjoy it for as long as she possessed it. "Well, I love this ring. Thank you for letting me wear it during our—'cough'—engagement."

Raphael smiled down at her, holding her hand, running his thumb along her finger and around the ring. She looked up into his eyes and they kissed. Just like they were really engaged and in love.

The clerk behind the register at the sunglasses place loudly cleared her throat until they broke the kiss and started moving through the basement again.

Francine was going to have to put the brakes on her feelings. She knew she'd be crushed when the time came for their fake engagement to end. Even if they kept dating, the engagement was only a farce. *Right?*

It didn't matter that her heartbeat sped up each time their lips came into contact. Once they returned from Pru's wedding and whatever side trip he needed to take, the engagement would be over. That was exactly what she should prepare herself for. The thought of preparing for reality made tears well up in her eyes, so she focused on the here and now. She had almost two weeks to enjoy being treasured by a worthy man instead of being made to feel like she was a creature so vile she had to be removed posthaste and exiled immediately from any family gathering.

Not for the first time, Francine pictured what it might be like to receive her family's approval and welcome at Pru's wedding, albeit with grudging acceptance by her parents as they exited the ceremony before heading to the reception. On Raphael's arm, she'd be able to go through the receiving line at the reception without fear of being cast out. She couldn't wait to see her parents' faces when she introduced a member of Ichor-Delta royalty as her fiancé and showed them the big honking ring she had on her finger.

At Drucilla's wedding, Francine had skipped the receiving line on the way into the reception and lined up with the servants to file into the cheap seats, as they called them on Earth. Fat lot of good that did.

"Where to next?" Raphael asked, breaking into her unpleasant reverie.

Francine looked around. "We should go into downtown Alienn and hit a few places. Cosmos Café so that Aunt Dixie can help get the word out, maybe the Earthbound Travel Company to pretend to look at trips to Niagara Falls. That should set the town's tongues to wagging. Maybe even a trip to Lovers' Lane to really cement things."

"Lovers' Lane?" A predatory smile appeared, making her wonder if he even knew what that was.

She grinned. "Well, maybe not. No need to go crazy, right?"

He shrugged. "I'm game either way."

"We'll see how our day goes."

"Because you have to work tonight?"

Francine blinked. She'd forgotten. "Yes. That's right. I'll be working by the time we could go to Lovers' Lane."

"We can't go there before dark?"

"Nope. Those are the unwritten rules, no daytime hanky panky on Lovers' Lane."

"I see." She didn't think he believed her, but it didn't look like he was going to give her crap about it.

"Let's head for the Cosmos Café."

"Lead the way, fiancée of mine."

Francine really loved the sound of that, but reined in her exuberance. She was his *fake* fiancée, not a real one. It took effort not to sigh dramatically.

Chapter 5

Raphael spent two days planning the journey with Francine. He arranged transport and lodging for all the stops on their whirlwind trip, including the stopover on Alpha-Prime the day after the wedding on Ichor-Delta, although they wouldn't disembark the transport ship. It would help with the follow-on trip to the Ossuary Valerian Space Station. He booked a house there for a week, though he didn't plan to stay that long. He didn't want to be too clear about their travel plans, in case anyone was watching him or taking note of their itinerary.

He didn't know what sort of clothing Francine planned to wear, but added two extra days to the front of their journey for a trip to an exclusive designer on Ichor-Delta. They both needed all the trimmings for the proper wedding guest attire befitting a royal. They certainly couldn't dress as servants. He hadn't kept any of his more regal clothing after leaving his family home. Bounty hunters, as a rule, weren't trying to make any fashion statements. It was always best to blend into the surroundings and not be noticed.

Raphael wanted to acquire several more casual yet regal outfits for their journey after the wedding celebration, searching for a fake wedding reception or honeymoon destination. Royals, at least on Ichor-Delta, changed into fresh clothes with every separate event during the day. He'd changed seven times on one particularly busy day when he lived at home. He did not miss that life even a little, but he'd have to mimic his past to ensure his royal cover held up under close inspection.

After the reception and before they reached the space station, he hoped to discover more information on how much trouble Victor was in. If he didn't get a message to the contrary when they stopped at Alpha-Prime, Raphael would know Victor was still in hiding. He didn't expect Victor to attempt to leave any safe haven unless forced to. If anyone caught Victor, word would spread across the galaxy like the induction force at the edge of a black hole.

In any event, he made his travel plans as if he and Francine truly were the epitome of a royal Boudreaux couple about to be married, touring potential places to hold their wedding or enjoy their honeymoon before returning to Earth, his possible new home base. If any or all of the visits weren't needed, they'd go as planned to keep their undercover engagement viable until their return to Earth.

If he and Francine stayed together after this adventure, he would certainly consider making the Alpha-Prime Earth colony his base of operations.

The thought of having someone to come home to after long journeys for work was appealing on many levels and an idea he truly hadn't considered practical before now. Or perhaps he'd never met anyone he wanted to make any huge sacrifices for until a certain kitten-owning redhead had fallen into his life.

Meeting Francine—and especially kissing her—gave him a new goal to reach for. He never would have taken a chance on interacting with his family if it weren't for her. Was this a sign of something deeper? Should he seek a private meeting with Will and discover his elder brother's frame of mind regarding Raphael and his life choices? Maybe Will wasn't like their father. Maybe Raphael could have some, if not all, of his family back. Once he arrived on Ichor-Delta, he'd consider initiating a private meeting with Will after the wedding and reception.

This was the first time he'd looked forward to attending a wedding, all because of the possibilities it offered regarding closing the door on his past and opening another to a future with Francine and his estranged family.

While arranging their itinerary occupied a large portion of Raphael's time, he also kept tabs on Edgar. So far, the slobbish bounty hunter hadn't done much in the way of attempting to track down

Victor. Mostly he'd hung around the Big Bang Truck Stop, spending the bulk of his time at various sub-surface drinking establishments each evening until they closed. He'd often drunkenly make his way back to his quarters, sometimes with a woman in tow.

While he and Francine had told friends, acquaintances and strangers alike about their engagement, they didn't tell a soul they were leaving Earth soon. Francine thought it best to just show up at the wedding with the invitation he'd managed to snag for them to attend as an envoy from the Boudreaux royal family. No notice was better than giving her parents time to check things out. He agreed.

The only other possible problem would be if any of his close relatives saw the ring Francine wore. His father, and possibly his elder brother, might cause an uproar if the discovery were made public. Raphael decided he'd burn that bridge once he crossed it. As far as he was concerned, the jewelry was his to do with as he wished and he dared anyone to disagree. That particular ring was the last thing his mother had ever given him. Speculating about a confrontation over the ring made him wonder if he secretly wanted a confrontation with his family. Maybe. Maybe not. He would be ready either way.

He got out of his borrowed vehicle, strolled to Francine's door and knocked. He couldn't wait to kiss her. When she didn't immediately answer, an edge of concern slid through him. He knocked again. Had she overslept? Decided not to go through with this fake engagement?

The moment he pressed the doorbell, she popped the door open, looking beautiful, but frazzled. Angel sat curled in one hand, chewing on her thumb.

"I have a very bad kitten," Francine said in lieu of a greeting. She looked down at her little black ball of fur and said, "You have been so naughty."

Beyond the entryway, he saw chaos in her relatively spartan home. A potted plant lay on its side leaking small clumps dark soil onto the carpet. One of the chairs at her dining table was on its back, and what looked like the shredded mass of an entire box of tissue paper had been strewn all over the visible floor space.

"You could still rename her Troublemaker. I'm sure she's not used to Angel yet," Raphael said.

Francine thrust the hand with the kitten at him. "Could you take her for a minute while I attempt to clean up the biggest part of the mess?"

"Sure. We have a few minutes."

Raphael tucked the young feline against his chest and watched as she righted the plant and the chair, then swept and quickly vacuumed the space. "Looks good as new," he said when she finished.

"Well, I don't expect it to last long, but after I leave, it will be my landlady's chore. Maybe she'll put Angel through some sort of kitten obedience class while I'm gone."

"Does kitten obedience class even exist? Seems like an oxymoron to me, given the little I know about kittens."

"You could be right." Francine shook her head in resignation and retrieved Angel from him. "For now, I'm going to close her into the bathroom where her litter box is with some water, food and all her toys. I'll put her scratching post in there, too. My landlady said she'd come over every day at least once, probably more. I'll leave her a note as to where Angel is and what she's capable of if left out and about unsupervised."

"Are you packed?" he asked.

"Yes. I'm ready to go."

"Great. I'll grab your bags and put them in my vehicle."

"You got a vehicle?"

"I borrowed one for today."

She nodded and pointed through the living room to a doorway. "In my bedroom. I have one large and one small bag on my bed."

He nodded and walked to the room she directed him to. Stepping inside her private space took him off guard. The air in the room smelled just like her—sweet and soft, with a hint of spice. He shook off the distraction, grabbed her bags and hauled them out to the vehicle he'd borrowed from Axel Grey.

Raphael hadn't wanted to make her walk to the Big Bang Truck Stop. He thought of the casual way Axel offered up the SUV when he learned they were taking the same shuttle from Earth to Ichor-Delta for the wedding. Every one of the Grey brothers was consistently a better friend to him than his own family. He envied their close relationship.

Francine exited her home, locked the door and met him at the back hatch as he finished loading up her bags. Once he shut the hatch, she moved close, lifting her face to his with a mischievous grin.

"We should share a kiss for luck before heading on our way, don't you think?"

Raphael responded by pressing his lips to hers gently. He knew she didn't want a quick kiss for luck. She wanted a full-blown, *we are engaged, and we want everyone to know it* kiss. He obliged gleefully.

When she pulled away, he asked, "Was that for your neighbors?"

"Sure. Okay," she said. Her impish expression made him smile. She walked to the passenger door and he followed to be a gentleman, opening her door.

They arrived at the Big Bang Truck Stop right on time to greet Axel and Lucy before boarding. They sat apart on the flight, but planned to sit together at the reception after the wedding. Lucy agreed they should keep a low profile at the ceremony and not go out of their way to let their parents see them until they joined the receiving line at the reception.

Before long, they were buckled into the commercial spaceship headed for Ichor-Delta and on their way to a ten-day galaxy trip with nothing stopping them. Francine told him repeatedly how elated she was to be heading to this special wedding for one of her favorite sisters. She thanked him profusely for the privilege.

Raphael hoped she didn't regret it.

He had set this in motion, unsure of what he'd discover when he arrived. He'd reserved expensive lodging for them near the wedding venue and contacted a lifelong confidant about securing not only the precious invitation to the wedding, but also information regarding any pushback he might get as a result of this bold action. Unfortunately, the invitation for Prudence's wedding and reception had arrived without any note attached.

He'd have to wait to receive any further information once they landed on Ichor-Delta.

They'd spend a couple of days getting properly outfitted before attending the wedding. A fancy coach would pick him and Francine up from the shuttle area on Ichor-Delta, while Axel and Lucy would have to follow whatever itinerary the sisters' mother had organized.

Raphael wanted to wow Francine. Aside from their accommodations and the designer clothes fittings, he'd arranged for a very luxurious and expensive coach to take them to the ceremony on the day of the wedding. No royal would be caught dead in anything less than the best.

Once the charade for her family was done, they would take a less public form of transport to Alpha-

Prime and on to the Ossuary Valerian Space Station before heading back to Earth.

Victor's situation worried him. He hoped his old friend stayed safe and free until they could meet. Knowing that at any moment he might receive news of Victor's capture weighed on him.

Raphael wasn't certain what he could do for Victor, but he owed him the chance to explain. They had a long history, one that included Victor doing him a huge favor when his father kicked him out of the family. It was a kindness Victor had never expected to be reciprocal, but Raphael had.

Given their past, there wasn't much Raphael wouldn't do to help Victor escape this situation. He just hoped he wouldn't have to give up his own life.

He glanced at Francine, squeezing her hand to reassure himself she was safe and sound in his care. Was he a fool to bring her along on this trip? No. He mentally crossed his fingers. He wanted to do this for her. He was grateful she'd agreed to help him with his own mission and planned to protect her with his life against any and all foes, including her parents.

Once they landed on Ichor-Delta, he summoned the fancy pre-arranged transportation to take them directly to the designer's shop. He looked forward to seeing Francine's reaction when they reached their destination. She thought they were headed to an out-of-the-way hotel.

The expression on Francine's face as the liveried

driver stowed their bags, then held the door for them, was a sight to behold. He could only guess she'd led a rather pampered life before being kicked out of her family, but he'd noticed she acted with extra gratitude when anyone did the least thing for her.

"Where are we going?" Francine asked as the driver took a turn toward downtown.

"It's a surprise."

She grinned. "I hope it's a good surprise."

"I hope so, too." Raphael wanted her to enjoy her trip.

They arrived in an exclusive area beneath one of the finest shopping areas on the planet. The driver eased the vehicle to a stop and got out to open the door. Francine's eyes widened when she saw the store with the well-known name.

"I haven't been to a place like this since I lived with my parents. I was here once before, but it was quite a long time ago." A wistful expression crossed her lovely face.

"As a part of our overall disguise, we need to look like royalty, so I set up fittings for us to get not only wedding clothing, but also casual outfits to wear once we leave the reception and head off to look at honeymoon destinations."

Her face went through a myriad of expressions—surprise, realization, acceptance—before settling on worried. After a long silence, he was about to reassure her when she nodded and said, "Right. Good call."

"Also, it's my treat."

She looked uncomfortable. "No. I'll pay my own way."

Raphael took her hand, kissed her knuckles gently. "This particular designer owes me a debt. That's why I chose him. I promise we won't be spending a single credit today."

Francine mulled that over. "Okay. Thank you so much, Raphael."

"My pleasure, Francine."

They stared at each other, moving closer and closer until their lips met. They kissed passionately, only breaking apart when the waiting driver cleared his throat.

They got out and Raphael guided Francine into the shop of one of the most exclusive designers in this part of the galaxy. Raphael had made a private appointment in his name to be sure there would be no interruptions.

As soon as Francine entered, the designer and proprietor exclaimed, "Why, you're Miss Francine Duvall from Alpha-Prime. I haven't seen you since—" Abruptly, he stopped speaking, as if just realizing her former status had been stripped away, never to be returned. He stood, mouth open, eyes wide, frozen in apparent horrified distress at having spoken to someone who was supposed to be erased from time.

Raphael followed Francine in. "Hello, Mr. Jacques Pierre."

The other man's mouth slammed shut and his face paled further. "Mr. Boudreaux," he managed after a long silence. His gaze went back to Francine. "If you'll excuse us, Miss Francine. I'm not sure I have anything you would like today."

"She's with me," Raphael said loudly. He lifted Francine's hand, showing the smaller man the large engagement ring she wore. For added measure, he wrapped his arm around her shoulders and gave her a small, affectionate squeeze. "Francine is my fiancée. We both need attire for a wedding we're attending in a couple of days and several casual outfits each for our further travels."

Jacques Pierre squinted. "You are engaged to—" He looked at Francine in horror. "Her?"

"Yes. Isn't she beautiful?"

At long last, the designer seemed to come to his senses and understand what was going on. He nodded his agreement with Raphael. Several deep breaths improved his color, but not by much.

"Can we get started? We only have a couple of days." Raphael herded Francine to a table where several very rich fabrics had been laid out. "Do you like any of these, love?" he asked her, running his fingers across the fanned display of silken cloth.

Jacques Pierre swallowed hard. "I'm sorry, Mr. Boudreaux. I don't know if I can help you today, either."

·✦·

Francine understood the problem immediately. Mr. Jacques Pierre would not be allowed to even acknowledge her existence if he hoped to have any further business from her prestigious family. Everyone knew what happened when an unfortunate family member was permanently ostracized from a prominent house, even if that house's seat of power was on a neighboring planet.

"Give me a moment, love," Raphael said to Francine and stepped away to discuss in loud whispers how basically the cow was going to eat the hay.

Mr. Jacques Pierre was resistant until Raphael, with a quick look over one shoulder at Francine, pulled him out of range of her hearing.

Francine wondered if there was about to be a fistfight, but the two men had what looked to be a civil conversation.

At one point, Mr. Jacques Pierre's eyes got very wide, but eventually he dropped his head and nodded. More loudly, Raphael said, "Excellent. Thank you for your cooperation." His tone was slightly exasperated, almost snarky. The designer didn't look happy, but whatever Raphael had told him clearly convinced the man to help them with their wardrobes.

Francine had brought a nice dress she'd planned to wear at the wedding and reception. It was a never-worn gown donated by Lucy from a large trunk she'd brought to the Earth. It was a sleeveless, jet-beaded, jade-green, form-fitting affair with a short, see-through yoke cape trimmed with the same jet beading. Stunning, but fashion from a couple of years ago. She didn't care, but others might.

Lucy said it was a fancy dress for her Fancy sister. Francine smiled in memory. It would have worked for her purposes, but even the lowest priced dress in a place like Jacques Pierre's shop would be so much better.

Mr. Jacques Pierre stalked across the room to the front door. He put the closed sign facing out and pulled a shade down so no one could see inside.

"Now," he said. "What did you have in mind?"

"In addition to the royal wedding attire we need in two days' time, I'd like wardrobe enough for a week for each of us," Raphael said.

The proprietor sighed. "The good news is I can get you each a week's worth of clothing for travel easily enough. The challenge will be getting your wedding clothing made in such a short time."

"We can start right now with fittings." Raphael shrugged out of his jacket and dropped it on the back of an ornate chair.

Jacques Pierre didn't look relieved. "I assume you are planning on attending the Duvall-Roth wedding, yes?"

They both nodded.

"I made the wedding dress and all the clothing for both families."

Raphael shrugged. "Great. Then you know exactly what to make so we'll fit in."

Francine understood what the designer wasn't saying. "He can't make clothing for us that will rival what's already been created."

"Why not?" Raphael asked, but his expression said he knew why.

"I'm merely saying your fabric choices will be extremely limited." The designer pointed to the table. "All of these were used in various designs for Miss Duvall's wedding."

"Then why are they all front and center in your store?" Raphael asked.

Francine put a hand on his arm. "In two days, directly *after* the wedding, whatever my family wore will be a hot product for everyone else with the means to pay for it. Right?" she asked the proprietor.

He nodded.

"Now I remember one of the reasons I hated—" Raphael cut himself off and turned to Jacques Pierre with a manufactured smile. "Please show us what our choices are."

Jacques Pierre motioned them toward the back of the store, and led them through a set of lacy curtains and down a hallway with five doors on either side, likely the dressing rooms. They all filed through an open door at the end of the hall. Francine stared in amazement at the trove of what could be every fabric ever made in the galaxy.

The room was large, at least three stories high, with library ladders to reach the highest shelving that housed material from corner to corner. She'd never seen so many bolts of fabric in her life. She'd been to a number of fancy designers throughout the galaxy, when she'd been one of the Duvall Five.

Jacques Pierre led them to the left-side corner, where he climbed the ladder to the third row and pointed to a shelf. "From this shelf down will be your only choices."

Francine scanned the shelves and saw several possibilities.

"What about those fabrics over there?" Raphael gestured to an open shipping container lodged against the only other door in the room.

Jacques Pierre frowned. "Oh, no. Impossible. That's next month's premier selection for my preferred clients."

"Perfect," Raphael said. "I believe we qualify."

"No. Please. I can't have those out in society. Not yet."

Raphael was indignant. "Why not? The wedding party didn't use them, did they?"

"No. However—"

"I like the emerald-green fabric," Raphael said, turning to Francine. He gazed lovingly at her. "It matches your eyes."

Jacques Pierre huffed and climbed down from the ladder. "Fine. Ravage my business, why don't you?"

"Jacques Pierre, you owe me a debt. When I helped you—for free, I might add—you told me anything, anytime, for any reason. I'm calling in that promise. Perhaps you never expected me to collect."

The proprietor's shoulders sagged. "You're right. I never expected you'd want or need anything I could provide." Jacques Pierre straightened and a new expression shone on his face, one of determination. "However, I am a man of my word. You shall have whatever you want for the coming nuptials. I'll do my best to see you are the talk of the wedding."

"Thank you, Jacques Pierre."

Francine moved closer to stroke her palm over the emerald-green fabric Raphael had selected. It was lovely. Similar in color to her jade dress, the fabric had a golden shimmer. "I do love this fabric," she said, not sure if she should upstage her family. "Perhaps a simple design would suit it best. I'm certain if my mother was involved in the selection of the wedding trousseau, the designs were complicated or very intricate."

"You *do* know your mother's style, Miss Francine," Jacques Pierre said. "Let me show you a book I have of elegant designs your mother didn't bother to entertain."

"Perfect."

Francine flipped through several pages of unique designs with her chosen fabric in mind, and found the perfect one. "This one."

The design was a long sheath dress with a sweetheart neckline and black lace-covered cap sleeves. Simple. Elegant. Understated. Exactly Francine's style.

Jacques Pierre nodded his approval. "It will be lovely, and original. I haven't made a dress like this yet and with the new shimmer fabric you'll have a one-of-a-kind dress, at least until it's seen at the wedding."

The designer found an equally nice suit for Raphael, then moved the wheeled shipping container aside to reveal another door. Inside, the large adjoining room held racks and racks of readymade high-end clothing. They selected several outfits to wear while searching for their fake honeymoon destination. Francine had forgotten how much fun clothes shopping could be and lost herself as they tried on various items.

Once all their selections had been made, Jacques Pierre promised to have them packaged and sent to the Borg Stein Slot, the ritzy place Raphael had arranged for their stay on Ichor-Delta.

Outside the designer shop, the driver waited to whisk them to their lodgings. She wasn't sure what to expect, but her mouth fell open when she saw where they were staying.

"This is a castle."

"Yes. It's an old castle, but recently updated to play host to rich folks who want to pretend to be royals of old."

Francine looked down at her traveling clothes. "They will take one look at me and send me to the maid's quarters or possibly the kitchen to be a dishwasher for the cook staff."

"No, they won't. You're with me. Everything will be fine. Besides, you look great." She wished she'd worn one of the outfits they'd selected from Jacques Pierre's ready-made collection to walk through the lobby of the extravagant establishment.

The fancy vehicle pulled through a set of ornate iron gates and stopped beneath the curved archway of a stone porte cochere. As she waited in the vehicle, Raphael paid the driver and arranged for castle staff to take care of their bags. He opened the door and took her hand to assist her out.

He offered her his arm and they strolled inside, heads held high, just like they *were* royalty. Half of pretending to be rich was attitude. Stone carvings swirled across the cathedral ceiling. Every inch of the lobby space screamed privilege or possibly "poor people beware—if you break it, you can't afford it." Even so, Francine pretended she was still a member of the Duvall Five. It was like putting on an old shoe, not a comfortable one, per se, but a familiar one.

No one at the registration counter blinked an eye at them. She didn't know if Raphael had acquired this lodging because someone owed him a favor or if he'd actually paid a king's ransom for it, but once they were on their way to their room, she relaxed. Clearly, no one was going to grab her and thrust her into any hotel service position for looking out of place.

They followed a porter down a luxurious hallway graced on either side by shallow alcoves filled with historical coats of arms and paintings of ancient royals.

The porter unlocked their door just as Francine heard another door open nearby, turned to look, and froze when she spotted the elderly gentleman leaving the room next door.

Uncle Bandore! The Duvall Five's favorite uncle and a supreme gossip like no other in the family.

Would he recognize her despite her new haircut and cinnamon color? Probably.

If he did, their carefully laid plans might incinerate here and now.

Chapter 6

The sight of the distinguished-looking gentleman made Francine instantly pale. She turned her back on the new arrival as vivid panic registered in her expression.

Thinking quickly, Raphael grabbed her, swung her around to block her with his body and put his back to the man. He lowered his head and pressed his lips to hers in a kiss he hoped would conceal her identity. It was not a chore to kiss Francine. Seconds into the passionate display, Raphael forgot why he was doing it.

"Say there," the gentleman said, sounding both disgruntled and amused. "Your room is merely steps away. Take advantage of it, why don't you?"

He harrumphed and then muttered, "Young people these days. No sense of propriety." A few moments later, Raphael heard the man harrumph again, but it sounded like he'd moved further down the hall.

Raphael stopped kissing Francine and checked to ensure the man was leaving.

He looked into Francine's dazed eyes. "Are you okay?"

"I think so. That was close."

Seeing her freshly kissed lips made him want to kiss her again. He held himself in check. "Who is that man?"

"Uncle Bandore. He was very close to our family growing up. I'm not even sure he's related by blood, but I was afraid he'd recognize me and the jig would be up before we even stepped foot into the wedding venue."

"Good thing I kissed you."

"Good thing."

Raphael gestured for her to enter their suite as he took the key and compensated the porter. He closed the door and followed Francine into a stately living room that held enough furniture to fill her entire apartment and have enough left over to store in her garage.

He wanted her to be impressed. She deserved it.

"This place is amazing," Francine said. "I've never seen anything like it."

"That's surprising."

She sent him a dazzling smile. "Don't get me wrong. I've stayed in some really nice places, but this is truly fit for a king."

"Or a princess, in this case."

Francine tilted her head to one side. "Oh, I'm no princess."

He shrugged. "You should be treated like one."

"You're very sweet."

"What would you like to do next?"

"Kiss you some more in our lodging fit for kings and princesses."

"That's a given. What about dinner? And after dinner? Should we attend a museum to pass the time tonight? The theater? What is my lady's pleasure?"

"How about dinner in our room tonight, since I want my arrival at the wedding to be a surprise and Uncle Bandore—gossip tsar of the galaxy—is right next door. As for later," she said with a meaningfully pause, "I'm sure we can think of *something* to do here in this luxurious room."

Raphael stopped mid-stride. He could think of lots of somethings to do. What did *she* have in mind?

Her lashes lowered in a sultry expression. "I mean, to the world around us, we are engaged to be married, aren't we?"

He watched her carefully. "Yes. We are, for all intents and purposes, engaged."

"Perhaps we could talk about the wedding and reception we are about to attend. We can discuss what-if scenarios and what comes after that on this journey."

"Sure. Great idea." He tried not to sound disappointed. It was good to discuss strategy and ensure they were on the same page if their engagement story was tested.

Francine's gorgeous face took his breath away. "Why don't you order dinner? We can discuss our plans and strategy for Pru's wedding and reception.

We need to expect pretty much anything and be prepared for it."

"True."

"I'd also like to know what we're doing after we leave the reception. What plans you've made and the like. I want to be ready."

"Sure. I'll tell you all." He told himself to calm the heck down and headed to the communication station on the ornate glass-topped desk.

It was reasonable for Francine to want to know where they were going and what they were doing. He'd tell her what he could. Some things about Victor would have to remain secret. He had no reason to feel disappointed. She was being very practical, while he had visions of the bed fit for a king they probably weren't going to share. He hoped the sofa in the luxury living room was as comfortable as it looked.

He picked up the communication device and prepared to order a nice dinner to go with their coming practical conversation.

Francine gifted him with a beautiful smile and said, "Excellent. Then after dinner we can discover if the bed in this place is fit for a bounty hunter and his bride-to-be."

Francine had been thinking about spending the night with Raphael since he scooped her up from a nasty fall and kept her from crushing Angel a week ago. No. That was a lie. She'd been thinking about it since before she was introduced to him in Valene and Wyatt's foyer. The bounty hunter had been on her mind for months.

She'd wanted him the instant she saw him strolling through the Big Bang Truck Stop basement facility with the Grey brothers, plotting their strategy to capture the infamous Indigo Smith.

Raphael kissed her like he wanted to do all manner of wicked things to her and with her, but ultimately always held himself in check. Never went too far. Never crossed the line. Never acted like a wolf unable to be tamed in any rapturous moment.

When she suggested they discover the viability of the bed, his whole body went rigid. He sent her a wildly scandalous gaze followed by one with an equal amount of uncertainty. He bobbled the communication device in his hand and almost dropped it.

"What do you mean?"

Oh, you know exactly what I mean. "I mean," she paused before continuing, "...we are *engaged*, right?"

His expression shuttered. He set down the communication device and approached her. He looked resolute, like he planned to tell her how he intended to keep holding himself in check. She had news for him. It wasn't going to work this time.

"Francine." He stopped short of her personal space.

"Raphael." She closed the small distance between them and slid her palms up his chest until she settled her arms around his neck. "I have plans for you."

His eyes narrowed. "Do you?"

"I do. Please stop being so gentlemanly and start thinking about later tonight when we're all alone together in a bed fit for a king or a bounty hunter and his bride-to-be."

He wrapped his arms around her slowly, molding her body to his frame. "I haven't thought of much else."

"Prove it." She pressed a cheek to his chest, imagining she heard the tempo of his heartbeat increase.

"Right now?" He nuzzled his face into her neck, placing a kiss below her ear. It tingled even after he pulled away.

"Unless you're too hungry."

"Food is not what I hunger for."

"Good." Francine kissed his stubbly cheek. She kissed his jaw, equally prickly. She kissed the corner of his mouth, tantalizing her lips. He tilted his face to align their lips and kissed her like she ruled him, heart and soul. She closed her eyes and sank into him, giving herself over to his control.

She lost all sense of time and place. When she opened her eyes, Raphael had carried her into the enormous bedroom. Her gaze went to the luxurious oversized bed, complete with regal canopy and lush decorative curtains framing the pillow-strewn surface.

He kicked the door shut behind them and resumed the scorching kiss. The back of her legs hit the edge of the bed and he stopped moving, but didn't end the kiss.

Francine leaned down, pulling him with her until her back nestled into the silken comforter, maintaining the exuberant kiss. She barely had time to notice how comfortable the mattress was before he joined her on it.

His weight pressed deliciously into her, but then he rolled onto his back, taking her with him, depositing her on his chest.

She broke the kiss. "Nice bed," she said, feeling breathless.

"Very nice."

"Fit for a king."

"And a princess," he added, placing a soft kiss on her cheek.

"And a bounty hunter."

His passionate gaze intensified. "And my bride-to-be."

They kissed again until she didn't care where she was, as long as he didn't stop.

Francine woke with a start and tried to remember where she was. When her parents left her behind on Earth after she didn't marry the groom they had arranged for her, she stayed at Valene Grey's place for a short time before moving into her duplex next to Mrs. Greenstone.

Every morning for several weeks, both in Valene's spare room and her new duplex home, Francine woke in the same manner, wondering where she was. The inevitable crash of memories would always surface, letting her know exactly where she resided. Every morning was the same. Shock and wonder, followed by memory and acceptance, followed by the relaxing notion that she was right where she was supposed to be.

Now, like then, she had to allow a few seconds for her to establish her location. Super comfy bed. Unfamiliar sheets. An ornate canopy over her head. She squinted. *Where am I?*

Recognition of the deep inhale and exhale of masculine breath next to her made her widen her eyes. Intense heat warmed one side of her body. She was not alone in bed. Her recollection of the night before came rapidly and, with it, a powerful surge of joy.

Raphael.

She sighed, charmed to be exactly where she was. Raphael truly was an archangel. Gentle. Tender. Amazing. He was perfection. Francine turned toward him and snuggled closer to his warmth. She drifted back to sleep as wonderful memories of their evening encompassed her mind, heart and soul.

Raphael woke briefly when Francine burrowed against his back. He was unable to wipe the smile from his face and gave up trying. She was a princess. A sweet, beautiful princess with a gentle hold on his soul.

His new plan was to ensure she became his fiancée in truth. He'd never been more certain of any decision in his life. She belonged with him. He belonged with her. They belonged together.

This was a turning point in his life, previously only filled with hunting bad people, chasing bounties and a certain amount of loneliness experienced during those times when he lay in wait for the criminals he chased to show themselves. He couldn't wait to start their life together. His mind stumbled briefly to Victor and he had to forcefully set that problem in the back of his mind, well away from attending the coming wedding with Francine. There'd be time enough for that worry later.

He dozed for a few hours until his empty belly woke him with a loud rumble. Francine was on her back, still pressed against him. She mumbled in her sleep, which he found adorable, then she said a few clear words before falling quiet again. After watching Francine for a long while, he slipped from the very comfortable bed and headed out to the living area before his beastly loud appetite woke *her* from a deep slumber.

Checking the ornate clock, he realized it wasn't as late as he thought. He ordered several selections of food for them, in case she woke up hungry, too.

Raphael contemplated their night together. His eyes drifted shut in memory of the spectacular events that had taken place in the adjoining room. He never would have instigated what transpired, and was so grateful she had. Francine wouldn't take no for an answer. Raphael hadn't put up much of a fight and what little resistance he offered hadn't lasted long.

The memory of her snuggling up to him in the middle of the night shaped his lips into a smile.

After last night, it would not be difficult to convince anyone who witnessed their ardent affection for each other that they were a couple. After they'd gotten through the wedding and reception for Francine's sister, and done whatever was possible to help Victor, perhaps he'd broach the subject of a permanent relationship between them.

His mind shifted to tomorrow afternoon's nuptials. Francine had shared her previous wedding-crasher strategies with him. She'd arrived early, hidden nearby and inserted herself into a large group entering the venue. That way she could blend into the crowd, seating herself toward the outer aisle on the groom's side of the divided space. To the best of her knowledge, no one had noticed her attendance during either ceremony.

As with the two Duvall weddings she'd crashed, the Duvall-Roth reception would take place directly after the nuptials. This time, however, instead of a separate site on the other side of the city, well away from the wedding venue, the attendees would be directed out a side door and down a covered walkway to the reception in the posh building next door.

There would be a formal reception line where he and Francine would be announced to the room, followed by a short walk to the wedding party's receiving line, where they could offer congratulations to the bride's parents, the bride and groom, the groom's parents and the few attendants.

Basically, they'd have to face Francine's parents straight away. For that reason, he planned to have the usher announce him initially and then give only Francine's first name as the guest accompanying him.

When he'd outlined it for her, Francine approved of his plan. She said her parents would be delighted to have a surprise royal in their midst and would hopefully keep quiet about her appearance with him.

He didn't know Francine's parents personally. He was fairly certain he'd never met them, but hoped his former title would hold up to scrutiny after so many years away from the bosom of the Boudreaux royals.

The wedding he'd attended with fellow bounty hunter Elda "don't ever call me Esmerelda" Lark had been much less formal. No ushers announcing folks, just a mad rush of all the attendees to enter the reception hall to get a good seat close to the buffet table or dance floor, depending on personal preference.

He and Elda had chosen seats at the table right next to their target. The man had been completely unaware of their intent even after they lured him outside the reception hall. He'd been clueless until they'd clapped handcuffs on him and led him away. No one at the wedding even noticed he was gone, or at least no one sounded the alarm over his absence.

This would be a different sort of operation. Their goal was to keep from getting kicked out of the reception or shackled by Royal Guardsmen. They also didn't wish to be sent out of the galaxy on a pricy shuttle and billed for the extravagant ride.

Francine was all for the plan, but he knew she worried about her parents' pride being stung. She didn't want them to react vocally and unfavorably to a surprise visit from their former and very disobedient daughter in public.

The lengths she'd gone to attend her younger sister's wedding had benefited him immeasurably, but she continued to insist how grateful she was for his help.

The invitation he'd garnered only had his name and a plus-one guest of his choice. If the usher slipped up and announced Francine by her full name, Raphael was prepared for that. He hoped she was, too.

Raphael would have to be his most charming and royal self. More charming and royal than he'd ever been in his real former life. If the elder Duvalls balked at Francine's entrance, he'd have to insist they treat his fiancée with the esteemed regard that befitted a future royal wife. Would they bite their tongues and play along? Or would they make a gigantic scene?

Only time would tell.

He heard the bedroom door open and a very sleepy looking Francine stepped out. She trudged across the room to where he sat waiting for breakfast to be delivered.

"Good morning," he offered when she seated herself next to him.

"Okay," she said and laid her head on the table.

She was completely adorable. "You don't have to get up yet if you don't want to, you know." He leaned over and kissed her cheek.

She smiled, but her eyes didn't open as she mumbled, "You're so sweet."

Before he could say anything else, there was a knock at the door. Francine's eyes popped open wide, she sat up, swaying in her seat. "Who is that?"

"Relax. It's the breakfast I ordered."

"Oh, good." She slumped forward and put her head back on the table beneath a bent arm.

Raphael didn't even look through the peephole, just popped the door open.

It wasn't their breakfast.

Chapter 7

Francine was not used to getting up early. Working nights had transformed her schedule. It wasn't even about being an early bird or a night owl. Even before she'd made Earth her permanent home and gotten the swing-shift grocery store job, she'd rarely needed to get up early.

Last night, she'd slept well, just not quite long enough in the great scheme of things to compensate for her abrupt routine change.

Raphael answered the door, opening it only partially. She hoped he'd ordered coffee, because she needed some. No, she needed all of it.

"I say, old chap. The communication device in my room seems to be broken, and I need to contact the front desk urgently." The sound of the familiar voice made her sit upright in a hurry and come to life.

Uncle Bandore!

"Sorry, my fiancée isn't up to receiving. What's your room number? I'll call the concierge and have someone sent to your room."

Uncle Bandore didn't retreat. From her vantage point she could see one richly cobbled shoe and part of a pinstriped suit leg. "Stand aside, man. It won't take but a few moments and I won't even look at your fiancée," the older man insisted.

Once Uncle Bandore had made up his mind to do something, it was nearly impossible to dissuade him. Usually, everyone just got out of his way. It was easier. Francine saw the shoe lift and move to step across the threshold. She stood up from the table, banging her knee on the edge hard enough to make her eyes water. She muffled a groan and crouched to run—or limp quickly—into the bedroom.

Raphael shoved the door, forcing it almost completely closed to keep Uncle Bandore in the hall. "No. You may not enter."

"How rude!" Uncle Bandore harrumphed loud enough to be heard back on Earth.

"That's right. *You*, sir, are being very rude." Raphael slammed the door on his angry retort.

Francine stopped limping. Her lips parted in surprise. Her eyes opened wide. She couldn't believe he'd closed the door in Uncle Bandore's face. She bent to rub her battered knee.

Raphael shook his head. "Your uncle is quite a piece of work."

"That is the truth. However, perhaps you shouldn't have thwarted him."

"He deserved it."

"He did. Trust me, I know. He always does. I just

don't want him to be another issue we have to deal with or watch out for during this trip."

Raphael shrugged. "Okay. I'll call the concierge and report that he needs help. Maybe that will earn me some points."

"Doubtful, but I appreciate your willingness to help out when he's been such an entitled, spiny little crust fish."

He laughed out loud. "I haven't heard that term in quite a while."

Francine smiled, realizing she'd never seen Raphael laugh so boisterously. And for something she'd said. He was even more attractive when he laughed. She melted.

Raphael crossed the room to use the communication device to call the front desk. Her uncle would likely never appreciate the gesture, but she did.

The next knock at the door was the food he'd ordered. Once they'd been served, Raphael made sure the delivery boy went next door to check on Uncle Bandore.

They'd just finished their lovely late breakfast when Jacques Pierre called to inform Raphael their wedding apparel was ready to be delivered, along with an outfit each for their coming travels. The rest would be delivered early the day of the wedding, before their departure from Ichor-Delta.

Once the wedding clothing and accompanying accouterments were delivered, tried on and laid out for tomorrow's festivities, they pondered what to do with the rest of their afternoon and evening.

Raphael asked, "Have you ever seen an unobstructed view of Scharffjell?"

"No, but I've heard it's beautiful, in a brutal sort of way."

The most famous mountain range on Ichor-Delta was the tallest range on the planet, according to an article she'd read during her efforts to learn about all things Ichor-Delta, due to her interest in a certain bounty hunter.

His brows lowered. "Who told you that?"

Heat crept into Francine's cheeks. Her former love, H.R., had furnished that tidbit long ago. "No one important," she responded quickly.

If he saw her flush, he didn't mention it. "Would you like to see it for yourself?"

"Yes. I would." She could make her own judgment about Scharffjell's beauty and perhaps create her own adjective to describe it.

She and Raphael left by way of a side exit to lessen the chance they'd see anyone either of them knew. The problem with a large, well-attended upscale wedding was that lots of invited guests were likely staying at establishments in the area. Being seen by other wedding attendees was socially desirable, so others knew one was important enough to secure invitations to the most exclusive events. Lucy and Wyatt were staying at the Duvall's temporary residence on Ichor-Delta, as were all the close family members. Except Francine. She refused to be affected by the slight. She had made her own way here with the perfect man to accompany her. As far as she knew, her parents didn't have a clue that she planned to attend.

Hand in hand, they walked casually toward the closest lookout. Ichor-Delta's terrain was as mountainous as Alpha-Prime was arid and desert-like. Some part of the Scharffjell mountain range was visible from many places, but few offered such a pristine, unobstructed view. A barrier prevented rockslides from battering towns at the foot of the mountains. The barrier featured special viewing areas inside the structure as well as spots along the parapets, with long, winding staircases to platforms for the masses of residents and visitors to enjoy the wild beauty.

Other than the one visit to the exclusive shopping area in her youth, and that had been at night, Francine had never spent enough time on Ichor-Delta to explore it. At best, she'd caught obstructed glimpses of the mountains from the shuttle landing port.

Not everyone appreciated the jagged, dark terrain of these mountains the way its people did, according to the material she'd read.

Raphael took her to an uncovered viewing place by way of a mechanical lift that rose up the side of the rampart instead of forcing her to climb hundreds of steps. Her sore knee appreciated that gesture.

Once they reached the platform, Raphael guided her to one of several open viewing stations with metal viewfinders. They looked like large binoculars on a stand, the larger end pointed at the Scharffjell range. Raphael adjusted the stand lower so she could look through the small end of the viewfinder.

"What does Scharffjell mean?" she asked, pressing her brows to the rim of the viewer and focusing on the jagged mountain peaks. It looked like shards of dark quartz had been pushed up through the terrain at various angles to form peaks and valleys. They weren't all dark, but a very deep purple so dense that only help from the solar light near the summits emphasized the color. Ichor-Delta was known for its limited yearly sunshine. Some viewed it as a dark and mysterious planet.

"Savage mountain, I believe."

That was an apt description. "Do people ever climb the peaks?"

"Not this northern range, the surfaces are too slick. There's a place in the southern region where the peaks aren't as tall, slick surfaced or jagged. There are lots of climbing places and hiking trails there. Would you like to go?"

"No. I just wondered."

Francine stepped away from the viewer so Raphael could have a looksee. "This is one thing I miss seeing on a day-to-day basis when I'm away."

"I can imagine. It's magnificent."

"Do you miss the desert on your planet?"

"Nope. Not even a little. Living in a sphere all my life, I never really spent time in the deserts of Alpha-Prime, but there are no mountains to speak of there. And if you step one toe out of a sphere, it's windy and sand blows in your face all the time. I was never a fan."

"Earth certainly has a varied terrain."

"Indeed. My favorites are the tall trees and all the lakes and rivers of water everywhere."

"Mine, too." He turned toward her. "Have you learned how to swim?"

"Yes. It's easy. Do you know how?"

He nodded. "I learned a long time ago, while hunting one of my earlier bounties."

"Oh?"

A wry smile shaped his lips. "I also learned the hard way."

"Meaning?"

"I had to chase my quarry into a very cold river on an ice planet I'd never visited before. Haven't been back since, come to think of it. The water wasn't over my head at the start, but as I chased him, it got deeper. It was either learn to swim as I went or lose my bounty and sink beneath the surface."

"And you got your quarry even though you had to learn how to swim?"

"Of course. I wasn't going to let a little bit of brisk, chilly water slow me down."

"Good for you." Francine could picture it. He was not the kind of guy who gave up easily. Bounty hunters, from all she'd read, were a unique blend of bravado, strength and a heightened resistance to failure.

"I'm surprised that you never learned when you were younger? You didn't live on a desert planet. Wasn't there water enough on Ichor-Delta to swim in?"

"Yes. However, my father didn't think it was necessary for his offspring. Apparently there's not enough money in it."

"Hmm. Interesting."

Raphael crossed his arms and leaned against the waist-high wall beside the viewer. He got an inquisitive look in his eye when he asked quietly, "What's your story, Francine?"

"My story?" That put her on her guard. Was he expecting her to confide her deepest secrets? "You already know my story. I didn't marry the man my parents chose for me and I was exiled from my family."

"That's not your whole story, though, is it?"

She shrugged exaggeratedly. "I don't know what you mean."

Francine suspected she knew *exactly* what he meant. Had he heard a rumor about her? Did he know about the unfortunate incident from her youth? The cruel betrayal she'd suffered in silence to avert scandal, only to be banished for a different reason much later.

The nemesis she reviled, H.R., the man she'd loved who deserted her for money and power and a more lucrative bride than she would ever have been. The first and last man to let her down in the love department, she'd sworn to herself.

Francine began walking toward the lift, hoping to end Raphael's questions.

"Who is Howard?" he asked.

She froze. Her stomach roiled sickly. He knew! How did he know? How could he *possibly* know that name?! She thought she'd been so careful. Apparently, not careful enough.

When she slowly twisted around to stare at Raphael, half afraid of what she would see, he didn't have a sinister expression on his face. Of course not. He was not Howard. He was not cruel or mean or hateful. He was good and kind and her own personal archangel. His expression was only curious. Like that name was simply a mini mystery he'd recently discovered and now needed to solve.

"Where did you hear that name?" she asked. She could have been walking on glass she felt so unsteady. Who had ratted her out? Who had told him? Even Lucy didn't know that name, only the initials.

Raphael uncrossed his arms and approached her. He slid an arm around her shoulders and squeezed her against his side. The hug was a surprise. He didn't seem angry. He leaned in to whisper, "Did you know that you talk in your sleep, Francine?"

Francine closed her eyes, mortified. She'd spent the night with Raphael and said another man's name in her sleep? How stupendously impolite.

"Oh, no. I'm so sorry."

He tipped her chin up, looking her straight in the eyes when he said, "You never have to say sorry to me, Francine."

"Thank you." She swallowed hard to keep from weeping in relief. "What did I say?"

"You said, 'Howard, no. Please, Howard, don't.' There was more, but I couldn't make out all the words you spoke, just that you seemed distressed."

That was accurate. They were the last words she'd spoken to Howard when she discovered what he'd done, what he was about to do to her.

No. She hadn't known she talked in her sleep.

"I feel an obligation to ask what he did to you."

"An obligation?" The horror of the scene that filled her memory was cut short by Raphael's next unexpected query.

"Did he assault you in some way?" he asked carefully. "Do I need to exact retribution on your behalf? Because, trust me, I will."

Francine snapped out of her reminiscences and shook her head. "No. He didn't assault me. But he did betray me. To add insult to injury, he was cruel and hateful about it when he most assuredly didn't have to be. It took me a long time to get over him, but I did."

"Are you truly over him?"

She grabbed Raphael by his coat lapels. Staring deeply into his eyes, she said, "Yes. I promise you, I am completely over him. It's been years."

"Why do you think you said his name last night?"

"Probably because you are the first romance I've had in my life since…well, since that time way back then."

"You haven't had a romance with any other man since?" He sounded surprised.

She shook her head. "No. Axel Grey certainly doesn't count. Though I liked him, I knew from the moment we met that Lucy was in love with him. He was like a brother to me from the start." She wondered how naive Raphael might think her if she told him he was the first man she'd ever been intimate with.

Francine hadn't been with Howard intimately, but she'd been close. Several witnesses could attest to what she'd been about to do. She might as well have done what she'd been silently accused of. It was a miracle her parents never found out. If they had, they'd been as silent as a grave about the matter.

A sudden grin shaped his lovely mouth. He wrapped both arms around her even tighter, lifted her in the air a few inches and said, "Are you saying that I was the one who helped you get over this dreadful man from your past?"

Yes. You made me believe in love again.

In his warm embrace, she felt secure, relaxed and optimistic with regard to the possibility of love. "I suppose so. You were the first guy I couldn't stop thinking about after I saw you."

"At Valene and Wyatt's house?" He lowered her to the ground, but kept his arms securely around her.

"No. Walking through the Big Bang Truck Stop with the Grey brothers when Indigo Smith was on the loose on Earth...the first time."

"Is that so?"

"It is. I've had my eye on you for months."

"I saw you that day, too."

"You did?"

"You were with your sister. I recognized you as two of the five Duvall sisters. And you hadn't changed your hair color yet."

"Did you like me better as a blond?"

"I really like the red. But, truthfully, you're beautiful either way."

She slid her arms around his middle, gazed deeply into his eyes and said a heartfelt, "Thank you."

He shrugged. "It's just hair color."

"No. For the other."

"The other?" His eyes narrowed. Francine wanted to kiss him.

"For not being difficult about my sleep talking. I can't imagine every man would be as understanding."

"Oh. Well. I guess I don't find it productive to be *difficult* about unimportant things that can't be helped."

She kept her arms around him and he propped his chin on her head. They stood that way for a long while.

Francine was falling in love with Raphael. She didn't panic in the least at that revelation. She delighted in the fact she'd found love after all this time.

True love.

Chapter 8

The Ichor-Delta Wedding

Raphael eyed the narrow path toward what he considered a rather ostentatious wedding venue. He offered Francine his arm. She grasped his elbow and together they walked slowly toward the entry in the center of a large throng of wedding guests. No one seemed to notice them.

As they moved at a snail's pace, several conversations from a multitude of directions impinged on his awareness. He listened only enough to ensure no one recognized Francine before their grand entrance at the reception.

He flashed a smile at one of the ushers standing at the door welcoming folks inside. He held up the decorative invitation and got the nod from the usher, who pointed to an electronic register on the wall. Raphael waved the invite at the register. When nothing happened, he decided they were golden. He would have been stunned if a siren or alarm had gone off, disrupting the event.

Beside the usher, a teenaged girl dressed in a pretty peach outfit handed Francine a program. Raphael secured the invitation in his pocket, as they'd need it to get into the reception. They strolled inside the opulent building like they belonged. In his opinion, they did. Well, *she* did. He was simply protection. Raphael would protect her from any and all problems, no matter what happened.

Francine had feared she'd be on some sort of wedding watch list or there would be wanted posters of her tacked up around the event, that if anyone spotted her, she'd be kicked to the curb. Raphael wasn't worried. There were so many details involved in these wealthy public spectacles that he was certain the required invitation was all the security there'd be to keep out unwanted party crashers.

No expense had been spared on the décorations. Raphael blinked at the variety of adornments scattered absolutely everywhere. Peach tones covered every wall. Every surface. Every conceivable place in the room. Everywhere he looked, peach.

Peach streamers flowed in an arch above where the couple would exchange their vows. More streamers flowed from the ceiling and decorated the Gothic windows that lined each side of the spacious room. On either side of the central walkway, rows of very nice cushioned chairs had been lined up like a regiment of soldiers ready for parade. Attached to the aisle chair of each row was a bouquet of—wait for it—peach-colored flowers wrapped in a peach ribbon. He thought if he looked underneath, there would probably be some sort of peach glue used to stick the bouquets to the chairs.

Shockingly, the chairs were covered in white, perhaps to mitigate the head banging sea of peach spewed around room. Otherwise everyone would be peach blind.

They found a place toward the center on the right side. Francine wanted to move all the way to the far edge of the row, but Raphael seated them closer to the center aisle, with Francine on his right. He wanted her to be able to see the ceremony. He gave her a wink of reassurance and they sat down. The venue filled up quickly and a time check told him the ceremony would start soon.

Francine kept her head bowed. She held the program, staring at it intently as if studying for an exam on the material. He didn't blame her. She had been highly embarrassed at the last wedding reception and it would be foolish to assume there wouldn't be someone looking for her at this wedding. Or perhaps she was shielding her vision from the room's blinding peach decor.

"You look beautiful," he whispered as he watched for anyone who might point Francine out or embarrass her. The shimmery emerald-green dress Jacques Pierre had created was perfect for her. She looked like a goddess. Well, to Raphael she always did. He'd thought her worthy of worship as she'd sleepily staggered around their suite that morning in her wrinkled, slept-in jammies.

"Thank you. You look amazing, too." She kept her hand on his arm, perhaps for added tactile support. He was fine with that.

Music flowed from unseen speakers throughout the gigantic room. He didn't know the tune, but assumed it had the word "peach" either in the title or listed in the lyrics somewhere.

In an aisle seat a few rows ahead, a man with dark hair and piercing silver eyes turned to look up the center path, perhaps taking in the peach runner lining the walkway. As he twisted to face the altar, he did a double take and sent a glare in their direction.

Raphael glared back. The man didn't notice. His gaze was fixed on Francine, his expression malevolent as he stared rudely for several seconds. Raphael leaned forward, blocking the man's view of Francine. Mr. Silver Eyes directed his animosity toward him. That was fine. Raphael returned the man's spiteful gaze with one of his own until the other man faced forward.

"What's wrong?" Francine asked.

"Someone was looking at us. I just stared back."

She glanced quickly around the area. "Who was it?"

"Don't know. Don't care."

Her worried gaze found his.

"You don't have to worry, Francine. I won't let anyone near you."

She squeezed his arm. "I know. Thank you, Raphael."

The music changed to a more traditional wedding song. The families, first the groom's and then the bride's, walked down the aisle to take their seats at the front. Raphael thought Francine should be there, too. He caught her wistful, delighted expression as people filed past them. She was happy just to be here, and that was all he wanted.

The groom stepped from a side door at the front of the room, next to the altar. The music changed, signaling the bride was about to make her way down the aisle.

Prudence Duvall walked down the center aisle wearing an enchanter veil that hid her features completely. It was a wonder she didn't stumble into every chair that lined the aisle, given the level of density sewn into the hairpiece. The bride must have been practically blinded by the opaque veil. It was typical of an arranged marriage and he supposed tradition was very important to some folks.

Raphael met Francine's gaze. Her happy tears and giddy grin made him soft in the head with love for her. She held his arm with both hands and squeezed him, as if to settle her excitement.

The ceremony was simple and short, surprising in comparison to the over-the-top level of peach decoration. He'd expected to spend a couple of hours at the least immersed in the fruity light orange color. Soon enough, the service was over. The smiling bride, finally free of the blinding veil, and her beaming new husband made their way down the central aisle as the attendees stood and clapped. Raphael ensured Francine was blocked from view until the wedding party passed.

More guests from the front rows began exiting up the aisle one by one. First the left row, then the right and so on. Mr. Silver Eyes cast another constipated look his way. Raphael didn't know if it was because he couldn't see Francine or if he knew she wasn't expected to attend the wedding. Either way, Raphael was on guard.

They followed the stream of people exiting the wedding venue, walking en masse to the reception. Raphael wondered if they'd be drowning in peach at the reception venue.

"Do you see the man who stared earlier?" Francine asked, keeping her face lowered.

"Nope. We're good." He searched the nearby crowd, but couldn't see anyone paying particular attention to them. The guests seemed ready and eager to get into the reception, possibly to sample all the surely extravagant food and beverages awaiting them.

"Okay," she said in a tone that suggested she was bearing up to be kicked to the curb by her family as soon as they saw her.

Raphael watched as guests ahead of them were announced and directed toward the receiving line.

First in line were the bride's parents and the true difficulty. If Francine's parents didn't make a scene, they were home free.

Next in the receiving line were the groom's parents, then the bride and groom, followed by the immediate members of each family. He knew Francine most wanted to hug her sister Prudence and wish her well. Raphael was poised to do whatever it took to make that happen. He didn't know the groom personally, only by family name. The Roth family was well placed in the upper echelons of Ichor-Delta, but not quite as lofty as the Boudreauxes. Aside from being a great match, Antonio Roth was by all accounts a worthy man for Francine's sister, Prudence.

Raphael handed the usher his invitation. "My plus-one is my fiancée, Francine," he said in a low voice.

The man didn't look up, but asked, "And her full name?"

He took a breath, exhaled, and said, "Francine Hayward Duvall."

He heard a scuffle behind him and some whispered conversation. Someone said, "No, we don't mind at all. Please, sir, you two go next."

Raphael looked up to see what was going on and stiffened in shock.

Francine must have felt it, because she squeezed his arm and followed his gaze to the last person he expected to see here.

"Is it really you, brother?" William Boudreaux asked, staring at Raphael and Francine as if just as surprised to see them.

Francine looked away from the usher announcing the guests. If he'd been forewarned or given any notice of her possible arrival and instructions to keep her out, she missed it. The two men who'd cut in line behind them looked very familiar.

What especially caught her notice was the way the younger man said "brother" as he stared at Raphael in obvious shock.

"William," Raphael said. His voice was cool. Guarded. Unsure.

"Luther! Why are you here?" asked the elderly man who stood with William. He wielded an ornately carved cane, the head of which depicted a bear-like creature. Violet diamonds filled fierce eyes above a gaping mouth filled with gleaming teeth, as if ready to bite. He leaned heavily on the cane as he spoke, the contempt in his icy tone palpable.

"Father, don't," the younger man said quietly. "Now is not the time or place."

"Please welcome Luther Raphael Boudreaux of the Ichor-Delta Royal House Boudreaux, and his fiancée, Francine Hayward Duvall," announced the usher in a voice loud enough to carry to the end of the receiving line.

She looked into Raphael's startled face and whispered, "You're really a royal Boudreaux?"

Before he could answer, Francine heard her mother's sharp inhalation of breath and turned to see her equally shocked expression.

"Francine?" The older woman sounded truly stunned. She put a hand to her chest as if expecting pain to erupt there any second.

Raphael's palm pressed gently into Francine's back, pushing her toward her mother. He greeted her with a winning smile. "Mrs. Duvall, I must tell you that the wedding was beautiful, as were the ceremony's decorations."

Francine's mother slid a smile in place like she'd done a thousand times before and took his extended hand. "It's a pleasure to meet you, Mr. Boudreaux." Her gaze turned to Francine. "I can't imagine where you two met, but I'm certain it's an interesting story." The smile on her lips did not come anywhere close to her eyes.

Raphael slipped an arm around Francine's shoulders, drawing her into the shelter of his warm, solid frame. "We met off planet, but I'm in love with Francine and we plan to be married very soon. I hope we'll have your blessing on our nuptials."

Francine was trying to wrap her head around the distinct possibility that Raphael was truly a royal Boudreaux and not some random bounty hunter with a good name. The pair of men who'd cut in line behind them both bore an exceedingly strong resemblance to Raphael. The younger man, William, had called him brother. That was...unexpected. He'd lied to her very convincingly.

Had he lied about anything else?

Her mother's eyes widened slightly, searching Francine's face, then Raphael's and taking in the angry older man behind them. "I can't imagine that we wouldn't welcome a royal Boudreaux with open arms." Her gaze fell on Francine again. This time, her expression seemed curious, but some rancor remained in her tone.

"Thank you, Mother," Francine said, keeping her response as appeasing as possible.

"You say you're marrying very soon. I hadn't heard anything about a royal Boudreaux wedding. It must be a small, private affair, yes?"

"Yes," Raphael said.

Francine's father extended his hand to Raphael and they both shook.

"Congratulations to you and your family," Raphael said.

"How soon will this private wedding be?" her mother asked, leaning forward as if to sniff out the accuracy of their fake engagement. If she discovered the truth, she wouldn't hesitate to shout it to the world and the assembled guests.

Raphael and Francine looked at each other. They had not rehearsed for this possible line of questioning, not expecting even her mother to demand a timeline while they held up the receiving line.

Whatever Francine expected, this was not it. She expected her parents—especially her mother—to be either cowed into silence by Raphael's name and unwilling to make a scene or sparked into acceptance by a possible link to a royal family and overly conciliatory for the rest of their time together. She'd misjudged her mother, not for the first time.

These questions regarding their not up-and-coming nuptials were a surprise. Her mother glanced at the queue where William Boudreaux and his father waited to be received.

In a low voice meant only for her parents' ears, Raphael said, "Given what Francine has told me, I anticipated we would keep our ceremony private and then have an after celebration at a later date. Of course, you will be invited to the post-wedding festivity."

"That's so very nice of you, but I have a better idea," said her mother, a sly glint in her eye. "Why don't you get married right now? Today?"

"What?" Francine and Raphael said at the same time.

Francine's father took his wife's arm. "Adeline, what are you doing?"

"I'm facilitating." She yanked her arm out of her husband's grasp. "The officiant will be here all day. I'm certain he'd be delighted to perform another service for us. What do you say?"

Francine couldn't believe what she was hearing.

Her mother was calling their bluff. She was *daring* them to get married.

Raphael tightened his grip on Francine's shoulders and said, "We'd be delighted. However, we'd never want to take a single bit of focus away from Prudence and Antonio's day."

Francine looked down the receiving row at Prudence. Her sister winked at her.

"That won't be a problem. Once the reception luncheon is completed, the bride and groom are leaving for their honeymoon. Trust me, we'll have plenty of time for another ceremony." Adeline Duvall's gaze was directly on her wayward, ostracized daughter.

Francine was about to concede and tell her mother the truth, but Raphael said, "Well, if you're certain it won't take away from the current marriage festivities, we'd be grateful and delighted to accept your generous offer." Raphael leaned down and pecked a kiss on Francine's mouth. "Wouldn't we, love?" He winked at her as if to tell her, "Play along and let's see what happens."

"Yes," she said. "We'd be delighted. Thank you so much."

Adeline's sly expression didn't waver. "Excellent. We'll announce it during the reception luncheon and everyone who is able to do so can stay on for a reception dinner."

"Is that possible?" Francine asked.

Adeline Duvall was going out on a limb with this

plan. Francine wasn't certain what her mother was up to, but heaviness gathered in her belly. Raphael, estranged from his royal family or not, was likely not expecting to actually take a wife today.

"Yes, of course, dear. We planned an after-wedding dinner for all the guests who came from out of town and off planet. Why not add another wedding? We'll be the talk of the season."

"Right. Why not?" Francine saw through her mother immediately. She wanted to embarrass Francine even more than she had the last time she'd crashed a Duvall wedding. "Before that happens, though," Francine said in a low tone, leaning toward her mother, "you'd have to reinstate me back into the family. How long will that take, do you suppose?"

That got a reaction. Her mother's eyes widened even as her mouth shrunk down to an unhappy O shape. "Don't be silly, dear. You have always been part of the family."

Francine wanted to snort and roll her eyes. She wanted to shove the exorbitant bill she'd received from her forced trip out of the last wedding into her mother's tightened fist. Instead, she took a cleansing breath and managed to form a small smile.

Her mother was about to press her advantage. Instead of being dragged out of the elaborate reception by two Guardsmen and placed on an expensively rapid shuttle bound for Earth, Adeline Duvall wanted to give the guests a show with the heightened probability that either the bride or the groom in the second ceremony would leave the other at the altar. What a grand display of embarrassment for each of them to endure, regardless of who won the game of chicken before the ceremony even started.

A ripple of whispers rose from the queue behind them. The closest guests had obviously heard about the additional wedding ceremony plans and shared the news with those further back.

"What's that?!" The shocked yet irate and very loud demand came from the elderly gentleman, presumably Raphael and William's father. "Luther is getting married? Who's he marrying? What's her name? Is his prospective bride worthy of our title?"

"Father, lower your voice," William said. The two Boudreaux men had yet to be announced. Francine thought the elderly gentleman could give the usher a run for his money as far as voice projection went. They could be present for the later declaration of another recently reinstated daughter being wed to someone important. It was win-win for her mother.

Either Raphael or Francine would bow out publicly or they'd be married in front of nearly every important connection of the family, including Raphael's brother and father who were, in fact, royalty.

So is Raphael.

Francine lifted her hand, seeing her fake

engagement ring in a whole new light. He hadn't received it as payment for a job. He'd given her a royal Boudreaux family ring worth a literal king's ransom.

Adeline looked at the ring on Francine's finger and sucked in another sharp breath. "The royal violet diamond from the Boudreaux family collection." Her sharp-eyed gaze went straight to Raphael. "Are you truly engaged to my daughter?" she asked, as if just realizing the magnificence of her scheme to force them to wed today.

She grabbed Francine's bejeweled hand, drawing the ring nearly to her face to inspect it. The look on her face was hungry. Power hungry.

"I'm not your daughter anymore," Francine said, snatching her fingers away. "I was kicked out of the family, remember? Because I certainly do."

A growing cacophony of voices rose from the queue behind Raphael's father and brother. Francine took a step away from her mother, and said, "We're holding up the receiving line."

The usher announced, "His Royal Highness, Lucius Grant Boudreaux, and his heir, William Wellington Boudreaux."

Francine turned to her father. He wore a sheepish expression, but she hardened her heart. "Father," she said briskly, nodding at him once as she continued past him.

Her feelings were so jumbled she had to forcefully set all her concerns aside to revisit later. If she didn't, she'd break down in a crying jag right in the middle of the reception. That would not do. She refused to let her mother see her shaken, despite the fact she was completely off the edge of reason.

Her chief issue among many was not even possible reinstatement into her family. That was something she never thought would be possible. No, her primary thought was to wonder why Raphael lied to her about being a royal Boudreaux, followed by why he'd lied about the ring.

She shook hands with each of the groom's parents, uttering platitudes she wouldn't be able to remember later, hoping she sounded sincere.

Francine stopped in front of Prudence, leaving Raphael engaged with her parents. "Pru," she said with a sincere smile. "You look grand. I hope you two have a wonderful life together. I'm so glad I got to see your wedding."

Pru practically glowed with happiness. "Thanks, Francine. I'm so elated that you were able to come." They hugged tightly. Francine breathed deeply. Her sister always smelled like flowers fresh from a garden, even though flowers were a rare commodity on Alpha-Prime.

Francine had to stifle a tear as yet another fierce emotional rush moved through her. According to Lucy, Pru and her new husband had fallen in love as they made their way through the arranged marriage process, and it showed. Pru introduced Antonio. They shook hands, then Francine hugged him, whispering, "Thank you for making my sister so happy." He nodded and looked at Pru like she hung the moon in the sky.

Pru said, "You certainly know how to bring life to a reception, Francine. Dragged kicking and screaming out of the last one by Royal Guardsmen and then engaged to Ichor-Delta royalty and set to wed your fiancé directly after our reception."

"You know me, always needing to be the center of attention."

Pru laughed, because Francine was the exact opposite of that. Raphael finally extracted himself from her parents, shook hands with the groom's parents and hugged up beside Francine in front of the bride and groom.

"Congratulations, Prudence and Antonio. I hope your life together is filled with joy and laughter," her royal fiancé said.

Francine was having a hard time being angry with Raphael for not telling her the whole truth. Admitting to herself that she hadn't shared her whole truth, either, she softened. He hadn't even been mad when she said another man's name after they made love.

Antonio said, "Thanks. It looks like you'll be joining my entrance into the married-man club later today yourself."

Raphael smiled widely and nodded. "Looks like it."

Pru took Francine's hands in hers, twisting their joined fingers to see the royal Boudreaux violet diamond better. "Your engagement ring is exquisite, Francine."

"Thank you." *I wonder if I get to keep it.*

Next up in line was, of course, her sister Ardelia and another possible battle ensued. "Hello, Francine. I'm uncertain if I should recognize you or not." Her gaze wandered from Francine's face and down the line to where their parents chatted with Raphael's father and brother. They were likely getting an earful about the coming surprise wedding.

"Well, since I'm getting married during the dinner service at Mother's insistence, I gather I'm back in the family."

Ardelia's gaze glittered, whether in jealousy or anticipation of a coming social humiliation, Francine wasn't certain. She wasn't certain who was more likely to embarrass her and Raphael, her mother or her eldest sister. Ardelia's husband, Percival, was a short, squat, balding man who was also very rich and very entitled, much like her eldest sister. He spoke fervently with another guest ahead of them in line, not paying any attention to either Ardelia or anyone else.

A memory of her eldest sister's extravagant wedding came into her mind. The bride and groom had both expressed a very loud, embarrassing hissy fit at the reception line when a guest had accidentally stepped on the edge of Ardelia's dress. The poor guest had departed the reception then and there, clearly humiliated, as Ardelia and her groom both smiled in satisfaction.

Francine hadn't witnessed the incident, as she'd been hiding among a throng of servants headed to their assigned tables, but Lucy and Axel had been close by, seeing the whole foolish event. She had long ago decided Ardelia and her husband, Percival, deserved each other.

Raphael joined her once more. This time, he settled his arm around her shoulders to keep her close. "Ardelia," he said, nodding once at her.

"Luther," she replied.

"I go by Raphael now."

"Do you?" Ardelia shrugged, sounding entirely unconcerned about him or what he wanted to be called.

Francine sent a questioning look at Raphael while her sister's eyes fixed on the front of the receiving line. She hadn't known the two were acquainted.

"I did some work for your sister once," Raphael said by way of explanation. "But it was a while back."

Francine's eyes narrowed in surprise. She asked Ardelia, "You hired a bounty hunter? What for?"

"None of your business," her sister hissed, grabbing her arm and squeezing hard. Francine snatched her arm away. Ardelia turned her venom on Raphael. "And you'd better not tell, either."

"Of course not. I'm a man of my word."

His word. Was he capable of keeping his word? That, of course, was debatable in light of what she'd just learned. She had to stuff her doubts way down inside to keep her fragile countenance acceptable for this venue.

Relax. He deserves a chance to explain.

Her biggest worry was that he would be the one to halt the pending surprise wedding. Francine didn't want to stop it. Even knowing he hadn't told her the whole truth about who he was, she believed he was a good guy. She was falling in love with him. She knew, given the chance, she would gladly and gratefully marry him. What did that say about her? That, for a second time in her life, she was too trusting. Was she letting her escalating love for this man get in the way of her reason?

Today had proven to be more surprising and difficult than expected and now she had to contend with Raphael not being entirely forthcoming about who he was. That, and the unplanned wedding at the end of this reception, had thrown her.

Seriously, what could go wrong next? As soon as the thought appeared in her mind, she should have banished it and cast a spell of forgiveness to keep any and all demons away.

Francine moved and Raphael stayed with her, nodding and smiling at the rest of the family members and attendants in the receiving line, including Lucy, Axel, Drucilla and her new husband.

Ushers waited at the end of the line to seat them at assigned tables. Apparently, it wasn't a first-come, first-served sort of reception.

Problematic, as she'd prefer to sit next to Lucy

and Axel, but whatever. Perhaps not knowing their lunch companions would make things easier.

Raphael hugged up close and said softly in her ear, "While I sense your annoyance with me and deserve your supreme irritation, we still need to present a united front, not only for—"

"Francine," a voice she never expected to hear again, interrupted her fake fiancé's lecture on how they should act. She turned to see a silver-eyed gaze boring into her with clear distaste.

Chapter 9

Raphael was slightly off his game after Francine's mother called their bluff and pushed them to prove they were truly engaged by getting married today. That after seeing his older brother and father for the first time in a decade attending a wedding they had not publicly announced their plan to attend. It was truly a banner day for shock and awe.

Even worse, Francine found out things about him that he should have told her himself.

He'd given Francine a story about the ring that, while true, was not the *whole* truth. He had gotten it *back* after performing a job for someone clever enough to acquire the precious family jewelry through trickery. Instead of returning it to his family, Raphael had kept the treasure for reasons he couldn't even explain fully to himself.

Besides, the ring had always been marked as his to give to a future bride, even though, at the time, he hadn't had anyone in mind. He hadn't met Francine yet and it was perfect for her.

The ring had slipped out of the family coffers through no fault of his and he'd completed a job to reacquire it. Now Francine assumed he'd lied to her about the ring and why he had such a treasure. Plus, he had for all intents and purposes outright fibbed and misled her about his role in the royal Boudreaux family, never expecting his relatives to show up at the Duvall-Roth wedding. Never expecting his brother to treat him civilly. His father, predictably, was furious from the word go. *Some things never change.*

He was about to tell Francine everything in a whispered report, hoping to win her forgiveness.

Until a man's voice said venomously, "Francine."

Raphael felt Francine shiver against him and looked up to see who had spoken. The silver-eyed man, a black scowl on his face, blocked their way. *Where did you come from?*

"I hadn't heard you were engaged, Francine," the stranger said in a mean voice.

"Well, now you know." The words were confident, but Raphael heard the uncertainty in her tone. The doubt he'd put there by not being as forthcoming as he should have been.

"I'm Raphael Boudreaux, Francine's fiancé. And you are?" Raphael moved, placing himself partly between them, and extended his hand. He'd love the chance to crush this man's fingers.

"Howard Reginald." He declined Raphael's hand, so Raphael dropped it.

"Is that so?" Raphael smiled thinly. *I know a secret about you, sir.*

Howard had an evil glint in his eye when he leaned into Raphael's personal space. "Does Francine still have the crescent moon-shaped beauty mark below her navel? I always wondered if it was real or fake."

Francine sucked in a horrified breath and her eyes glittered with unshed tears.

Raphael leaned to within inches of the other man's smug face. "Given that you betrayed her so brutally and cruelly, I don't really care if you ever learn the truth as to that private information." At normal volume, certain to be heard by anyone nearby, he added, "Bad bit of news about your cousin's escape. Has he been found yet?"

Howard's eyes widened as he took a step away from Raphael. His lips slammed shut until they formed a straight line. "No. They haven't. I mean…how did you…? I mean…I don't know what you're talking about."

His expression congealed so quickly, Raphael expected it to crack off his head. Howard shot Francine a fearful look, opened his mouth and then closed it.

Raphael straightened. "You owe Francine an apology, don't you, Howard? Why don't you tell her how sorry you are for all you've done?"

Howard looked like he'd rather swallow a barrel filled with glass. He drew in a huffy breath and frowned, clearly not ready to acquiesce. Raphael leaned in and whispered another threat. "I will see to it that every law enforcement agency in three galaxies knows who you are related to and suggest the authorities search your extensive properties with a fine-tooth comb. Do not test me, Howard. You will lose."

After several expressions flashed over his face, Howard finally said, "I'm sorry, Francine." The harsh whisper wasn't the apology Francine deserved, and Howard certainly didn't sound like he meant it, but Raphael decided it was as good as they would get under the circumstances.

Francine's lovely lips parted in surprise, but she didn't speak. Howard gave Raphael a sharp look, nodded once, turned on his heel and walked away like he had a stick shoved all the way up in a place where the sun never shines.

"How in the world did you do that?" Francine stared after Howard's retreating figure. "He never backs down. I wasn't certain he even knew the word 'sorry,' let alone ever allowed it to escape from between his lips." A look of awe shaped her features. "Whatever did you say to him?"

"Knowledge is power. I had some knowledge about his family and I shared the fact I knew it. Then I threatened to reveal the information to everyone and anyone." Raphael hoped he'd won back some points with her. Given her reaction to Howard and what he knew about the man, he had a good idea of what had taken place between them.

"Who is his cousin?"

Raphael said close to her ear, "Indigo Smith."

She gasped. "What? Is that true?"

"Yep. It's a distant connection, but the Reginald family spends a healthy batch of credits each year trying to keep that link out of the public eye whenever someone stumbles across any record of it."

"Huh."

"Shall we go sit down and discuss some things?"

"What things?"

"Today's wedding, perhaps?"

"The wedding?" She seemed confused.

"You know, *our* wedding."

"Oh, that." She sounded so disheartened, he could have kicked himself.

Raphael slid his arms around her. Softly, he suggested, "Or we could discuss my sordid past. I want you to know that I'm sorry I wasn't as forthcoming as I could have been about my family history. I thought I'd have more time to explain it to you."

Francine hugged him back. "Please, you don't have to explain anything to me. My parents are the ones forcing us to get married today. Before they can, they have to claim me as their daughter. I don't know how complicated that will be, especially given how I was treated at the last wedding."

Before he could reply, an usher approached to guide them to their assigned seats.

Raphael produced the invitation, the usher scanned it using a nifty device the size of a fat pen with a display that showed numbers and letters, likely their seats. He led them to a table in the front of the large room near the wedding party, as warranted by the Boudreaux family name. He expected his brother and father would join them at the premium spot for an even more uncomfortable discussion about the last estranged decade, his and Francine's surprise wedding, or any number of topics he wouldn't want to discuss with anyone, let alone William or his father.

Raphael checked the other four names indicated on the place settings as he and Francine circled to their seats, and breathed a sigh of relief when he didn't see his family's among them.

While they were still alone, Raphael took Francine's hand in both of his. "My father kicked me out of the family a decade ago for not bending to his every demand about the way I lived my life and my staunch refusal to wed the rich royal he'd chosen. I totally understand about arranged marriages, by the way. But that was the final straw for my father. He said I had to marry this horrid woman or I was going to be kicked out. I was delighted to go, although I knew I'd miss my brothers."

Francine's expression softened. "You truly don't have to explain, Raphael."

"You're sweet, but I do need to at this point. I always intended to tell you all of this after we made it through your sister's wedding. I didn't want to add to the stress of what was already on your mind."

"Okay."

He held the hand with his family ring. "This engagement ring is one of many in the Boudreaux family collection. It is the ring I was supposed to give to the woman I intended to marry. Several years after I left home, I discovered someone had sold it. I set up a plan to retrieve it from the person who'd purchased it. He wanted a favor to not only keep our transaction quiet, but also to return the ring. I *did* bring in a bounty to get the ring back."

Francine's smile made his heartbeat do double-time. "Okay. I'm glad you explained that to me."

"Good."

"Even though I'd already decided that whatever else, you are a good man. I know that much is true."

"Thank you. But don't let that get out. I'd be summarily dismissed from the biggest and baddest bounty hunter club in the galaxy."

Francine's laugh made his insides glow with love.

"What if we do get married today?"

"What? You really want to marry me?" She looked surprised.

"I do. I've never met anyone like you, Francine. I know it's rushed and not what we planned, but would you do me the honor of becoming my wife? It's only a matter of time. One way or another, I want to marry you. The when isn't as important as ensuring we spend the rest of our lives together."

Several expressions crossed her lovely face, surprise, confusion and then joy. "I would love to marry you, Raphael."

A harsh voice intruded on their sweet, forever-love moment. "Too bad he's already married to someone else."

Francine was absolutely exhausted from all the machinations at this wedding and reception. Her mother, with the *I'm calling your bluff* surprise marriage ceremony. Raphael's family showing up unexpectedly. Learning her fake fiancé truly *was* a member of a prestigious royal family on Ichor-Delta.

Seeing her ex-idiot boyfriend, Howard, after all this time, yet not having to face his attitude or his inherent cruelty because Raphael saved her. He'd even managed to force the idiot man to apologize to her. A miracle if there ever was one.

And now Raphael's father had just spitefully announced that Raphael was already married.

Drama. Drama. Drama. Totally exhausting.

Raphael stood up, his grip on her hand firm. "I'm not already married, Father. Stop trying to make waves where there are none."

Francine stood up beside Raphael. His father's tone was like that of her mother when her pride had been pricked. Much like her attitude about today's wedding.

"You might as well be married," the elder Boudreaux said. "The arranged marriage papers were signed when you were five years old. They are still binding."

"Except you kicked me out of the Boudreaux family a decade ago and your new spare son, Alex, can fulfill *that* obligation. Surely you resubmitted the paperwork when you booted me out."

His father tilted his head to one side as if looking at a curiosity in an Earther circus sideshow. "You didn't return here today intending to grovel your way back into the family?"

"No. I'm a bounty hunter. I plan to keep my job."

He pointed a gnarled finger at Francine's engagement ring. "Where did you get that family heirloom?"

"Well, after you allowed it to be stolen from the Boudreaux collection, I made a point of getting it back."

"How?"

"What does it matter? I did a favor for the person who purchased it, unaware it was stolen. I got it back. You're welcome."

"I did not say thank you, Luther." The man looked angry that Raphael had reclaimed a prized piece of family jewelry. Curious.

"I go by Raphael now."

"Well, *Raphael*, you still didn't return this family jewel after reacquiring it."

Raphael's eyes narrowed. "Was this jewel stolen or did you sell it?"

His father's expression hardened.

"Or worse, did you use it to pay someone off? A blackmailer, perhaps? A gaming enforcer?"

"How dare you?!"

"That's exactly what I was thinking when I found out it wasn't in the family safe anymore. Either way, I'm keeping the ring. It was given to me a long time ago."

"The ring wasn't hers to give."

"You're wrong. It was the only thing Mother did have to give to me."

Raphael's father narrowed his eyes and turned to Francine. "If you marry him, you'll regret it."

"No, I won't. I'll never have any regrets. Raphael is the finest person I know."

The old man laughed. It was a grating, unappealing sound. "That's not saying much, is it? Aren't you the same Francine Hayward Duvall who was kicked out of your family for doing something disgraceful? That's why you stick up for him. He helped you get into this little wedding affair so you could get back into *your* parents' good graces again, didn't he?"

Raphael released her hand and stepped forward, going toe to toe with his father.

The old man stood his ground, but his expression faltered.

In a tight voice, Raphael said, "Get away from her and do not speak another word to her, ever. Do not ruin this wedding reception because of your misplaced arrogance. You are a sad old man who gave away your chance to make amends with me long ago. You've spent over a decade furious that you were unable to bend your middle son to your will and too proud to ever back down or apologize for driving me away. That's all on you."

Francine put her arm around Raphael, wanting to comfort him. The sorrow in his tone as he spoke his mind to his father was hard to miss, even though he said it in a voice low enough that she barely heard him.

Raphael was a good man. He was trying to keep Pru's wedding from becoming a gossipmonger's dream come true. The elder Boudreaux sniffed a couple of times, refusing to look at Raphael. He walked away without another word.

Raphael sat down and took her hand in his. He sucked in a deep breath and let it out slowly. A smile surfaced soon after. He winked at her and asked, "Now, where were we before we were rudely interrupted?"

"We were deciding whether to get married today. But—"

"But?" He looked wounded.

"But I'm not going to let my mother bully us into it. We can get married today or wait to do it in our own good time."

Raphael smiled. "You are absolutely right. We can do whatever we want."

"Indeed. Because something else occurred to me just now."

"What's that?"

"If we get married today, I'm certain the news will get out like rocket-fueled missiles all through the galaxy."

He shrugged. "I don't care."

"Won't that ruin the rest of our trip? I don't know where we're going, but I know we're supposed to be looking for wedding, reception and honeymoon destinations. Right?"

His eyes widened with realization. "You're right. I can't believe I forgot about that." He looked around the room. Most of the seats had filled up and the bridal party was moving from the receiving line to the designated table at the front of the room.

Lucy and Axel walked by on their way to the family table, stopping to hug and congratulate Francine and Raphael.

Once they were alone again, Francine told Raphael her plan. "We'll wait until after Pru and her husband are safely away before letting my mother know we've decided to go ahead with our small private affair and not bother her with a wedding tonight. If she puts up a fuss, I'll tell her she won't be invited. That should keep her from acting out or making a scene. Trust me, her ultimate goal is a link with the Boudreaux royal name. I don't believe she'll risk that in order to press us if we turn her down."

"Okay." Raphael kissed her hand. "Good plan."

The other two couples at their table were strangers to both of them, but clearly knew each other. They chatted and made light, harmless conversation throughout the meal without making Francine or Raphael uncomfortable. It was a needed respite after moving through the receiving line, fraught with tension and gossip, to get in here.

Francine was relieved not to have to fight off any further drama or fake a smile throughout a horrid, long wedding luncheon with mean people.

Applause sent Pru and her husband off on their honeymoon trip as small birds with black and purple feathers, representing the color of the Ichor-Delta mountains, were released to fly over an old-fashioned crystal carriage pulled by four Ichor-Delta beasts called brays.

The equine-like creatures were smaller, shorter and stockier than horses and they had thick, dark fur like an Earther bear. The fur had been trimmed into elaborate designs highlighted with glittery powder. One side featured the groom's family crest, the other, the bride's family crest. After the wedding celebration, the brays would be shaved so their fur could grow long enough in about a month to be trimmed for the next wedding.

Raphael explained the Ichor-Delta custom to Francine as they followed the crowd outdoors to see the newly married couple off on their journey together.

Francine took Raphael's hand as they made their way slowly back to the reception hall. Her mother had told all the guests right before exiting the room to be sure to return promptly for a surprise. Except her mother was about to be the one surprised.

Right before they entered, Raphael pulled her back and said, "Want to make a run for it? I don't think they'll be able to catch us."

Francine laughed, put a forefinger up to her mouth and tapped her upper lip a few times as she pretended to think about it.

Yet another familiar voice cut through the murmurs of the straggling guests entering the reception hall to yell, "Francine!" Uncle Bandore.

At least she didn't have to run and hide from him this time. Francine turned. "Uncle Bandore," she said, trying to sound happy to see him.

"Good heavens, girl. What have you done to yourself?" He pointed to her hair and wrinkled his nose, making clear his distaste. Whether he didn't like the short style or the new color or both was anyone's guess.

"New life. New hair," was all she said with a shrug.

Uncle Bandore looked at Raphael. "Say, I know you. You're the wretched crust fish staying next door at my hotel."

"Uncle Bandore! That's not nice."

"Well, he wouldn't let me in to use the comms."

"The world does not revolve around you." Francine stared him down.

He looked affronted, but his expression softened.

"I did call down and have them send someone to you," Raphael said in his own defense. "Did they fix your device?"

Uncle Bandore made a face. "Yes. Eventually they came up and fixed it."

"Seconds after the call was made, then?" Francine asked.

"Don't be impertinent, young lady. The good news is that your hair isn't terrible. Your mother probably had a fit over it, though, didn't she?" He laughed and added, "What is this surprise, anyway? Do you know?"

"Surprise?" Francine asked, buying time.

"I mean, this wedding has been an endless affair already, hasn't it? The ceremony drenched in peach, the endless reception line, the nine-course luncheon seated with strangers, lengthy explanations about traditions from both sides of the family. It's been exhausting and now we have to go back for more?"

"Well, there is a dinner planned, which is an Ichor-Delta tradition." Francine turned to Raphael, who nodded in confirmation.

As expected, that perked her uncle up. Uncle Bandore always loved a free meal. "You don't say. Well, that's grand. I guess I could go in and see about this surprise and try out more tasty dishes.

The lunch was very good. Didn't you think it was good?"

They both nodded.

Uncle Bandore gave a little salute and headed back into the reception hall. Francine and Raphael followed a few paces behind him. Raphael was quiet as her mind raced a thousand miles an hour, trying to figure out what she'd say to her mother about the surprise wedding.

Two steps from the threshold, Raphael leaned close. "Last chance to run for it."

"She'd hunt us down."

"Do you know what you plan to say?"

"Not exactly. Do you have any suggestions?"

He shook his head. Francine thought maybe she could feign illness or tell her mother she hurt her knee and didn't want to limp down the aisle. "Maybe I have an idea."

"Awesome. You should definitely do the talking then." He laughed, turning the sound into a cough when her mother hurried to stand in front of them.

"I have terrible news," she said, looking genuinely distressed.

"What is it?"

"You won't be able to get married today."

"We won't?" Francine and Raphael said at the exact same time.

"We don't have the official form filled out and stamped by the wedding authority here on Ichor-Delta. On Alpha-Prime it wouldn't be a problem, but here the marriage authority is very strict about such things. Worse, the place to get the official form is closed for the day and the officiant refuses to marry anyone without it."

"That *is* bad news," Francine said, desperately trying to keep the relief out of her tone. Not that she didn't want to marry Raphael, she did. She just wanted to plan her own wedding in her own way.

Adeline sniffed, looking quite distraught.

"What's wrong, Mother?"

The older woman's gaze lifted. "I wanted to say… Well… I'm so truly sorry for how we treated you at Drucilla's wedding, Francine. How *I* treated you. It was too much."

Whoa! That was a surprise. Her parents did not believe in being sorry or expressing regret. First Howard and now another miracle in her mother saying sorry. Raphael must have an aura that forced others to express overdue forgiveness or something.

Raphael's expression was quizzical, as if he couldn't understand her mother's distress or apology. If Francine didn't know better, she would think her mother was about to cry.

"I'm not going to lie, Mother. You really hurt my feelings. I wasn't bothering anyone. No one noticed me except you."

"I know. I was horrid. Can you ever forgive me?" A tear rolled down her face. Adeline Duvall never cried.

"I suppose so."

"Will you let me come to your wedding?"

She exchanged a meaningful glance with Raphael. "Yes. If we have a wedding, you will be invited."

"*If* you have a wedding?" Her mother's voice turned harsh. "What do you mean by that?"

"We might elope," Francine said.

"Elope?" She looked aghast. Rich people like her parents and their peers loved all the pomp and circumstance of a complicated wedding. An elopement was unthinkable in their world.

Raphael spoke up. "Actually, we planned an extension of this trip. We're going to look at a few wedding venues and honeymoon destinations on the way back to the Earth colony."

"I see." She looked relieved. No doubt she thought even a small wedding was better than eloping. "Well, please let me know if you need any help. Even if it's a small wedding, I know that we could make it beautiful."

Francine nodded. "I'll contact you once we get back to Earth when we decide our exact plans."

"Thank you, Francine. That would be lovely." She brushed the tear from her cheek. "Would it be all right with you both if I announce your engagement and coming wedding to the dinner guests?"

Raphael cleared his throat. "As long as you don't tie us down to a particular date. We aren't certain with our schedules exactly when we'll get married."

She nodded, hugged them both and turned to go back inside.

Raphael lifted Francine's hand and kissed the backs of her fingers. "I feel like we just escaped certain death and adrenalin is still pumping through my veins. Not that I didn't want to marry you today, I would have, but I truly need to visit the places next up on our trip to help a friend."

"No worries. I feel the same way. Like I've just run Ichor-Delta fast around the planet a few times."

Raphael smiled at her reference of running Ichor-Delta fast, adding, "After dinner, we'll head back to the hotel. Our flight isn't until early afternoon, so we can sleep in."

"Awesome."

"We can take our time, lounge around and have brunch delivered to the room. What do you say?"

"Sounds like my fiancé—who's not fake anymore—has figured out that the fastest way to my heart is sleeping late along with room service brunch. He's a smart man."

"We just like the same things."

"I'm so glad. So, what will we do tonight, back in the room, all alone together?" she asked with a mischievous grin.

Raphael's gaze simmered with intensity. "I'm sure we'll think of something," he said in a sexy voice.

Chapter 10

Early the next afternoon, Raphael helped Francine into the vehicle he'd hired to take them to the spaceport. The morning had been a whirlwind of activity, even though they'd slept in and had a long, luxurious brunch in their room.

They stayed up late talking about all the unspoken things they'd held back. He told her how and why he'd been kicked out of his home and family. She told him about Howard and what he'd done to her long ago. If Raphael had known what an unmitigated villain he'd been to Francine, he might have announced the man's relationship to Indigo Smith a little louder at the reception and then invited him outside for a thrashing.

It was late when Francine finally fell asleep wrapped in his arms. He swore to himself he'd never lie to her ever again. Not for any reason.

Once he figured out if he could help Victor with his bounty problem, he pondered the impact of Francine being in his life. Kissing her forehead as she sighed in her sleep, he wondered how he'd managed to live without her.

Being a bounty hunter was often a lonely profession. Until recently, he hadn't minded it so much. He rarely slept in the same bed more than two nights in a row. He spent lots of time traveling, tracking and trying to figure out and find his quarry as quickly as possible. Then it was on to the next bounty, the next hunt, the next lonely trip.

Cam's offer of a security position on the Earth colony at the Big Bang Truck Stop was becoming more and more appealing. Sure, he'd miss some aspects of being a galactic bounty hunter, but having Francine to come home to each and every night was something he looked forward to.

They could get a house or he could move into her place and help take care of her little black kitten, Angel. He could maybe take a couple of interesting bounties a few times a year to keep his skills sharp and he could look forward to seeing Francine when he got back.

The life he painted for them was truly an idea he hadn't realized he was interested in until all the unusual aspects of this trip gave him something new to consider. Something new to look forward to. Something new to end an adventurous life he was growing tired of continuing anyway.

Maybe it *was* time to settle down. Maybe he would make a life on Earth with Francine and never look back.

The vehicle slowed to a stop, throwing Raphael out of his reverie. The driver said, "Here we are, sir."

Raphael exited and held the door for Francine as the driver removed their bags from the back of the vehicle.

"How long is the flight?"

"Not long. We're headed for Alpha-Prime first, but just to pick up some travelers there. We don't even have to disembark unless you want to. Then on to our final destination. Total time will be less than three hours." He expected a message to be delivered once they docked on Alpha-Prime.

"Good." Francine looked very relaxed this afternoon and it suited her.

Raphael had sent his questions to a friend in the bounty hunter office dispatch on Alpha-Prime. Bly Zendorr was a cousin of a well-connected family, but as a poor relation he didn't have access to the kind of wealth his relatives did. Even so, many friends of his exalted family confided in him. He was often in possession of *extra* information that he'd add to special dossiers for various bounties.

Well, not for just anyone. Raphael and Zendorr were friends. They came from similar circumstances, as Raphael was formerly from a lofty family and making it on his own. Zendorr often gave him surprisingly helpful tidbits of information that aided Raphael in tricky captures.

They were right on time for their departure. He'd procured first-class tickets, not only for the comfort, but also to ensure anyone noticing them would only see a rich couple on holiday and all that implied.

The spaceship jetted out of port a minute early. In no time, they landed on Alpha-Prime to take on additional passengers.

The steward opened the door to the outside dock. An official Alpha-Prime security messenger waited with an electronic clipboard and a flat package. The messenger handed the steward the clipboard to sign, then the package. The steward brought the package immediately to Raphael.

Francine quirked an eyebrow as he looked around for a private place to open it. A small study next to the restrooms held a desk along one wall and a square table centered in the room with a chair tucked beneath one side. He went inside, locked the door behind him and ripped open the security seal before even sitting down.

He'd hoped Victor might have sent a message to let him know exactly where he was located on the Ossuary Valerian Space Station. It wasn't from Victor.

Inside was Zendorr's carefully crafted dossier covering the events that had taken place, explaining what had happened and why there was a giant bounty on Victor. Zendorr wasn't able to add any information that Raphael didn't already know, but he appreciated that his friend had made the effort.

The bounty was staggering, ten times the highest he'd ever heard of. It probably set a record. If it were anyone but Victor, Raphael would be on the hunt and ready to accept the riches. That was bad news, because it meant every bounty hunter in every known galaxy would be on the hunt for his friend.

Raphael sighed, read through the entire document one more time to commit it to memory, then put it in the room's flash-burn device. He pushed the button, reducing the contents to ash in half a second. No one else needed to have such a comprehensive list of information about Victor.

He used a fresh digital message pouch from the supply in the desk to send a return message to Zendorr, thanking him for his information. He also mentioned he might stay on the Earther colony and to send any further messages to him there; he'd pick them up as he was able.

He sealed the pouch and left the room to give it to the steward, who swiped and pushed several times on his electronic clipboard, sending a digital receipt to Raphael's comms device.

Raphael returned to his seat in time to see five new travelers enter the first-class area. Two couples were dressed smartly for intergalactic first-class travel. The fifth, a very tall, large woman, wasn't even dressed for third class. Her clothes looked dirty, dusty and hopelessly filled with cuts and holes, like she'd made her way to the port by way of the Outer Rim on foot in a lashing windstorm filled with glass particles. The steward tried to direct her to the next section down the hall, away from first class, but the woman frowned and whipped out her ticket, shoving it in the steward's face.

"See? I belong here!" she said in a deep, angry voice.

The steward backed down immediately. "Of course you do, madam. Let me show you to your seat. May I bring you a refreshing beverage?"

Once the two couples and the angry woman were settled and all sipping refreshing beverages, the transport ship sailed into space, headed for a short refueling stop on the Ossuary Valerian Space Station. All the passengers would disembark at that time as a safety precaution.

Raphael and Francine planned to pretend to do some shopping in the spaceport. Once the spaceship had left for its next destination, Raphael would ensure no one had followed them. Once he was assured they were truly alone, he would escort Francine to the small home he'd rented for a whole week.

Hopefully, no one would expect them to leave the Ossuary Valerian Space Station in only two days on a late-night—or middle of the night—transport back to the Earth colony with a short stop at a more wedding and honeymoon-friendly destination. Their original flight plan included, the Gothic Ice Floe Planet. The one they were truly taking included Lava Rock World instead before heading back to the Earth colony.

Raphael had conceived the intricate travel plans

to ensure he didn't lead anyone to Victor. He wanted to help his longtime friend, not make things worse.

The rental house was situated in the heart of the city, within walking distance of several places to eat and shop. The homes on either side of the pricy rental were not so close that they could hand a cup of sugar to each other through aligned windows, but still within shouting distance. They'd have to be careful not to raise their voices and accidentally give away any relevant information about Victor.

A waist-high iron fence surrounded the property.

Francine alighted from the transport looking not a bit travel worn in her soft, gauzy white blouse and emerald-green slacks. She looked like a rich debutant on holiday. Her lovely red hair brushing her shoulders made him want to forget what he was doing and plunge his fingertips in the soft tresses and kiss her senseless. The driver took their luggage from the back of the transport and carried it through the decorative iron gate all the way to the small porch at the front door.

Raphael barely paid any attention to the driver as he stared at Francine. She was his future. His love. His reward for living alone for so long, feeling like he was unworthy of anyone good.

"Sir," he heard from what seemed like a long distance. "Sir?" the driver repeated, zipping him out of his daydreams. "Will that be all?"

"Yes. Sorry. Yes." Raphael needed to pay attention. He had a job to do. Help Victor.

"I'll contact you again in a week when we're ready to depart."

"Yes, sir. I'd be happy to set that up now."

Raphael hesitated. He glanced in Francine's direction. She stood looking at the house, seemingly captivated. A breeze ruffled her beautiful cinnamon hair. This engineered space station asteroid was exactly like being on a small planet.

"Sure," he said absently. He gave the driver a date and time without taking his gaze from his fiancée, the first real one he'd ever had.

"Very good, sir. I'll be here promptly."

Raphael gave the man a generous tip and approached his bride-to-be. "What do you think?"

"It's charming and very historic looking."

"It's one of the oldest homes still standing in the city. I gather there was vast repair work on the outside to make it look exactly like it used to and equally massive renovations inside, of course, to make it modern so they can charge more." The stone façade in varying shades and sizes of burgundy with tan stones forming the trim made the two-story home look stately, even if it was an older house.

She grinned. "Of course. Historic often means very expensive."

"Shall we go inside?"

At her nod, he grabbed her hand and led her down the central walkway, up four steps to the landing under a small overhang. He unlocked the burgundy door and opened it, gesturing for her to enter as he moved the bags from the porch to just inside.

"Wow," she said, crossing the threshold into the two-story entryway.

The home was relatively small, only three bedrooms, with three-and-a-half bathrooms. The large master bedroom was downstairs on the other side of the house from the living room, dining room and kitchen areas. There was a full bathroom directly off the living room.

The other two bedrooms, each with a full bathroom, were upstairs. From a small alcove next to the kitchen, an old staircase led to an unfinished storage space in the basement. The only finished spot down there was a half bathroom that looked like it was original to the house.

As lovely as it was, Raphael had rented the house with a specific purpose in mind. It suited his needs perfectly.

After a quick tour of the main level, Raphael left Francine in the master bedroom while he fetched their luggage from the foyer. He'd been out of her sight for less than a minute when Francine's heart-stopping scream pierced the air.

Raphael dropped the bags and raced toward the bedroom. Before he could reach it, her earsplitting cream cut off and silence filled the space.

The instant quiet sounded so much worse.

✦

Francine floated through her day like she lived on a cloud. The trip from Ichor-Delta to Alpha-Prime, then to this unusual space station created on an ancient asteroid had been idyllic. A small part of her wondered if she was dreaming, but then Raphael would kiss her hand or her lips and she knew it was real.

Prudence's wedding was behind them and Francine was very satisfied with how things had turned out. She had initially only hoped to escape her parents' wrath or being called out or, worst of all, kicked out of Pru's wedding, sent to Earth and billed for a second expensive trip to the colony planet. One she would be hard-pressed to afford.

Now she was engaged to a member of Ichor-Delta royalty, even if Raphael wasn't interested in being reinstated into the family he'd been separated from for a decade. He also seemed content with how things had turned out. He mentioned that his brother, William, had requested a meeting in the near future to catch up and set things right. "Whatever that means," Raphael said, but smiled as though he was eager to find out what his brother meant.

All in all, this trip had been an exuberant success for all involved.

Francine was charmed by the house Raphael had rented for their stay on the Ossuary Valerian Space Station, or rather the aged engineered asteroid. As a rule, she wasn't typically enamored with old homes.

Not because they weren't charming and nostalgic, but because Lucy—who read everything—once told her about a refurbished home on this space station that had been haunted, with specters popping up out of the floorboards to terrorize any and all who dared trespass.

The thought of someone popping out of the floorboards gave her a chill, though she didn't truly believe in such things. Did she?

No, she did not.

Shaking off her foolish fears, Francine peeked into the adjoining master bathroom, noticing a beautiful double-sink counter and a lovely large tub she planned to make use of later. Perhaps she'd invite Raphael to join her for a good, long soak.

The creak of a floorboard behind her sent her pulse pounding. She banished the stupid fear to the back of her mind...until she turned and saw the menacing strange man looming over her, dusted in white chalk from head to toe with what looked like a planet full of spider webs clinging to his frame. The shriek came from the very depths of her terrified soul. She closed her eyes and bolted for the door.

The ghost grunted as she tried to pass him, grabbing her faster than she could move out of the way. A big, meaty, dusty hand covered her nose and mouth, cutting off not only the scream, but her air supply. The specter's other arm wound around her body and yanked her against him, struggling, horrified and quickly losing the ability to breathe.

Francine heard thunderous footsteps coming from the direction of the front of the house. *Raphael!*

The man closing off her precious oxygen intake spoke in her ear, "I'm sorry I scared you. Please don't scream again, okay?" He sounded less ghost-like and more…like a reasonable, corporeal being. What was going on?

Raphael charged into the room, the expression on his face murderous. The minute he saw them in an intimate position, Raphael stopped cold. He squinted, like he couldn't believe what he was seeing.

"Victor? What are you doing here?"

Victor?

Francine didn't have time to think about who might have arrived for a visit, she was dangerously close to passing out from lack of air. She sagged in her captor's arms. He released his hand from her face immediately. She staggered, taking a wobbly step toward Raphael and sucking in deep breaths of air.

Raphael was by her side in a flash, holding her up, running his hand thorough her hair, uttering question after question, asking if she was okay. She couldn't immediately speak. She was trying to breathe.

"I'm so sorry," Victor said. "I panicked when you screamed."

Francine nodded. In a weak voice, she said, "That's okay. I'm okay now."

"No, it's not," Raphael said angrily. "I told you not to appear until after dark."

"I couldn't wait."

"Why not?"

"Someone found me."

"Who?"

"Don't know. That's why I scurried up here."

Francine was confused. *What is going on here? Where had Victor been hiding? How had he gotten into the room? Was she really dead and only dreaming all of this?*

The sudden and very hostile pounding on the front door made Francine jump. At least she was in Raphael's arms. He squeezed her tight, once. "I'll go see who wants to break our door down, okay?"

"Yes. I'm fine. Really. Just had a good scare, you know?"

"Again, I'm really sorry." Victor, who looked like the Ghost of Christmas Past, did look and sound sincere.

Pound. Pound. Pound. The front door practically rattled in its frame.

"Good grief, what are they knocking with, a tree trunk?"

Raphael released her and strode out of the room, leaving her with Victor Campion. How extraordinary.

Francine looked down at her white shirt, liberally coated in pale gray dust and whatever Victor had all over his clothes. She brushed her palms over her shirt and slacks, trying to dislodge what she could. Victor looked sheepish and started doing the same thing to his clothes. After a few pats of his large hands, it looked worse.

"Stop. That's not helping. You're going to need soap and water to clean up," Francine said, pointing to the bathroom. "Or perhaps you could just burn your outfit and start over."

His low bark of laughter was unexpected, but he took a step in the direction of the bathroom.

Pound. Pound.

Francine heard Raphael open the front door with an exasperated greeting. She had gotten most of the dust off, but decided not to appear next to Raphael, at least not until she heard the unmistakable voice of a woman echo in the foyer.

Who could that be?

Without thinking it through, Francine walked purposefully toward the front door in time to see an achingly beautiful woman with raven-black hair and blazing blue eyes throw her arms around Raphael's neck and hug him. When the woman looked like she was about to kiss him on the mouth, Francine made a noise somewhere between a growl of fury and a grunt of warning.

The woman stopped her assault on Raphael to flash fierce baby blues in Francine's direction.

Raphael, arms at his sides, had not moved to hug the woman in return.

Francine marched forward, shot her hand out and

said, "Hello, I'm Francine Hayward Duvall, Raphael's fiancée. And you are?"

"Raphael?" she said. Even her voice was beautiful.

"That's the name I go by now," Raphael said, taking a half step back from the most beautiful female Francine had ever seen.

"Really? Why?"

"Because I didn't think he looked like a Luther. So he changed it for me. His fiancée." Francine tilted her head to one side. "I'm sorry. I didn't catch your name."

"I'm Elda Lark. Pleased to meet you." The woman nodded once in Francine's direction.

"She's the bounty hunter I told you about," Raphael said.

"The fake fiancée bounty hunter?" Raphael nodded.

Francine was aghast. "You pretended to be engaged to *her*?"

Raphael and Elda looked at each other. He said, "Yes. Why?"

Francine sighed. "But she's so...beautiful. I'd been hoping she looked like an oily, stink-reeking crust fish that'd been left in the sun too long. But she doesn't."

Nobody said anything for a full count of three. Then Elda laughed, long and hard, even bending at the waist in her mirth.

Raphael smiled. "Are you jealous of Elda?"

Francine's eyebrows rose in sudden embarrassment. "Maybe."

"She's like the sister I never had. I promise, Francine. You do not have to be jealous. Right, Elda?"

Elda straightened up, nodding because she was laughing too hard to answer verbally. After she settled, she said, "He's like the brother I never wanted. No worries. But I'm stealing that oily, stink-reeking crust fish line. That's hilarious."

Francine laughed along with her for a moment, but her mind spun furiously. She figured out quite a few things in the next few seconds that passed. Elda was a bounty hunter. She was looking for someone. Victor was mere steps away in the master bedroom covered in dust and spider webs, clearly hiding in a dusty, horrid place. He was on the run with a bounty on his head. It didn't take a genius to put two and two together and arrive at four.

What would happen if Elda discovered that Victor Campion was here? Nothing good.

Chapter 11

Raphael closed the front door. Now that he'd headed off the jealousy train, it wasn't a stretch to imagine why Elda Lark, the fierce female bounty hunter, was here, but he asked the question anyway. "What are you doing here, Elda? How did you even know where I was?"

Elda's expression hardened, all amusement gone. "What if I told you I'm on the hunt for a bounty?"

"What bounty?" He could guess.

Elda's features flattened. "Victor Campion."

"What makes you think that I know anything?"

"You two are best friends. At least you used to be. Let's call it a hunch. I figured that if I followed you across the galaxy, you might eventually lead me to him." *Yep. Right again.*

There was an appropriate saying on Alpha-Prime for this very situation. *Space Potatoes!*

"Bad luck." Raphael shook his head, trying to figure out a way to get her to leave. Not that it would do much good. Even if she left, she'd likely still tail them to the ends of the galaxy.

"What's bad luck?"

"You following me here is a big waste of your time. I just escorted my fiancée to her sister's wedding on Ichor-Delta and now we are searching for a wedding and honeymoon venue for our own nuptials." *Plus, I won't let you take Victor. No matter what.*

"A wedding on Ossuary Valerian? That's odd, isn't it?"

Raphael shrugged. "We like the unusual. Don't we, Francine?"

"That's right. My sister Lucy used to tell me all kinds of spooky stories about this old space station built on an ancient asteroid. I've always wanted to come here and to do something special. A wedding seemed perfect."

Elda snorted. "Where are you going on your honeymoon, Lava Rock World?"

"No," Raphael said. "The Gothic Ice Floe Planet." He looked at Francine and winked.

She immediately perked up. "Really? That was supposed to be a surprise, wasn't it?"

"Yep."

His lovely and very smart fiancée turned to Elda and said, "And you had to ruin it."

"Me? I didn't ruin anything." Elda looked put out.

"Sure you did. You had to make fun of our special day by being a pest until Raphael told you what we were doing. I think you should leave." Francine pursed her lips and looked genuinely unhappy.

Elda made a face. "I'm sorry if I ruined anything, but I'm looking for a big bounty."

"Oh, and you think we have some big bounty here? For crying out loud, we've only been here for five minutes. And we're trying to be alone, if you get my drift." Francine threw her hands up in total exasperation.

"I'm happy to leave. Just as soon as I take a look around this house." Elda's gaze went to the staircase leading to the second floor. "What's upstairs?"

Raphael was about to say, "Nothing," but before he could speak, Francine marched to the bottom step, crossed her arms and practically dared Elda to try and get past her.

"You are *not* invited upstairs." Francine extended an arm and pointed to the door. "Please leave."

"There's nothing up there anyway," Raphael offered.

Elda tilted her head to one side. Raphael knew what that meant. She was about to go into battle mode and mow Francine down in order to search the empty upstairs bedrooms.

"Elda," he warned. "Do not touch Francine."

"I won't," she said, moving swiftly across the foyer. "I can squeeze by."

Elda was at a dead run by the time she got to the base of the staircase. Francine dodged to the right for the block, but Elda had fast reflexes. She feinted right, darted left and went past Francine easily, not even touching her as she bounded up the stairs two at a time. Her laugh of triumph sounded as she reached the top stair and disappeared into the first bedroom. She stomped out of that room's en suite and entered the second bedroom and attached bathroom. They heard every step she took.

Raphael winked at Francine, who grinned and winked back.

He counted on Elda wanting to search the master bedroom once she'd scoured the second floor. Victor had surely heard them at the door and returned to his hidey-hole below the floorboards. A hatch led into a hidden basement that wasn't on the house's registered plans and not connected to the unfinished basement.

Victor had always said he'd never be caught dead in the former home of one of his Campion ancestors because of all the ghost stories associated with the place.

That is, until he came of age and learned the secret of the place. The hidden cellar under the master bedroom was a weapons room when the house was built, serving as an escape route if the enemy breached the building.

Raphael walked quickly and quietly to the master bedroom and peeked inside. Someone had placed a rug over the hatch. When Victor disappeared, he had left one corner folded up.

Raphael fixed the rug and rejoined Francine at the base of the staircase. "I love you," he said in a voice meant for her ears alone.

"I love you, too."

He lowered his mouth to hers, intending only a brief peck, but she licked his bottom lip and he couldn't resist a deeper, more thorough and downright passionate kiss.

Elda was stomping around the upstairs even more loudly, no doubt annoyed to discover they'd told her the truth. No one was upstairs. She trudged downstairs, nudging them apart as she passed by and breaking their passionate embrace.

"Hey!" Francine said. "Are you through? We have plans."

"Plans. What plans?" Elda said distractedly, glancing at the door to the master bedroom. "Is that another bedroom?"

"It's the master bedroom," Raphael said. "Trust me, no one is in there."

"Maybe I don't trust you when it comes to Victor Campion," Elda retorted and walked toward the master bedroom. Raphael followed her and Francine followed him.

Raphael entered the room and stood on the rug he'd just straightened. He crossed his arms and tried his best to look impatient. Mostly he was concerned that Elda knew about the hiding place and was about to uncover it.

Elda started with the half-closed bathroom door, popping it open, banging it against the inside wall. She looked around once before backing out. She marched to the walk-in closet and threw one door open, then the other. She was probably ready to say, "Ah-ha!" each time, but Victor wasn't there. Thankfully.

Francine seated herself on the padded chest at the foot of the bed and crossed one leg over the other. He could see a dusty spot on her shoulder where Victor had left a smudge.

Elda, thwarted by the empty closet, dropped to the floor and stuck her head under the bed. She stood up, her expression thoroughly annoyed. "Where is he, Raphael?"

"Don't know, Elda."

"And you wouldn't tell me if you did." Hands braced on her hips, Elda's gaze wandered around the room. She huffed, dropped her hands and stomped out of the master bedroom. Francine and Raphael trailed her.

"You've searched the entire home, Elda. I'm telling you, he's not here. You are wasting your time." He wondered how many times he'd have to repeat himself.

She whirled around. "Maybe I am for now, but eventually, I know you two will find a way to meet and I intend to be there." Elda walked to the front door. "You haven't seen the last of me."

"Thanks for the warning," Francine quipped as Elda slammed the front door.

Raphael locked and bolted it. He hurried back into the master bedroom, shoved aside the rug and opened the hatch. Victor waited on the ladder, suspended above the dirt floor of the hidden basement. He reached a hand up and Raphael pulled him into the room.

"There are no windows in the master bath, so you can go get cleaned up. And I've brought some clothes for you to change into."

"Thanks, Raphael. After this, I'll owe you ten times what you ever owed me."

"Don't worry about that now."

Victor moved into the bathroom and closed the door.

Raphael turned to Francine, who stood in the doorway. "I'm sorry we won't have any alone time this evening."

She shook her head. "Not to worry. You allowed me the joy of seeing my sister's wedding without being humiliated. I'll be eternally grateful." She added, "It just occurs to me that I'm the only one of the Duvall Five that's not married yet. There have been four weddings and now there's just me."

"Not for long." Raphael watched her as he dragged the case he'd brought with clothing for Victor toward the bedroom. She was beautiful. He stopped in the doorway and said, "I want you to know that if you decide you want a big wedding, I'm happy to oblige you."

"Really?"

"Of course."

"I'll think about it. Long ago, I did picture having a big production of a wedding, because I knew that's what my mother would do regardless of my feelings. After Howard, I didn't care if I ever got married or even who my husband would be. The arranged marriages didn't make a jot of difference to me."

"And now?"

"I guess…I'm not sure. I don't care if we elope or if everyone in an entire galaxy witnesses our ceremony. I truly just want to be married to you." She shrugged and grinned at him.

"Good, because I want the exact same thing."

The bathroom door opened and Victor stuck his head out. "I need the clothing you mentioned, unless you want me to run naked through the house."

Thus ending their sweet moment. Raphael planned to discuss the subject again to ensure she got exactly the wedding she wanted, whatever size or shape it ended up being.

Once Victor was suitably attired, Raphael ensured all the windows were closed and the curtains covered them in the living room. He turned on the perimeter fence security warning system. If anyone tried to get through the gate or any window or door, he'd be notified. If any breach occurred, a siren would go off.

"I'm not certain what I can do for you, Victor, but I'm willing to do anything to help."

"I appreciate it. I'm not certain what to do beyond hide."

"What happened? I read a limited dossier that didn't reveal much."

"Few people know what I'm about to tell you. There was an attempt on my father's life. I'm the heir and I'm an only child."

"The information I saw said it was more than an attempt. That he was assassinated."

Victor nodded. "My father survived, although he has not regained consciousness yet. I had that information circulated, hoping to buy time to figure out who ordered the attempt. Perhaps flush out the culprit. Then a bounty was placed on me, and I was blamed for the attempt. I did not do it."

"Of course not."

Francine said, "If your father was gone and you were jailed for his murder, who would the title go to?"

Victor smiled. "She's a smart one." Raphael nodded.

"The answer is complicated, and it depends who you talk to. There are basically two factions that would vie for my father's title if I were out of the way. Claudia and Roger are distant blood cousins. Each has a fairly equal claim if my father and I were dead or jailed for an Imperial crime."

Raphael crossed his arms. "My money's on Claudia. Roger is afraid of his own shadow and was always small for his age. He's allergic to everything, a hypochondriac or ill most of the time and rarely leaves home."

"True. But Roger's mother, Alvina, is the opposite. She could give Claudia a run for her money in the devious department, if you know what I mean." Victor's eyes narrowed and he added, "Weren't you supposed to marry Claudia?"

Raphael's gaze slid to Francine. Her eyes widened as he nodded. "My father wanted that arranged marriage, but I left home because I refused to follow through on it, among other issues."

"Maybe you should renew your acquaintance with her," Francine said.

"What?!" both Raphael and Victor said at the same time.

"It seems to me that if she's the one involved in this, and has gone to the expense and lengths she's had to in order to carry off the murder of a royal—or the attempted murder of one—and a frame-up for Victor, she's not looking to share her spoils with a co-ruler, right? She will want to remove you from the picture promptly. With that knowledge a possibility right up front, maybe you could set a trap and trip her up."

"She *is* a smart one. How did you get so lucky?" Victor asked with a certain amount of awe.

"I followed her around like a stalker until an appropriate meet-and-greet opportunity presented itself." Raphael winked at her.

"You did not."

"Oh, yes, I did."

Francine thought about the night they'd met outside the supermarket and how it had changed her life. "Well, I'm glad."

"Still want me to seek out Claudia and make a play for her?"

"No, but I think it's the easiest way to find out if she's the one doing this to Victor and his poor father."

The three of them spent another hour trying to think up other ideas, but in the end, Francine's was unanimously voted the best.

A piercing sound reverberated through the house. They all stood up.

"The gate alarm," Raphael said, shouting to be heard.

Seconds later, the pounding on the front door made all three of them freeze in place for a couple of seconds before they started moving. Victor had only taken two steps toward the master bedroom and his bolt-hole when a bright flash and a loud boom popped the front door wide, a burning hole seared through the middle of it.

As the smoke cleared, Elda Lark strode in with a large pistol in each hand, one of which she pointed at Victor, the other she moved between Raphael and Francine.

"I knew you were lying to me, Raphael," she said triumphantly. "Victor Campion. You are mine."

Francine's mouth dropped open when Elda burst into the house with what sounded like a bomb on the front door. The rental deposit wasn't going to cover that.

Elda kicked what was left of the front door closed and pointed the pistol in her left hand at it. When she pulled the trigger, bright blue, red and yellow striped foam sprayed out. She drew a straight line down the doorframe, then included the foot-sized hole where the lock used to be, filling that with foam in a circular pattern. Francine thought it looked like she'd shoved an Earther all-day sucker in the hole.

Raphael demanded, "What in the space potato farm are you doing, Elda?"

"Don't swear at me, Raphael," she countered. Once the foam hit the door and the frame, it swirled around, changing to a whitish-gray color and then, miraculously, started turning the same color as the door and frame, respectively. In seconds, it was indistinguishable from the red of the door and the brown of the frame. *Interesting. What is that stuff?*

Raphael's hands went up in the air. "You just blew the lock off the front door of my rental!"

"And I'm fixing it."

"Chameleon foam is not *fixing* it."

"Don't worry. I'll pay to have it properly repaired," she said, finishing up her foamy fill-in job. "Just as soon as I cash in my bounty. It's going to be huge. This will hold it in the meantime."

The lock was still missing, as were the doorknobs on both sides, but at least the foam sealed the door from the outside. Francine wasn't certain how they were supposed to get in and out without a handle, but they had bigger problems.

Raphael moved to stand in front of Victor, blocking the bounty hunter's view of her quarry.

"Stand aside, Raphael, or I will make my way through you."

"I'm not letting you take him, Elda."

Francine moved to stand beside Raphael and Elda's foam gun rose to point at her. "I already know that's a foam gun."

Elda turned it sideways and sighed. She stuck it back on her utility belt with a sheepish look, but leveled the other gun at Raphael's chest.

"Elda, my love," Victor said. "I took great pains to send you that secret message so you *wouldn't* hunt me down."

My love?

"Well, I tried to keep my distance. Things changed when I saw the price of the bounty on your head," she said, a lopsided grin forming as she looked past Raphael.

Victor moved around Raphael and Francine.

Elda lowered her gun, stowed it in her holster and ran to him. They met in the middle of the foyer and embraced like long-lost lovers and kissed like they were about to be parted forever.

"What is going on here?" Raphael looked perturbed. Francine felt for him. First the door blown to smithereens, now a new love connection complication at best.

Victor broke from Elda and told Raphael, "The reason I believe someone is trying to frame me for my father's murder is because I want to marry Elda. My father was not too keen on the idea, as you might imagine, but he was coming around. He didn't want Claudia or Roger to succeed him if I abdicated. Someone must have learned he was softening to the idea of a non-royal as my bride."

Elda kissed Victor's cheek. "I promise that I didn't hunt you down at first, as you requested. When I found out how much the bounty was, I knew you were in more trouble than even you could handle. By then I didn't know where to look. So I found Raphael and used him as my guide. My instinct was right." She looked at Raphael. "You would never hunt him, no matter how much the price on his head is." She pointed at him. "Say it, Raphael. Say I'm the best bounty hunter ever."

"Yes, yes. You're the best and baddest bounty hunter of all time, Elda. I'll ensure it's carved on your headstone one day," Raphael said. "Are you happy now?"

"A narrow victory, all things considered, but I'll take it." Elda looked at each of them. "Well, fill me in on the plan so I can help. The sooner we get rid of this ridiculous bounty on Victor's head, the sooner we can all get back to our regularly scheduled lives."

When neither man rushed to speak, Francine said, "Here is my idea." She filled Elda in.

"Wow. That's a great idea. She's a smart one, isn't

she? How did you get so lucky, Luther? I mean, Raphael."

He rolled his eyes, but Francine could see his amusement.

Elda said, "My plan was to take Victor in as my prisoner and collect the bounty, hide some battle tech on him so he'd be able to escape and meet up with me later. Francine's idea is better. It's easier to control the parameters and Victor doesn't have to go to jail. I don't know if he'd survive it anyway."

Raphael nodded. "You're right. He might be shot trying to escape. My guess is that's the way whoever is behind this would make it look."

The four of them refined their strategy until they came up with a viable plan everyone agreed was the best. Raphael would approach Claudia to make a deal, telling her he knew where Victor was so they could set a trap for her.

Victor and Elda left by way of the hidden escape hatch. Elda had a better place to hide him. They would meet the next day at the space dock for a private flight back to Ichor-Delta and launch their scheme to outwit Claudia.

Once they were alone, Raphael left briefly to ensure the front door wouldn't fly open in the night or become a burglar's wildest dream come true. While he was gone, Francine quickly changed into something more comfortable. An outfit she'd secretly selected from Jacques Pierre's shop when Raphael had been trying on his wedding finery.

When he returned, Raphael's gaze landed on her, seemingly noting the outfit change, but then he asked, "Are you sure you're okay with me doing this plan of ours?"

"Of course. It was my idea. Although if you don't have to kiss her, that would be a bonus."

"Trust me, I'm not going to. Besides, if it truly is Claudia who's behind this, she won't want to kiss me. She wants a power wedding with another royal family and the wealth that comes with it, but absolutely no physical relationship beyond what's required to continue the legacy."

"How do you know that?"

"Before I refused our arranged marriage, she made her feelings clear regarding the physical aspect of any marriage she would be involved in."

"When was this?"

"Shortly before I was kicked out of my family home a decade ago. I told my father I wasn't interested in a loveless marriage for the sake of power. He disagreed, told me it didn't matter beyond having an heir and a spare, which I also didn't want to do with Claudia. And she didn't even want to have a wedding night.

"My father told me that I needed to follow tradition. I said no way. I refused to honor the arranged marriage, so I was out. He expected me to come crawling back."

"Instead, you went out into the world and became a big bad bounty hunter. Also, you kept Claudia from criticism for being jilted, I'd imagine."

Raphael nodded. "Once I was out in the world all alone, I had help. Victor was the only reason I was able to change my life. He wasn't supposed to even mention my name. He said he'd likely be in the same boat someday. The names they were floating around for *his* marriage prospects were not to his liking, either. The difference was his father wasn't willing to kick his son to the curb as easily as mine was."

"Your father had an heir and two spares. Victor is an only child. That makes a huge difference in lofty circles."

"Maybe that's true." Raphael shrugged. They stared at each other. "I want you to know that Claudia makes my skin crawl."

"Noted." Francine untied the silk belt around her waist and let her robe slide off her shoulders, revealing a sheer black negligee she'd been saving for a special occasion. If his widened eyes and parted lips were any indication, he liked it.

"Let's make a few more memories while we have the chance," she said. "So that when you're with Claudia you can have a better vision of your true future."

"I love you, Francine. Don't ever doubt it."

"I love you, too."

Raphael grabbed her up into his arms and kissed her like he was afraid she'd disappear in a puff of smoke if he didn't hold her tight enough.

Francine kissed him back, with the warm thought that things were finally going their way.

Chapter 12

Raphael strolled into Claudia's home after the butler opened the door and led him deeper into what he considered enemy territory. The place hadn't changed much in the years he'd been away. Claudia had inherited the house after her parents died. She had no other siblings vying for it.

Francine, Victor, Elda and Raphael returned to Ichor-Delta on a privately acquired transport that only recorded three of the four of them on the official logs.

For a steep price, Victor had been stowed in a specially constructed place aimed at those seeking hidden transportation. They went their separate ways once the ship landed the day before, planning to meet after his appointment with Claudia.

Raphael made a show of being in public without Francine to discover who might come looking for him. A message arrived promptly at his hotel room.

Claudia was the first to make contact, asking for a

meeting at her house to discuss a special offer. The four conspirators further refined their plan, given the message and location of the meeting at Claudia's home.

"Luther," she said the moment he entered the greeting room. Her tone was polite, if not exuberant. He expected her to be a little more excited to see him after all this time.

"I go by Raphael now," he said without thinking.

Her brow crinkled. "Raphael?"

"Yes. My second name."

"I see. Well, whatever you like." She picked up a delicate cup, took a sip and returned it to her side table. "Would you like a cup of crystal liquor?" she asked. "A cookie?" She pointed to a decorative plate covered with bite-sized treats.

"No, thanks. I'm not hungry. Let's get to it, shall we?"

"Fine." Undaunted, Claudia pivoted easily. "I called you here today to make you a lucrative offer."

"You called me here today because you think I know where Victor Campion is, and until he's caught and put away, you can't make a claim to his title."

"Always right to the point. I like that about you, Luth—I mean, Raphael." Her gaze fastened on his face. "The years have been kind you. Surprising, given what you do for a living."

Raphael smiled. "You haven't aged a day since

the last time I saw you." He knew she valued flattery and his observation was sincere. She'd obviously spent a goodly amount to look younger than her years.

Her head cocked to one side as if she didn't expect him to be civil. "Thank you."

Raphael glanced around the room and noticed that things looked worn, for lack of a better word. Every surface was tidy and clean, but the furniture was not new, as he would have expected. Did she have financial issues? Was that why she'd concocted this plan to get rid of Victor?

"What's your offer, Claudia?"

"I'd like you to find Victor and turn him in to the authorities. I believe you have the best chance of making that happen."

"Victor is my best friend. Why would I ever do that?"

"Because once he's been captured and convicted for the murder of his poor father, I'm in line to inherit the title, of course. The longer Victor remains uncaptured, the longer the Campion affairs will languish."

"What about Roger Campion?"

"What about him?"

"He's got a claim to the title as well, doesn't he? What if he makes me a better offer?"

"He won't." Claudia's expression darkened. "He doesn't have a valid claim."

Raphael fixed his stare on her face, surprised she

didn't consider Roger a foe. "That's not what I've heard."

"Well, I have some information that ensures I'm the only heir. After Victor, of course. But he killed his father. Once he's executed or put into a gulag or whatever, the title is mine."

"What if he's found innocent?"

She shrugged. "I don't believe that is possible." She didn't question Victor's guilt.

"Okay. Let's say I'm willing to betray my lifelong friendship with Victor—and that's a big if—what could you possibly offer me that would be worth it?"

"Once I'm in charge of the Campion estate, I could help you, Luther—I mean, Raphael," she said. "You've done well for yourself after I'm certain was the heart-wrenching loss of your family, but I could be your champion. I could ensure you have the best of whatever you desire, once I'm confirmed as the Campion heir."

You don't want to marry me?

He didn't know whether to be relieved or insulted. Both feelings vied for attention. Something about her offer didn't feel quite right.

Claudia didn't act like she was scheming to gain a title she'd orchestrated a murder and subsequent frame-up of Victor to acquire. She didn't even have a calculating attitude. Instead, she had an air of expectation, perhaps desperation. Time to put his cards on the table.

He seated himself across from her, hearing the chair creak the moment his butt hit the cushion. "What makes you think Roger doesn't have a claim to the Campion title? It's my understanding that both of you have an equal entitlement. Won't a magistrate have to decide the fate of the Campion title once Victor is formally stripped of it? Perhaps you'll only get half, if any at all."

Claudia considered his question for a long time, as if trying to decide whether to trust him with whatever information she had on Roger that made his claim null and void.

Raphael tried again. "If I do aid you in your quest for the Campion title, Claudia, I'm not exactly looking for any help with my current profession. I'm at the top of my game. I already get my pick of the best jobs."

One of her thin brows rose in question. "What *do* you want?"

"I want to share in your good fortune."

"Share?" The word came out like a gunshot. "What do you mean by *share*?"

"We were once nearly engaged, but when I refused to honor the arrangement between our families, my father cast me aside." Raphael leaned back in the chair, eliciting more creaking noises. He hoped the chair would hold him and not collapse beneath his large frame.

Her eyes widened. "And you want to resurrect that arrangement?" She looked panicked. Clearly, she did not want him for a husband. Raphael had a whole speech memorized to align himself with her anticipated wish to marry him, in the vein of joining their families for the good of the kingdom, blah, blah blah.

Her eyes darted back and forth, as if it never occurred to her that he'd want to be her co-ruler and she desperately needed a response. Interesting. Raphael wondered why she'd never found another to marry. When he'd discarded their arranged marriage, he expected she'd be every eligible royal's next choice.

He expected her to be married before he even got off the planet. Her parents had died unexpectedly several years ago. Perhaps they'd left her enough that she didn't have to marry for funds. Then again, the worn look of the room made him wonder what she was up to.

"In the last decade, you've never married. Never even tried to find another suitable arrangement. Why is that?" Raphael watched her closely, trying to figure out what her plan was if not to marry him and strengthen her position within the realm. Having two powerful families bonded by marriage would ensure any children born to them would enjoy a powerful alliance for decades.

Claudia's eyes averted from his intense stare, lowering to the small cup in her hands.

The communication device on his belt buzzed, breaking the uneasy silence and the thick tension that had filled the room. Raphael stood up and pulled the buzzing comm from his side to read the display. Victor? Now what?

"Excuse me, Claudia. I need to take this call."

She nodded, looking so relieved at the interruption he almost laughed. He left her alone and exited into the hallway. He faced the front door and answered the call.

"It's Elda. No time to explain. Turns out that Claudia isn't the culprit. Roger, or more specifically his mother, is behind this. Get out of there before you end up married to the wrong woman." In the background of the call, Raphael heard gunfire, screams and explosions.

"How do you know? And what is going on there?"

"Alvina's family has just invaded Victor's home. We're in a gun battle, but they underestimated the pushback they'd get. They thought with Henry dead and Victor under suspicion for his murder, the guards would be either decimated or dismissed. They were wrong. The guards were doubled, prepared and motivated."

Raphael straightened. "What in the space potato farm are you doing at Victor's house?"

"Don't swear at me, Raphael. We thought it would be a good place to hide. We were wrong." Elda let loose a much viler curse than he'd said and he heard her gun fire three times in rapid succession. Her satisfied grunt likely meant she'd hit her target, as she so often did.

"Where is Francine?"

"She's fine."

"I didn't ask you if she was fine, I asked where she is."

"Relax. She's at your hotel room. She doesn't even know we came here."

Raphael exhaled the breath he hadn't realized he was holding. "Do you need me there?"

"No, I'm just letting you know what's up. Once we neutralize the attackers, we're going to sneak back out and head for a safe house not too far from here. I'll call you in a couple hours to reconnect. Now that it's clear who is behind the assassination attempt, we should be able to clear this all up pretty quickly, don't you think?"

"Let's hope so. Be safe, Elda. Thanks for the heads-up."

"Yep." She hung up and he ducked back into the room with Claudia.

"What do you have on Roger?" He kept his tone harsh and loud to let her know he wasn't going to brook any nonsense. He needed to know what was going on. Now.

"I—" She paused. "I have recently come into some information that explains something that was obvious from the start, but now I have proof."

"What information? Proof of what, exactly?" Raphael moved to stand over her, glaring down into her surprised face.

Claudia dropped her cup, which bounced on the rug and rolled away.

"Roger isn't a Campion by blood," she blurted. "Alvina was already pregnant when she married Victor's father's cousin. Roger wasn't weak because he was born a month early. He was sickly because his scheming mother was clearly sleeping with men who were not royals. She likely doesn't even know who the actual father is, but a recent blood test was brought to my attention, showing that Roger isn't related to his Campion father."

Raphael didn't share the same old-fashioned ideas about bloodlines and their strength or weakness based on royal bloodlines, but it was a waste of his breath to say so. "Why did Alvina think she'd be able to put Roger into the Campion title? They would have done tests to assure he was truly in the bloodline, wouldn't they?"

Claudia shrugged. "Perhaps. I couldn't take that chance. She's not below paying people off to curry favor."

Neither are you, he almost said. "What else are you hiding?"

She shrugged again.

"Why aren't you a contender for the title?" He moved closer, one inch more, and bumped her knee with his. His movement made her look up, lips parted in a sneer, ready for combat. "I'm the *only* contender after Victor."

"What does Alvina know about you that threatens your claim? There must be something."

"My claim is secure. I am a legitimate Campion. She simply has information that does not make me the best marital candidate, that's all."

Raphael wanted to scream the rafters down at her vague answer. "Tell me what it is!"

Claudia sighed. "If you must know, I'm infertile. I will never have children. Not that I wanted any in the first place—I most surely don't—but it doesn't make for a good marriage alliance when it's known that a woman can't bear children."

She sounded resolute about her inability to conceive. Accepting. She only wanted the security of a good marriage with a royal family. If she acquired the title this way, her infertility wouldn't be an issue. At least not as much as if she tried to find a royal husband who needed an heir and a spare, as was the custom.

If they'd married a decade ago, the odds were high she wouldn't ever have had to produce a child as the wife of a second born. Raphael was stunned. Was that why she'd insisted they didn't need to have a physical relationship? Had that been part of her rationale at the time?

"Okay, you seem to have come to terms with that issue. What else happened?"

He backed away, not feeling the need to hover so close. He reseated himself in the creaky chair.

Claudia's mouth shaped into a sneer. "Alvina found out about the pivotal examination my family had done years ago, confirming I would never be able to produce healthy heirs for any family. When the test said I was barren, my family hid the results, but not well enough, apparently."

"You never married because you couldn't produce an heir."

"Yes. But I'm not a pretender to the title like Roger."

Raphael almost felt sorry for Claudia. The truth was, she'd done him a favor by nixing any kind of physical relationship between them when they were younger. If she hadn't been so cold and unrelenting where sex in a possible marriage was concerned, he might have made a different choice. She did it for her own purposes, but any additional animosity he'd held all this time fell away.

He leaned forward, creaking again, wanting to let her down gently. "I'm afraid you will not be inheriting the Campion title, Claudia."

Her gaze narrowed. "Whyever not?"

"You'll find out soon enough, but trust me on this."

"I don't trust anyone, least of all you."

"I'll see myself out. Good luck to you, Claudia," Raphael said as he exited. She might need luck. But she was not his problem anymore.

He was determined to head to Elda's hideout. Raphael didn't regard it as very safe, but at least no one would think to look for Victor in a former orphan hospital for desperate girls, abandoned as it was to the elements for longer than two decades.

Before Raphael got into the vehicle he'd acquired, his communication device buzzed again. He'd used this device more in the past two weeks than in the past two years.

Surprisingly, the call was someone who'd never contacted him before.

Someone who was supposed to be in a coma. Victor's father.

Henry Campion.

Francine had practically paced a hole in the rug as she waited for Raphael to return from his meeting with Claudia.

Although it seemed like forever, he'd only been gone an hour when he entered the room, gathered her in his arms and kissed her senseless. "We need to go."

"Where?"

"Victor's house. I'll explain on the way."

He hailed a transport outside their new hotel. He'd wanted to go back to the Borg Stein Slot, but they claimed to be booked solid. This hotel was nice, though Francine would have been happy to sleep in the vehicle, as long as Raphael was with her.

"How did it go with Claudia?" she asked.

"Surprisingly."

"What does that mean?"

"She didn't want to marry me."

"Why not?"

Raphael told her about Claudia's offer subsequent secret infertility, Elda's call during a gun battle and the unexpected contact from Victor's father.

"That's quite a lot of news. You were only gone an hour," she said.

"Seemed like longer."

"Tell me everything."

Raphael took her hand in his, lacing their fingers together. "Henry Campion called me as I left Claudia's home, confirming Roger's mother Alvina as the culprit who'd tried to kill him. He woke up in the hospital, heard about the exorbitant bounty on Victor's head and his subsequent disappearance from polite society."

"Let me guess. He knew you were friends and wanted you to find his son, right?"

Raphael squeezed her hand. "Yes. I explained what had gone on and what we'd done. He was relieved and grateful. He's also about to do a public conference from his hospital bed, explaining that he is still alive and reveal who tried to kill him and frame his only son."

"That should instantly revoke the ginormous bounty on Victor's head. Alvina and her family have all been arrested, including Roger, but he probably didn't have any active participation in the plan to steal the Campion title from Henry and Victor. I suspect he'll eventually be let go."

"Wow. That's huge."

"Victor invited us over to celebrate with Elda. Henry has even told Victor he can marry Elda with his blessing."

Raphael kissed her again. "Now that Victor is safe, we are free to do what we want."

"It's not like we haven't already been doing exactly what we want to do."

"True, but now we can do it without any disruptions or getting ready to leave the planet for the next meeting to plan our wedding and reception."

"What about *your* family?"

"What about them?"

"Don't you want to see them before we leave? Maybe we could meet up? Chat?"

Raphael made a face, but didn't respond.

"What does that face mean?"

"It means that I don't want to subject you to my father again. He's likely to be difficult where you are concerned. He won't care that Claudia kept her barrenness a secret and turned out to be a bad match. He will simply select the next available royal on his list of appropriate marriage partners for me and begin the haranguing." Raphael lifted one shoulder, his expression guarded with a hint of pain.

She held up her hand to show him her engagement ring. "Not even if I'm sporting this ring?" Francine didn't care what his father thought of her. As long as

Raphael loved her, she would ignore the older man and any negativity he spouted.

He gave her an endearing smile. "I don't want you to get your hopes up."

"What about your brothers? William was decent to you at the wedding. Surprised to see you there, but nice."

Raphael looked at the ceiling. "Well, I wouldn't mind seeing Alex. And you're right, William wasn't a bore at the wedding. I did plan to meet with him soon anyway."

"What if I said that I'd like to meet and talk to your brothers? Does that sway you any?"

"Maybe." His half smile made Francine's heartbeat speed up. "I'll call and see if they are free for dinner. Does that make you happy?"

"Being with you makes me happy."

"And making nice with my family also makes you happy?"

"Yes. Not only that, but my family has welcomed me back into the fold. They even made it public. Lucy sent me a notice from yesterday's Alpha-Prime society section. Not only am I back in the family, but they announced I'm engaged to a royal member of the Boudreaux clan from Ichor-Delta."

Raphael's smile widened and Francine's knees went weak. "Good."

"I also got a notice that my debt has been cleared. Seems my family decided not to bill me for the pricey ride back from the last wedding I attended."

"Even better."

"Best of all, though…" She stared at him.

"What?"

"You loved me even when I was a nobody grocery clerk from a backwater Earther colony. Then you changed my life."

"Francine, you were never a nobody grocery clerk. Besides, you changed my life even more profoundly. You helped me save my best friend by thinking up the plan for me to make nice with my ex-fiancée to discover who the true villain was. There are not many women who are all right with that sort of sacrifice."

Francine shrugged. "It wasn't a chore. You clearly didn't care about Claudia. You left your family and their fortune rather than be stuck in a loveless marriage with her."

Raphael called William to make plans. A few hours later, they were dressed, out the door and on their way to a Boudreaux family dinner.

Raphael followed her as they were led through the upscale restaurant to a private table in the back of the large establishment. William and a younger man who looked like a Boudreaux were already seated. They both stood as she approached. Raphael introduced her to Alex, who seemed pleased to meet her.

When Alex turned to Raphael, his smile dimmed. "Brother," he said, sounding reserved as they shook hands.

The conversation throughout dinner was polite as

the three men talked about growing up together and caught each other up on their lives over the past decade. Raphael told them about some of the bounty hunter predicaments he'd gotten himself into and out of.

"...So Charlie Adler manages to grab hold of our quarry's leg before he runs. Charlie is a big guy, too, but it didn't even slow the guy down.

"Our bounty was from Paludion-Epsilon, where they run like the wind is continually at their backs, even faster than we can on Ichor-Delta. Poor old Charlie held tight with both arms and was dragged quite a distance through the sand, across a river gulch with no water and into the brush along the edge before I was able to catch up and shoot our bounty with a tranquillizer. Charlie didn't stop cussing through the entire ride or after it stopped. He might still be cussing up a storm right now whenever he remembers it."

Raphael was absolutely the most gorgeous man she'd ever seen and never more so than when he was telling stories about his bounty hunter adventures. Francine hadn't been introduced to Charlie. Was he the bounty hunter who stole Raphael away from her the night of the party at Valene and Wyatt's place?

Everyone was amused by the story, certainly picturing the funny scene of a big bounty hunter hanging on for dear life as he was dragged across dusty terrain.

Francine looked at Alex. While he laughed along with everyone else, she could tell he held back, trying to be polite, but not exuberantly welcoming to someone he clearly loved, if the stories the three men shared from their childhood were any indication.

Before she changed her mind and left well enough alone, she asked, "Alex, are you set to marry someone arranged for you, or do you get to select your own bride?"

Alex's eyes widened. "At one time, I was supposed to marry Claudia. About five years ago, father squashed that idea and told me he would find someone else. To my knowledge, he never has. I'm in no hurry. I like being single."

The two elder brothers smiled as if they well understood their youngest brother's view of life.

"Are you married, William?" Francine asked.

"Not yet," he said with a grin so similar to Raphael's she was momentarily transfixed. "But the woman my father wants me to marry is very sweet, very nice and we are friends. Maybe that's the best way to start out anyway."

The waiter arrived to refill water glasses, take further drink orders and offer the dessert menu. Once they were alone again, Francine was compelled to discover why Alex seemed so somber. Had he been upset when Raphael left home? Could it be as simple as that? She tried to see things from his point of view and decided it was worth a question.

"Have you missed Raphael all these years, Alex?

I'd imagine in the same situation, I might have been rather miffed to be left behind."

Alex's eyes widened. He looked at her, then at Raphael and then back at her. "How did you…?"

"I'm truly sorry, Alex," Raphael said, seeming to understand what Francine had figured out. "Father kicked me out and I didn't look back. I should have tried to contact you, but I was afraid if Father found out, he'd take it out on you."

Alex stared at Raphael for long moments. "I was devastated that you left without saying goodbye. I waited to hear from you for years, but you never contacted me. I guess I always understood why, but it still hurt."

"I am sorry—" Raphael started to say again, but Alex put a hand up.

"No. You already apologized." He took a deep breath and a bright smile appeared. "It's okay, Rafe. Now that I'm older and have spent more time with our father, I understand how unyielding he can be."

"And unrelenting," William added.

"And unforgiving," Raphael said.

"The three of us shall be united going forward, yes?" William asked.

"Yes," they all said together.

Glasses were raised, clinked together and sipped in order to solidify their brotherly reunion and understanding.

Dessert was delivered and consumed. As they were saying their goodbyes with promises not to wait another decade for their next meeting and dinner, Raphael's communicator buzzed.

He ignored it until his brothers were gone, snapping it from his belt only as they waited for transportation back to their hotel. His face hardened as he read the message.

"What's wrong? Who sent the message?"

"Diesel," Raphael said quietly. "It just says, 'call me,' but there's no other information. I think we both know what—or who—he's calling about."

"True." Francine was sorry that her vacation was basically over, but she did miss home and wanted to get back to her little black kitten. Now that Raphael was coming with her and would be part of her future, she was anxious to return to her *regularly scheduled life*, as Elda had put it.

Raphael contacted Diesel as soon as they got back to their hotel room. Francine kissed his cheek and headed for the bedroom, whispering she would be taking a quick shower and getting ready for bed. The mischievous grin she sent over one shoulder as she walked away warmed his heart—and other parts.

He planned to make this call as fast as possible.

"Diesel," he said when the other man answered. "What's up?"

"Nothing is up and that's what worries me. There haven't been any sightings of Indigo Smith.

There hasn't been any gossip about him. The silence unnerves me. He's out there. I know he wants his treasure back. The quiet and lack of any information is alarming, don't you think?"

Raphael hid his amusement and recited something appropriate from the Earther phrase book he'd read. "Don't borrow trouble, Diesel. I say no news is good news."

"Whatever. When will you be back on Earth?"

"Our flight leaves tomorrow, going the scenic route by way of Lava Rock World. Three days."

Diesel wasn't happy, if the long-suffering sigh he sent over the communicator was any indication. "Fine," he said, but added, "Lava Rock World? Really?"

"My bride-to-be wants to see it. I'm just along for the ride. I know you understand."

Diesel's woeful second sigh said he did. "Yeah. I understand. My wife would also like to visit Lava Rock World and the Gothic Ice Floe Planet. I see those destinations in my near future."

"Gothic Ice Floe Planet is a future trip. Want me to pick up a brochure for you?"

"No, thanks. I already have several."

"See you in a few days."

"Right."

Raphael had hoped Indigo Smith might beat them back to Earth and be a nonissue once he and Francine returned. No such luck. It was frustrating to have to recapture the wily criminal. Would this be the last time? Or would Indigo Smith escape as he always did? He understood that no one fully understood the criminal's shapeshifting capabilities.

Supposedly, the gulag he'd been assigned to had been warned of his unique skills. They should have taken better precautions to hold on to their prisoner, in Raphael's humble opinion.

The shower started up in the next room and Raphael's focus on wily, escaped criminals changed quickly to more carnal activities.

He was on vacation. He planned to enjoy it.

Raphael put his communication device on silent, forgot about everything else and headed to join his love, Francine.

Chapter 13

Raphael and Francine held hands and reclined in their first-class seats. They were nearing the end of the trip. He was both happy and sad about that. He was happy to have had this time alone with Francine to forge a bond that would carry them into their bright future, sad it was coming to an end too quickly.

All of the passengers got on the flight at the Lava Rock World departure platform. It was a direct one-day flight from there to the Earth colony with no stops along the way, not even for refueling.

He'd eyed the others in the first-class lounge to discover if there would be any troublemakers like the large, tattered-looking woman on the flight from Ichor-Delta to Alpha-Prime. One man was as large as she'd been, but he was older, graying. Unlike the loud woman's ragged appearance upon boarding, the man was well-dressed. Something about him seemed familiar. Raphael studied his face and couldn't place him.

The man's traveling companion was a tall woman who wore expensive clothing and even more expensive jewelry that did nothing to sweeten the frown on her face. She also struck a familiar chord with Raphael. Perhaps it was her foul attitude that twigged his memory. Some people refused to be content, preferring to seek out drama and irritation every single day of their lives.

Raphael did not like excessive drama.

No one seated in the premium section had made any scenes, although the couple he'd noticed seemed particularly unhappy. Since boarding, they hadn't spoken a single word to each other. They didn't look at each other. It was as if each pretended the other didn't exist. Trouble in paradise? Unfortunate, and not his business.

Francine squeezed his fingers and he snapped out of his reverie. "Ready to get back home?"

"I'm sort of torn on that one. I'm anxious to see my kitten and sleep in my own bed, but it was a lovely trip and I appreciate you taking me. Lava Rock World was better than I thought it would be."

"It was my pleasure. I left with a fake fiancée and I'm coming back with a real one. That makes me happy beyond words. And I also liked Lava Rock World more than I expected to."

Francine turned in her seat and leaned close. It was intimate and he liked it.

"I also want to give you a special thank you for taking me to my sister's wedding and quietly enduring all the drama surrounding that affair."

Raphael moved closer to his love. In a low tone, he said, "Well, thank you for understanding my little brother's feelings and sharing them so we could get past a difficulty I hadn't even been aware of."

He kissed her with gratitude, she kissed him back with desire, so he didn't stop. They kissed until the speaker system announced that the flight would land in less than half an hour and to gather belongings near their seats.

Raphael glanced at the silent couple one row ahead of them on the opposite side of the aisle and was surprised to see the woman staring at him with a menacing expression. She saw him watching and turned away. *What's her problem? Maybe kissing in public is against her moral code. Too bad.*

Once the transport landed, he and Francine walked behind the angry couple until they reached the base of the stairs and entered the Big Bang Truck Stop's underground facilities.

It was night on this little slice of Earth, so he didn't have to fish his sunglasses out of his bag. When the other couple got to the bottom of the staircase, they each headed in a different direction, marching with hard, fast steps like they couldn't get away from each other fast enough. *Good riddance.*

Raphael had arranged for Francine's bags to be delivered to her home, so she wouldn't have to lug them around in the crowd.

Before he got two steps from the first-class stairway, Diesel appeared seemingly out of nowhere to block his path. "'Bout time you got back here."

Raphael hid his surprise. "Why? Do you have news?"

"No, but now we can sit here together and worry about what's coming."

"Oh, joy. Just what I've longed for," Raphael deadpanned.

Diesel flashed a quick grin and nodded at Francine in greeting. "How was your trip?"

"Wonderful!"

"I'm glad to hear it. What did you think of Lava Rock World?"

Her eyes brightened even more. "It was awesome. I'd love to go back and explore other places we didn't have time to visit."

"Good to know. Juliana wants to go," Diesel said. "I promised to take her in a weak moment."

Francine laughed. "You might like it."

"I don't know about that, but I do like to see my wife happy."

Raphael cracked a smile at how obviously in love Diesel was with his wife and the lengths he'd go to make her happy. He would certainly do the same for Francine. "Let me take Francine home and I'll come back and be miserable with you."

"You don't have to take me home. I can get there all on my own, I promise."

"Are you certain?"

She glanced at her wristwatch, a ceramic bangle bracelet with a digital clock embedded in it. "Of course. It's not too late to get a few chores done."

"Chores?" he asked.

Francine looked amused. She was so beautiful. "Well, I've got to go and let Mrs. Greenstone know I've returned. I will probably have to clean up whatever trouble Angel has gotten into while I've been gone. Then I need to call to see what my work schedule is next week. Lots to do before it gets too late. No worries. I'll see you later, okay?" She kissed his cheek, sent a finger wave to Diesel and disappeared into the mass of travelers spilling into the basement shopping area.

He watched her leave, easily able to follow the bright color of her hair. It was visible even in a throng as she moved through the energetic basement area. Memories of sifting his fingers through her soft cinnamon locks while she slept or when he kissed her overrode any other thoughts in his head. The urge to follow her rose up so fiercely he took a step in her direction.

"Francine is very sweet."

Diesel stating the obvious shook Raphael from his reverie. "She is."

"You're a lucky man."

"I am."

Diesel cleared his throat. "I heard a rumor you might be staying on Earth or at least making it the home base for your bounty hunting business."

Raphael took in Diesel's hopeful expression and said, "Yep."

"Because of Francine?"

"Yep."

Diesel grinned. "Good news for us. There will definitely be some more work for you on our trips north to Suspicion, Minnesota."

"Still working things out with the Secret Keeper?"

Diesel pushed out a sigh. "Indeed. A tough nut to crack, that one. More trips will definitely be coming. Wheeler is going next time."

"Oh, yeah?" Raphael narrowed his gaze.

"He's less volatile than Cam in any discussion."

"That has also been my experience." Wheeler was definitely calmer in temperament than Cam with regard to security issues. Last time Raphael had escorted Cam up to Minnesota, he'd had to act as the voice of reason when the Secret Keeper wasn't as forthcoming as Cam demanded. He'd had to physically hold Cam back at one point during the meeting.

Raphael lost sight of Francine and gave Diesel his full attention. "Good to know. I'm happy to have regular work here on Earth whenever I can get it. Cam mentioned that might be a possibility before I left." He sent his gaze back down the length of the Big Bang Truck Stop basement, wondering if he should have gone ahead and escorted Francine home.

It wouldn't have taken very long. Then again, she'd been doing fine on her own without him for months. She wasn't some shrinking flower he needed to protect and guard every second of every day. Although, if she did ever need that, or just want it, he was ready.

Diesel clapped him on the back. "Let me show you the file the gulag sent me on Indigo's escape. I didn't notice anything helpful, but maybe you'll see something I missed."

Raphael followed Diesel to his office, looking over his shoulder one last time, wishing he could still see Francine's cinnamon hair moving through the crowd. Five minutes out of her sight and he already missed her. Did that make him a sap? Probably. Did he care about that? No.

After being with her for the past ten days, he felt empty without her nearby, like he was forgetting something important.

"Come on," Diesel said. "It won't take long. You can read through it, memorize it like you always do and think on it for a while, at least until Indigo shows his face here on Earth. Then perhaps we have a chance. Once you look through the file, you can get back to Francine, where I know you'd rather be."

"Yep." Raphael followed Diesel to his office and visually scanned the file, thinking about Francine most of the time.

Before he finished reading, Axel and Cam came in to heap additional praise on him to ensure he understood that they wanted him to work for them all.

"You were invaluable when we caught Indigo the first time," Cam remarked.

"That's the truth," Axel said.

Cam shook his head. "It is beyond my capacity for belief that he was allowed to escape from a hardcore gulag like XkR-9."

"Oh, I expect Indigo had this planned long before he ever got caught." Raphael looked up, surprised to find them all staring as if in anticipation. "Listen, I appreciate your faith in me, but Wyatt Campbell—who was instrumental in Indigo's capture—should also be consulted, don't you think?"

"Oh, he has been. Trust me. He has a finer line to walk in the human world, but he's also on the lookout," Diesel said.

Raphael finally finished reading the file, but didn't learn anything he didn't know from all the news accounts of the daring escape from the gulag. No one had seen Indigo Smith or no one *admitted* to having seen him. Given that Indigo could change his appearance at will and look like anyone, catching him would be that much harder. The gulag had supposedly tried to hamper his ability to shapeshift, but clearly their efforts had been wasted or possibly even nonexistent.

They discussed strategy and ways to find and recapture the infamous criminal.

The next time Raphael noticed the clock, it had been over two hours since he had disembarked from the transport. He said his goodbyes to the Grey brothers, left the private administration area and made his way out into the public part of the facility, still lively with all the passengers from the recent transport giving their custom to the variety of restaurants and shops available belowstairs.

His phone buzzed. Francine's text said, "I'm very tired, I'm going to sleep. See you later."

Hmm. Interesting. He hadn't thought about whether he would stay with Francine once they got back to Earth. They'd been together every night on the trip, but that didn't mean she was ready for him to move right into her home.

His phone made a dreadful noise that meant it desperately needed to be recharged, so he mentally shrugged and headed for his small apartment. He did need to get his own travel bags squared away and check for any messages and mail delivered in his absence.

Raphael would make it a point to discuss their living arrangements with Francine the next time they were together. He made a note to pick up club sandwiches and chips for them from the Cosmos Café for lunch tomorrow, if she wasn't working later in the afternoon.

Perhaps he'd suggest they go to the justice of the

peace and get married as soon as possible. If it were up to him, the sooner the better. Her mother wanted to help arrange a small, beautiful wedding ceremony, but they could elope.

When Raphael finally laid his head down to sleep, he found it difficult to drift off. He would doze then wake with a start when he subconsciously realized he was all alone in bed. He'd have to reorient himself to his small apartment belowstairs in the Big Bang Truck Stop, where he'd always felt safe and sound. Until now.

After the fifth time he woke reaching out to the empty side of his bed for Francine, he huffed. *That's it!*

Tomorrow, Raphael would do whatever it took to convince Francine to elope. He never wanted to sleep alone again.

Early, the next morning

Diesel said good night to Cam, Axel and Raphael, but sat back in his desk chair worrying about there being absolutely no sighting of Indigo Smith. Not anywhere. It was like he'd turned into a ghost. That made Diesel sincerely unhappy. His gut roiled almost continually, apprehension growing like an out-of-control wildfire as each minute ticked by with no word, no sighting, no anything that could be connected, explored or discovered.

He didn't leave for home until well after midnight. He was back in this exact same seat less than six hours later. Still worried. Still without any new information.

Everyone told him not to worry. It was useless advice that only made him more concerned.

The phone on his desk rang, making him jump. He checked the time, noting it was still pretty early. He shook off his surprise and answered. "Hello."

"Diesel, it's Gage. Have you seen Wheeler?"

"No. Where is he?" Diesel answered without thinking. When one brother called asking about another brother, he wasn't willing to play telephone tree.

"Well, if I knew that, I wouldn't be calling you."

Diesel pushed out a sigh. His primary focus for the last several weeks was on an escaped criminal with the ability to shift into anyone, not his adult brother, Wheeler, who was prone to wandering off to paint or sculpt for a day or two without communicating his whereabouts to anyone. "He's probably working."

"Normally, I'd think that, too. But he was supposed to meet me an hour ago. Typically, he doesn't go down a rabbit hole of creativity if he has a meeting."

Diesel agreed. Wheeler was very creative and time wasn't a priority when he was working on a piece. However, he was also very dependable. Even so, Diesel didn't have time to worry about it right now. "In answer to your initial question, no, I haven't seen him. Yes, usually he's very prompt about meetings, but perhaps he got held up."

"This early in the day? Held up by what?"

"How would I know?"

Gage made a noncommittal grunt. "Well, if you see him, tell him I want to talk to him."

"Sure." Diesel would probably forget all about this call thirty seconds after he hung up, but he pretended to be cordial. He needed to find an escaped criminal, not herd his many brothers around on a day-to-day basis.

Indigo Smith was a danger to everyone.

Wheeler was a danger to no one.

Diesel went back to thinking about Indigo and where the escaped prisoner could be.

Last week, Wyatt Campbell had assured Diesel he had his good friend and fellow sheriff, Hunter Valero, keeping an eye on someone Indigo Smith might contact if he reached the area. Daphne Charlene Dumont had fallen in with his plans easily enough the last time he'd been in Alienn.

Hunter was the sheriff in Old Coot, Arkansas, but he patrolled all around the tri-city area, just like Wyatt did. Hunter, as a human sheriff, was not privy to all the alien details regarding Indigo Smith, just a general description and BOLO to contact either Wyatt or Diesel if he saw or heard anything.

According to her testimony, Daphne Charlene swore she had been tricked and led astray by the infamous criminal. Afterward, her memory had been painlessly removed. As an Earther, she didn't need to have any memory of Indigo Smith or Alpha alien information he might have let slip.

Diesel felt satisfied that fairness had been served and the bad guy had gone away to a gulag for his numerous crimes. Indigo's escape from the gulag had been a blow to anyone seeking decency.

Diesel had ensured the stolen gold ingots were hidden where no one out of the loop would ever think to look for them. He almost broke his arm regularly patting himself on his own back at the cleverness of his hiding place.

And then Indigo Smith escaped.

Every single transport that arrived at the Big Bang Truck Stop's belowstairs way station was scoured for any hint of the man, searched with trained dogs sniffing for the scent of anyone who didn't belong and every corner searched twice before being allowed to leave.

Diesel had even insisted some permanent storage lockers on the last cruise liner be opened—which needed a special tool—for scrutiny. Director Patmore, the point of contact on board, had been livid before they opened the panel and was nearly apoplectic when nothing was found because the flight was delayed by half an hour to put things right again.

Pfft.

Diesel didn't even care about the threat Patmore leveled at him, vowing to send a personal letter of censure. Whatever. Cam and Axel tried to smooth things over with the high-strung director, to no avail.

The word paranoid had been used several times in or near Diesel's presence lately, but he only rolled his eyes, having reinstated that abandoned policy a while back. Eye rolling was his only salvation of late. Juliana was worried about him. He tried to tell her not to worry, but that was a waste of breath.

In the depths of his gut swirled the feeling that he and the truck stop were on the precipice of something dire. How could he be prepared if he just threw caution to the wind and pretended the most notorious criminal in several galaxies wasn't on the loose and gunning for Earth?

He couldn't. He wouldn't.

The phone on his desk rang, making him jump like a nervous nelly once more. Maybe he'd cut back on his caffeine intake.

"What?" he barked into the phone, figuring he was about to have to apologize to the caller in his next breath.

"It's Wyatt. You need to come to the Skeeter Bite Sheriff's Office. And I mean right now, this minute."

Chapter 14

Raphael woke with a pounding, *I didn't get nearly enough sleep* headache to the sound of someone knocking loudly on his door. The inevitable disappointment at discovering there was no Francine in his bed put him instantly in a foul mood.

He stalked across his apartment barefoot, dressed only in exercise pants, and wrenched the handle to open the door, already feeling sorry for whoever was about to experience him in full-throttle fury mode.

Raphael was unprepared to see Lucy standing there, looking bright, cheery and clearly well rested. Unlike him.

Her ready smile fell away and her eyes widened when he loomed tall in the doorframe like a sand-claw beast woken from slumber too soon, ready to bite someone's head off for daring to knock on his door.

"Raphael?" she said in a quivering voice, taking a step back as both hands came up, palms out in an effort to ward him off or possibly fight off an imminent attack.

Instantly contrite, Raphael shrank back from the doorframe, ducked his head and plastered a fake smile in place as he beckoned her inside with a wave.

She did not move one eyelash.

"Sorry," he said in a quiet tone. "I didn't get much sleep last night."

Lucy's eyes went even wider. Her lips formed a small O, her cheeks went tomato red and she waved both hands back and forth as if waving away a car along a roadside. "I'm so sorry," she said, taking two more steps backward. "I did not mean to interrupt…you know…anything."

Raphael squinted. "You didn't interrupt…" *What is she talking about?* "…anything." He motioned again for her to come into his place, but was not convinced she'd step one baby toe inside his lair, since he'd been such an insufferable brute when he opened the door.

"Okay. Great. Well. Just tell Francine I stopped by to talk, okay?" She stared. He stared. She added, "Okay then. I'll just…go, now."

"Oh. Oh!" *I get it.* "Francine's not here." He figured out in that second what Lucy thought she had interrupted. He scraped his fingers through his hair along his scalp once, trying to wake up. He scratched his chest, and registered the fact he didn't have a shirt on. "Hang on a second," he said, turning to grab last night's T-shirt, which was draped over one of his two barstools, and slipped it over his head.

When he looked at Lucy, her brows were furrowed. "Where is she?"

"Francine?" Raphael had to stop and think. He really needed something to help him wake up. "She's at home."

"No, she's not." Lucy crossed her arms, head tilting to one side and looking past him into his small place, like he was lying and had Francine hidden in a closet or something. "I've already been there. I pounded so loud her landlady poked her head out and made a mean face. And Mrs. Greenstone is the nicest person in the world. Francine never answered, so I thought she was with you."

Raphael grabbed his phone off the charger on the bar countertop, unplugged the device and looked to see if Francine had messaged to say she was on her way to his place.

The only message was the one she'd sent last night about being tired and heading to bed.

He sent a quick text, telling her he was bringing club sandwiches and chips from the Cosmos Café for lunch, asking if noon was a good time. He waited for a response.

"Usually she answers pretty fast unless she's at work."

"True," Lucy said.

Nothing came through after a couple of minutes. Raphael handed his phone to Lucy with the messages on the screen to prove what he'd said.

Maybe he needed to invite her in to do a thorough search of his quarters. She could look to her heart's content. It wouldn't take long.

Lucy stared down at his phone screen, frowned, and handed it back. Then she pulled her own phone from her pocket. She swiped, punched the screen a few times and handed him her phone, open to a text. It said, "Hey, I'm back, but I'll be busy for a few days. Talk later." He also noted the three messages Lucy had sent in return, with no response.

"I tried to call her, twice, but she didn't answer."

Raphael handed over her phone and put both palms to his face, scrubbing furiously. Every word spoken and thought in his head was a struggle. "I'm not quite awake yet." He probably needed more sleep, but was unlikely to get it. He cleared his throat and tried to think of something intelligent to say. Nothing came to mind.

Lucy sighed. "No problem. I'm sorry to have disturbed you." She looked like a dejected puppy he'd just thrown to the curb.

"Wait, Lucy. Tell you what—let me grab a quick shower, and a quicker cup of coffee and we can go to Francine's place together. If she's not there, we'll hunt her down until we find her."

"You don't have to do that."

"I'm a bounty hunter. It's what I do and pretty much the only thing I'm good at. Besides, I know for a fact that she wouldn't want you to be worried."

A smile formed. "Okay. Why don't you go get

your shower and I'll fetch both of us a cup of coffee to cast away the cobwebs. Deal?"

"Deal. Thanks."

Lucy smiled and pulled his front door shut. He stripped his clothes off as he walked toward the bathroom and took the fastest shower he'd ever managed. Even so, Lucy was knocking by the time he'd dressed.

This time he opened the door with a big smile instead of the scowl of a deranged lunatic. She handed him one of the to-go cups she held. He noted with appreciation that she'd gotten him the largest available size.

He took a long pull of the hot drink, not caring if he burned his throat. He was surprised to find she knew he liked his coffee with lots of sugar and a shot of cinnamon dolce flavor.

"Have you been talking to Francine about me?"

"No comment. Why?"

"You know how I like my coffee."

She laughed. "Yeah, well, so does Katina at the Bean Me Up coffee kiosk around the corner."

Raphael cracked a smile, remembering that Katina took gleeful credit for forcing him to try the cinnamon dolce flavor. The word cinnamon made him think of Francine's hair.

Where are you, Francine? He grabbed his phone and apartment key off the counter, shoving them into his pockets. Together, he and Lucy headed out to find Francine.

Lucy's concern was starting to rub off. He'd feel better when they found out she wasn't answering because she'd silenced her phone for a meeting at work or something equally innocent.

Diesel arrived at the sheriff's station in Skeeter Bite faster than lickety split, expecting to face no less than three world-ending plagues as set forth in Earther biblical times.

He didn't even make it to the door when Wyatt, dressed in his uniform complete with gun belt, burst out and pointed to his cruiser. It gleamed from a recent wash as morning light bounced off the hood. Diesel hopped in the passenger side as Wyatt got behind the wheel, started the cruiser and took off like a shot.

"You gonna maybe tell me what's going on?" Diesel asked, hanging on for dear life as his brother-in-law sped through town like the devil himself was on their tail.

Wyatt shook his head. "This is something you have to see for yourself. Don't know that I could rightly describe it anyway."

They drove north for about fifteen minutes before Wyatt turned left onto an old county road and then right after a mile or so onto a dirt road next to a field of what looked like rice. Diesel's phone buzzed in his pocket, letting him know someone had texted him.

A second buzz sounded. He ignored it, making a mental note to check the messages when he got back to the truck stop.

After they'd bounced along the dirt road for a few minutes, Diesel looked out the window.

"Do you see the problem?" Wyatt asked.

"Yep." The careful rows of rice planted side by side in a large field—or paddy—that had to be at least a hundred acres square had been disturbed in what looked like a very violent way. The few remaining plants stood forlornly in muddy water.

Wyatt parked his cruiser and they got out for a closer look.

There were several untouched rows along the sides of the paddy. In the center, it looked like a large animal had burrowed through the field without plan or reason, uprooting easily a fifth of the crop.

"What in the world did that?"

Wyatt huffed. "You tell me and we'll both know. Could it be one of those alien beasts like what I found out on Lovers' Lane that time?"

Diesel squinted. "I mean, I guess it's possible. I haven't heard of any new beasts being registered by arriving transports. At least not anything that could do this. Then again, transports aren't always aware of what their wily passengers bring along."

"Not reassuring," Wyatt said below his breath, adding, "The other thing you might not notice in all the chaos out there is the rice is gone. There is not a single grain left in all that destruction."

"What?"

"Whatever did this either ate or took all that nearly ready to harvest rice from the plants that were disturbed. The green stalks were cast aside like so much chaff."

"That's a lot of rice."

"Yep. So one of those alien sand beast things or whatever *could* have done this, right?" He whispered the word "alien."

"It's possible, but not really credible."

"The farmer is beside himself, asking me what could have done this. I'll be honest, I'm having trouble thinking up any plausible way to explain it. Clearly, 'gas leak' isn't going to work. Any suggestions?"

Diesel shook his head. "Grizzly bear? I don't think that would work either. Do bears even like rice?"

Wyatt shrugged.

"Maybe a whole horde of wild grizzlies could accomplish this level of destruction, but even that's a stretch and where are the bears now?" Diesel asked the question, but knew there wasn't an answer.

"That was the farmer's initial concern, beyond the money lost for this crop. Where are the beasts responsible located now? Will they come back?"

"Wild boars?"

Wyatt nodded. "I would have said that, but there are no tracks. Boars leave lots of tracks coming and going when they are causing trouble."

"Right."

"There could be tracks under the water."

"Imprints that are now compromised by all the water, so that won't give us any clue as to what could be responsible for this." Diesel pushed out a sigh. He was flummoxed by this situation. Had never seen it before.

"Yes. Exactly."

"When did this happen?"

Wyatt tipped his head back. "Sometime in the night. An alien transport came in yesterday, right?"

"Yep. Last night."

"Any creatures you know of that consume rice like this?"

"Not to my knowledge, but that isn't saying much. Lots of alien folks don't always share every detail of their personal lives or intimate knowledge of what things they must do in order to survive."

"I get it. But have you ever heard of this before?"

"Nope. Never."

Wyatt hooked his thumbs in two belt loops. "I hate to say this to you, Diesel, but you're no help at all." His brother-in-law followed that observation with a big grin.

"I'll take that as a win, since you didn't call me paranoid."

"Oh? Has that been a problem for you lately?"

Diesel shrugged. "I'm worried about Indigo Smith roaming around here somewhere waiting to cause trouble."

"Yeah, I've been keeping an eye out." He pointed to the defiled rice paddy. "Could this have been him?"

Diesel started to shake his head, then stopped. "Space potatoes. I don't know if it was Indigo or hereto previously unknown rice-consuming space creatures or what. I'm not an authority on every single species in all the galaxies or all the proclivities of the ones I am acquainted with. Perhaps I should check with someone else."

Gage came to mind. Or perhaps he could find an authority on Alpha-Prime. However, letting their home planet in on any difficulties the colony faced always had to be measured against what they might do with the information. He didn't want to be singularly responsible for burning down the Earther colony's way of life, only to find out an unknown Earth bug infestation was responsible for the stripped rice paddy.

"Who would know?" Wyatt took his hat off to wipe his brow with his forearm, and replaced it square on his head.

Diesel cast about his semi-addled brain and said, "I have an idea."

"Want me to go with you?"

"Sure, why not."

They got back into Wyatt's cruiser. "Where to?" the sheriff asked, turning the key and gunning the engine.

Diesel pushed out a long-suffering sigh. "Let's go talk to my wily aunt Dixie."

Wyatt did a perfect three-point turn to reverse course and head back to town, laughing boisterously the whole time.

Standing on Francine's landlady's porch, Raphael didn't think he'd heard Mrs. Greenstone correctly and repeated what he'd said, hoping for clarity. "What do you mean Francine didn't come home last night?"

She frowned. "I don't think I can be any clearer than that, young man."

He snapped his fingers. "But she must have been here at least once because I had her luggage brought over from the transport. They sent me a text confirming it had been delivered."

Mrs. Greenstone shook her head sadly. "No. I took delivery of her luggage." She opened her door wider and he saw Francine's bags stacked neatly by the wall, the two she'd brought at the start of their trip and the two filled with the clothes they'd picked up from Jacques Pierre on Ichor-Delta.

"Did you see her last night? Did she talk to you at all?"

"No. I assumed she was with you."

Lucy gave him a worried look and his gut twisted in true concern for the first time since waking up.

He'd head to the Big Bang Truck Stop security office and file an official missing person form with Cam. Then he would call together as many folks as he could to search the area and discover what had happened to her.

"Maybe she had to go to work," Mrs. Greenstone suggested. "Usually she works nights, but since she's been gone so long, perhaps they called her in for a special shift."

Raphael actually exhaled in relief at the suggestion. That made perfect sense.

"Thank you, Mrs. Greenstone. That's probably what happened."

He and Lucy waved goodbye to Francine's landlady and got back into Lucy's vehicle. It was a large SUV, which Raphael appreciated, since he was tall and usually his knees rested against any other vehicle's dashboard.

Lucy drove to the Supernova Supermarket, parking in the first available space near the front entrance. They got out and headed into the grocery store.

Before they made it ten steps inside the door, they heard someone say Francine's name. He and Lucy shared a concerned look. They pivoted and headed in the direction of the female voice expounding on some dramatic story.

"...and then she said a bunch of bad words—I can't repeat them, of course, but you all get the idea—and then she quit. Just like that!" the cashier said with a flourish, snapping her fingers in the air like a flamenco dancer. Raphael had seen them in an Earther video.

"That doesn't sound like Francine," said the customer in line, an older woman in a loud, flowery print outfit.

The cashier shrugged exaggeratedly. "All I know is that even if Francine wants to come back and work here again, Mr. Petey probably won't let her. He's pretty chapped about the whole situation, know what I mean?"

"I want to know what you mean!" Lucy said angrily.

The cashier, whose nametag said, "Hi, I'm Roberta. How can I help you?" blanched when she saw Lucy.

"In fact, I don't believe a single word of that," Lucy added.

Roberta held her hand up like she was about to swear on a Bible before giving testimony in court. "It's *pretty* much exactly what happened," Roberta whined, making Raphael's back teeth ache.

The customer in the flowery print outfit snorted in obvious disbelief. Roberta sent her a dirty look.

"Oh? Pretty much? Don't you have anything better to do than spread gossip all over town?" Lucy asked, clearly about to vent her frustration on the gossipy cashier. Roberta looked puzzled by the question. Maybe gossip was her mainstay in life.

Raphael prepared to grab Lucy if she made any

move to launch herself at Roberta. He understood her fury, but didn't want her to end up in jail for assault.

"Well, she asked," Roberta said, throwing the customer under a bus.

The lady in the loud print floral outfit huffed. "All I said was that I hoped Francine had a nice vacation." She sent a frown at Roberta, adding, "She deserves it."

Lucy moved behind the cashier area, stalking within six inches of Roberta. "Tell me everything you know! Not gossip, just the facts. Now!"

Roberta backed up into the register. "Mr. Petey, the assistant manager, was handing me some change from the back office when he got a text from Francine saying that she quit and wouldn't be back. That's it. That's what happened. Mr. Petey got mad and stomped off, mumbling about calling her to get an explanation. That's all I know!"

Raphael asked, "Where can we find Mr. Petey, the assistant manager?"

Roberta blinked. Everyone queued up in line, including the lady in the loud floral print, pointed toward the back of the store and said in unison, "Manager's office at the back of the store, next to the bathrooms." He nodded his thanks and grabbed Lucy's forearm, pulling her away from Roberta.

He saw the sign for the bathrooms and followed that to a door labeled, "Manager."

Raphael didn't knock, just walked right in, Lucy

on his heels. A short guy with an almost mustache and long wavy hair parted on the side stood in front of a paper-littered desk. A female employee sat in one of the chairs in front of the desk.

"I'm looking for Mr. Petey, the assistant manager," Raphael said.

"I beg your pardon," the man said, brows furrowing.

"Are you Mr. Petey?" Lucy asked, coming around to stand beside Raphael.

"Who's asking?"

"I'm Francine's sister, Lucy." She pointed to Raphael. "This is her fiancé, Raphael. We want to talk to you about the text she sent you."

Mr. Petey's frown deepened. "Francine's text?"

The female employee stood up and skirted around Lucy, calling out over one shoulder, "I'll get back to work and let y'all talk." Mr. Petey went from annoyed to fuming.

"Now wait just a minute. You can't barge in here and interrupt an important employee meeting."

Raphael took a long step toward Petey. "We already did. Now tell us about the text from Francine."

"Why should I?"

"She's missing." Raphael towered over the assistant manager. "You didn't have anything to do with that, did you, Petey? Perhaps we need to call the sheriff to bring you to the station and help you cooperate."

"Missing?" Mr. Petey went from puzzled and uncooperative to frightened in a heartbeat. "Of course I don't have anything to do with that!" He grabbed his phone from a back pocket and began punching and swiping at the screen as fast as his thin fingers could work. He turned the screen toward them. "Here. *This* is the text she sent me after being on a ten-day vacation. I think it's rude that she didn't give two weeks' notice and I told her so in the return text, which she didn't bother to respond to, by the way."

Raphael read Francine's text. "Mr. Petey, I'm not coming back to work at the Supernova Supermarket. I've found someone to take care of me." *What? Is she talking about me?* Francine had never said anything about quitting her job. At least not to him. The night before, she'd even mentioned checking her work schedule.

She also never said anything about wanting to be taken care of. Raphael scanned the return message Mr. Petey sent. "This is a surprise, Francine. I'm assuming you know that Supernova Supermarket policy requires a two-week notice to resign your employment here. I find it rather rude after you were gone for such a long vacation to quit without notice."

"This doesn't sound like Francine." Lucy said out loud what Raphael had been thinking.

"I agree. Something sounds off about this message."

Raphael looked at Mr. Petey, who only shrugged.

"I didn't know her that well. She's only worked here for a few months."

He handed Mr. Petey his phone, but held on to the edge as the assistant manager tried to tug it from his fingers. "I'd like to have you take my number and call me if you hear from her again, okay?"

It wasn't a question, and Mr. Petey seemed to understand that. "Sure. Why not? I doubt she'll call me, though."

Raphael recited his number and watched as Mr. Petey entered it into his contacts. Lucy also insisted on giving Mr. Petey her number. They left, walking slowly out to Lucy's vehicle.

"Where to next?" she asked.

"Honestly, I'm not certain. My next stop would be your place."

Lucy nodded. "Let's go to my place. Maybe she's waiting for me there." Raphael got inside her SUV. He had hope, but didn't really think Francine would be there.

He was getting a really bad feeling in his gut. He should have taken her home last night instead of talking to the Grey brothers. Raphael spent the drive to Axel and Lucy's home thinking about the last time he'd seen Francine's cinnamon hair bobbing along in the horde of passengers disembarking from the transport. She turned left toward the outer civilian exit hallway.

Meaning she could be anywhere.

With anyone.

Where are you, Francine?

Raphael conjured the worst possible scenario from the depths of his nightmares in order to answer that question. Such as, *What if Indigo Smith took her to make a trade for his gold ingots?*

Chapter 15

Diesel pushed out a long sigh, wondering why he'd gone against his better judgment to come here. "Aunt Dixie. Beyond the fact that's not why I'm here, let me be very clear—the answer is no. I do not think we should mass produce the highly inappropriate Maxwell the Martian mugs where hot beverages poured inside makes our alien mascot appear naked with his hind end sticking out!"

Wyatt had a hand up over his mouth, not at all hiding his amusement over the elderly woman's scandalous question regarding a new marketing plan she'd drawn up for clever alien tech on coffee cups.

"We'd make a fortune, Diesel! And it's so funny." She turned to Wyatt. "Have you seen the mug?"

Wyatt shook his head as tears threatened to spill from his eyes.

"Once you pour hot liquid inside, a bubble above Maxwell also appears and says, 'Well, crack my crater, this cup is as hot as a naked alien!' Isn't that hilarious?"

Wyatt bent at the waist and nodded. "It is," he managed to say, not bothering to hold in his laughter.

"I don't care if we made all the money in the world or if it makes everyone in the world laugh like a loon. The answer is still no."

"Spoilsport." She mumbled a few other words under her breath that he ignored. He made a mental note to talk to Wheeler—who designed the illustration—and Gage—who invented the tech—about ensuring their aunt would never be allowed to mass produce that joke mug he'd received as a gag gift.

Diesel wiped one hand down his face and tried again. "The reason we are here is because of what happened at a rice paddy a few miles from Alienn."

"Rice paddy?" Aunt Dixie looked instantly contrite, her eyes shifting back and forth, as if she expected him to blame her for something.

Wyatt wiped moisture from one eye, cleared his throat and said, "There was a disturbance at a farm where it looks like some sort of wild animal plowed through the center of a large plot and either ate or carried off quite a bit of the rice about to be harvested."

Aunt Dixie's eyes went wide as saucers. "You don't say."

Diesel asked, "Do you know of any creature or alien being that could do that?"

"Let me think." She paced back and forth across

her floor. "I can't think of anyone or anything, but let me call Miss Penny."

"Would she know?"

Aunt Dixie shrugged. "I know she loves rice. In fact, it's her favorite food."

Diesel couldn't picture the frail, small-framed, elderly Miss Penny on hands and knees, plowing her way through a rice paddy to quench her love of rice, but maybe being a fan would give her special insight into other possibilities. He was taking any and all tidbits of advice.

"Great. Call her. See if she will come over and talk to us."

"Dandy. I'll be right back." His aunt went to call, leaving Wyatt and Diesel alone.

Wyatt wiped both eyes with the backs of his hands. "You sure have a fun family. And Aunt Dixie is very entertaining."

"You only say that because you're not responsible for managing her chaos. You know laughing only makes her bolder."

"Can't help it. Even you have to admit that the cup she talked about is pretty hilarious."

"I do not have to admit anything." That made Wyatt snort and start laughing again.

Diesel shook his head. His phone buzzed again. He pulled it out and glanced at the screen. It was Gage, probably looking for another of their brothers. Deciding he'd call him back later, Diesel pocketed his phone without answering it.

Wyatt calmed himself and asked, "Do you think Miss Penny will have any information we can use?"

Diesel shrugged. "I hope so. I don't know that being a rice lover will help, but I can't think of anyone else to ask. I also don't have a next step to try without some sort of direction to go in."

Aunt Dixie walked back into the room and headed for the front door. She got there as a light knock sounded. She popped the door wide open and let in Miss Penny, Aunt Dixie's cohort in crime.

"Good day, Miss Penny," Diesel started. He was about to ask his question, but Miss Penny's worried expression stopped him.

"What's wrong, Miss Penny?" Aunt Dixie asked.

"Can you describe the rice paddy that was in disarray?" she asked in a soft voice. Diesel knew she was stronger than she sounded, but was tempted to whisper his response to be respectful.

He and Wyatt told her what they'd seen.

"And the stalks were left behind?"

"Yes. That's what it looked like."

"That's worrisome."

"Why?"

"I suspect it's Indigo Smith."

"What makes you say that?"

"Rice is a pretty good food substitute for nutrients that shifters like me and him typically live on. It is the only sustenance on Earth that helps restore our power to shift."

"I told you rice was her favorite food. I knew she could help." Aunt Dixie grinned as if she knew she'd given them good information. She had. Diesel might admit it to her later.

"Why would he desecrate a rice paddy?" Wyatt asked.

Aunt Dixie said, "Well, he's on the run from everyone, right? So it's not like he can stroll into the Supernova Supermarket and shop pretty as you please without someone recognizing him. He's got to be undercover. He's hiding out somewhere. Plowing through a rice paddy sounds like the perfect solution."

"He didn't ruin any rice paddies the last time he was here."

"Maybe Daphne Charlene ordered rice for him from her restaurant," Aunt Dixie said. "She probably had a jumbo bag in storage ready to cook up and serve with her stupid, award-winning chili recipe."

Diesel looked at Wyatt. "What do you think?"

"I think it's worth a trip over to Daphne Charlene's to ensure she's not harboring an infamous galactic escaped criminal. Again."

"If Daphne Charlene was feeding him, he wouldn't need to destroy a rice paddy," Aunt Dixie said. Miss Penny nodded solemnly.

"What do you suggest?"

Miss Penny straightened. "He's probably hiding in plain sight. But if he ate a big patch of rice, he probably was in his shifted form for a long time and had to have a big feed in order to restore his shifting abilities. The way it works for me is that if I remain in my shifted form for a length of time, my shifting stores wind down like battery power. Once I'm at zero, my shift fails and I have to eat lots of rice to restore myself to full power, so to speak."

Aunt Dixie laughed. "Like when we took the trip on the luxury liner. You went through a forty-pound bag of jasmine rice the week we got back, didn't you?"

Miss Penny cackled at the memory. "Yep. That's about right. I was on empty after a two-week trip and jasmine rice is my favorite kind."

"He probably came in on the transport last night in disguise," Diesel said.

Wyatt narrowed his focus and asked Miss Penny, "Do you have any special skills or the ability to search him out?"

"No. I only know how to keep him from shift—" She stopped talking abruptly and a rueful expression shaped her face. She shook her head and pointed her gaze to the floor.

"You know how to keep him from shifting? That would be very useful knowledge for whatever gulag he ends up in. How?"

Miss Penny shook her head, gaze still on the floor. "Sorry. I can't say. It's a secret. I should never have revealed that. Curse my old age and running at the mouth."

"A secret?" Diesel didn't mean to sound obtuse, but he really wanted something in his arsenal to keep Indigo Smith from escaping so easily. "Can't you tell me the secret?"

Miss Penny stiffened her spine and said, "No. I'm sorry. I can't."

"Can you tell me why?" Diesel wished she'd quit staring at the floor. It made him feel like a bully, looming over a frail old woman he'd known his entire life.

"The thing is…it's a secret that could be used against me as well." She finally lifted her head. He could see the resolute demeanor in her expression. "I'm sorry, but no, that information is too dangerous to be out in the world. There are so few of my race left, that I can't in good conscious reveal it. I'm sorry, Diesel."

Diesel nodded. "Not to worry. I understand." He would be putting that factoid into his back pocket for possible use in the future, now that he knew it existed.

Wyatt said, "What if we got hold of the manifest from last night's transport? Perhaps we could narrow down our suspect pool."

"What are you thinking?" Diesel asked.

"We get a list, check the names and pictures of the passengers, crossing off anyone who already lives here or regulars that we know and search out the shortened list for potential folks that could be Indigo Smith shifted into a fake person."

"Didn't Francine Duvall and her bounty hunter fiancé come back last night?" Aunt Dixie asked.

"Maybe you could ask them if they saw anyone suspicious on the flight."

Diesel tilted his head to one side. "That's a great idea, Aunt Dixie. Thanks."

She beamed from ear to ear. "I have lots of great ideas, Diesel. Want to hear a few more?"

"No time. I've got to go find a criminal."

"Fine." Her faux dejected tone didn't sway him to stop and listen to any more of her "great" ideas. The thought of what else she might want to show in the nude for a moneymaking scheme made him shudder.

Diesel and Wyatt exited his aunt's home and hopped back into Wyatt's cruiser. "Where to next?" Wyatt asked, starting the car and revving it like he was about to stomp the gas pedal to the floorboard and try to win a stop-light race.

"Let me send a message to Raphael and see where he is."

The moment his phone was flat in his hand, it started playing his standard ringtone for a phone call.

"Hello?" he answered, wondering why his sister-in-law, Lucy, would be calling him.

"Diesel!" she said loudly. She started crying so hard he couldn't understand a single word she said after his name.

When Lucy burst into tears, Raphael put his hand on her shoulder to comfort her. It wasn't in his nature to cry and he rarely did it, but right now was the perfect reason. Francine was missing. There was no sign of her anywhere. No one had seen her and besides the three texts from the night before to him, Lucy and Mr. Petey, no one had heard from her. No one had seen her. No one.

He didn't understand any of the words Lucy was trying to say to Diesel, so he held out his hand and she gave him her phone.

"Diesel, it's Raphael. Francine is missing."

"Missing? Just since last night?"

"Yes. We've already looked in all the expected places. She sent a text to me, one to Lucy and one to her boss at work. She quit her job with no notice."

"That doesn't sound like her. I mean, I don't know her super well, but it seems out of character."

"I don't think she made it home last night after our flight." Raphael couldn't believe he was holding it together. His insides felt much like how Lucy was reacting.

"Space potatoes," he heard Diesel say under his breath. "I'm sorry, Raphael."

"I'm worried that Indigo Smith is somehow involved, even though I don't have a shred of proof." Raphael's insides started to shed the sadness as his anger built. He needed to have his sharpest focus for what came next: Indigo's apprehension. He vowed to make that a reality and soon.

"Well, I have a shred of proof," Diesel said. "I'm with Wyatt. We think Indigo Smith is here in town, hiding out. The two incidents could be related." He explained the issue with the rice paddy and what Miss Penny had shared about shifters like Indigo Smith.

Diesel asked, "Did you see anyone on the flight that looked out of place or suspicious?"

Raphael's heartbeat sped in concern. "Possibly. Where can we meet?"

"How about in my office belowstairs? I'd like to have you look at passenger photos from the flight manifest and see if anyone stands out."

"I didn't see anyone that looked like Indigo Smith, obviously, but in disguise he could be anyone."

"True. Still, I'd like to have you take a look."

"Sure thing. There was a couple a row ahead of our seats that I'd like to start with."

"We'll see you there soon."

Raphael hung up, told Lucy what Diesel had said and together they climbed into her vehicle to head back to the Big Bang Truck Stop.

"I should have gone home with her last night." Raphael kicked himself up one side and down the other for not escorting her home.

Lucy sniffed a couple of times. "Stop blaming yourself, Raphael. If she's missing because of Indigo Smith, he would have simply waited until you were gone to take her."

"Maybe."

"We don't even know for certain it was him."

"True." *Who else could it be?*

They drove the rest of the way in silence. She texted Axel from the parking lot and he was waiting in the conference room when they arrived. Lucy flew into her husband's arms. He whispered something in her ear and she calmed down as she clung to him. He stroked a hand down her blond hair, looking at her like she was the most important being in his world.

Raphael wanted to do the same to Francine. She *was* the most important being that had ever been in his world. He was probably even more motivated to find her than Lucy was, but he kept his feelings buried deep down. No need to fall to pieces in front of everyone. An outwardly emotional bounty hunter was bad for business. He also recognized that he'd fall to his knees and cry a bucketful of tears if it would bring Francine back right now.

Diesel and Wyatt sat at the end of the oval table looking at the passenger manifest pictures. Cam Grey, security guy extraordinaire, typed furiously on a different computer further down the table.

"Hey, Cam," he said, taking the empty seat between Wyatt and Cam. Lucy and Axel sat on the other side of the table next to Diesel.

At the end of the table opposite Diesel, a large flat screen blinked to life with an animated picture of Maxwell the Martian hanging from the Alienn,

Arkansas, water tower which was shaped like a saucer spaceship.

Cam pushed a button on his computer and Maxwell disappeared as surveillance video of the Big Bang Truck Stop parking lot started playing. He pointed at the screen. "This is a few minutes before the direct transport from Lava Rock World unloaded last night," he said, pushing another button to speed the playback.

Figures walked quickly across the pavement toward a parking lot on the far left of the screen, where Francine had parked her car before they left Earth for the wedding.

Raphael sat up straight. He couldn't believe he'd forgotten. "Is Francine's car still in the truck stop parking lot?"

"Yes," Diesel said. "I checked after you called. It's still here."

After they sped through ten minutes, Francine appeared on the screen. Raphael's breath stopped for a second or two, as if he expected to see a crazed, rice-munching monster appear out of thin air and spirit her away. Cam hit a button on his laptop and the film slowed to regular speed.

Francine had a sweet smile on her face as she walked. What was she thinking of?

A car pulled up, stopping just barely in frame. They could only see the dark front quarter panel of the vehicle. Francine stopped, looked at the car and smiled wider, waving at someone.

"Is there sound?"

"Nope. Just video," Cam said.

Diesel snorted. "That doesn't sound like you. When did you give up sound on surveillance?"

Cam rolled his eyes. "I have sound and even color on all the internal video surveillance. But the outdoors ones are video-only."

"Why video-only outdoors? Has it always been like that?"

"Yes."

Diesel crossed his arms. "Explain."

Cam's eyes narrowed as if affronted that someone dared to insinuate he wasn't completely on top of a security issue. "Because we need to look like a human business. Remember that foolish alien motto we have where we hide in plain sight and pretend that we're humans all the time so the indigenous population won't discover what we truly are?" The sarcasm was hard to miss.

"That doesn't explain why we don't have sound on the outdoor video cameras."

"It is cost prohibitive to record any usable sound on an outdoor surveillance video at a redneck, southern Arkansas gas station. There are those who would question why a truck stop had such sophisticated and expensive equipment and wonder what we were hiding."

"She's moving," Raphael said, hoping to head off a brotherly brawl.

Francine walked over to the vehicle, moving slightly out of frame as she bent down to look into the passenger window.

"She's not threatened by whoever that is," Lucy said.

"I agree."

There was thirty seconds where they only saw her back, perhaps while she had a conversation with the person in the car. She moved into the frame again briefly, but not enough to see her face. She opened the passenger door and got in the car.

Raphael leaned forward in his seat as if that would help them identify who was driving or offer a hint of what kind of car it was. Unfortunately, the vehicle backed out of the frame and that was it. There was no more.

"Where's the rest of it?" Lucy said and stood up. Axel put a hand on her arm, rubbing soothingly. Raphael wished Francine was here to calm *him* down.

Cam pushed a few buttons, but there was nothing more. "At least we know she got in a car with someone she clearly knew, but we have no idea who it is."

"Any other cameras with a different angle?" Raphael said.

"Nope. This is the only one."

"Did anyone else pass by the same area right before Francine who might have seen something?"

Cam backed up the video to the last person that went in the same direction as Francine, but it was a solid two minutes and twenty-four seconds before she showed up on screen.

Raphael stood up and walked to the screen. "What is across the street here?" He pointed to the edge of the screen.

Diesel squinted. "There's a bank and the Black Hole car wash and an empty lot."

"The bank," Raphael said, snapping his fingers. "Isn't there one of those machines on the street where you can get funds?"

"Probably. So?"

"Can't we look at their video for a different angle?"

"Not unless you're the FBI and on a case involving a felony."

"That's not true," Diesel said.

Cam huffed. "Oh? That's what Barney told me the last time I wanted to search his bank's video to find a pesky vandal."

Diesel said, "We can at least ask him. He might cough it up to help Francine."

Raphael straightened. "I'll ask him." Apparently, his growling, menacing tone was too threatening, because everyone at the table shook their heads.

Before they resolved the issue of who would approach the bank manager across the street, Gage bounded into the room.

"Why haven't you answered any of my texts?"

Diesel squinted. "I'm busy looking for an escaped prisoner and now a missing woman. I'll get to you eventually."

Gage looked worried, which wasn't usually his nature. He was hard to rile. "I suggest you get to me now. Wheeler was found knocked out cold behind the truck stop. He's unconscious. I thought you might want to know."

No one spoke. No one moved. No one blinked. And then everyone did. Then everyone around the table stood up, faced Gage or started walking toward him, all asking questions about Wheeler.

Raphael was sorry Wheeler Grey was hurt, but he didn't want anyone to lose focus about Francine being missing. Before he could say anything, Diesel whistled sharply, silencing the commotion. "Settle down everyone. Gage, you're the doctor. What happened to Wheeler?"

Gage sighed. "A garbage collector found him behind one of the bins picked up to dump in the truck. It seems someone knocked him in the head hard enough to keep him out for several hours. His vitals look good, but it worries me that he hasn't woken up yet."

Diesel turned to Raphael and Lucy. "Why don't the two of you try to get access to the video from Barney? Ask nice and maybe he'll look at it and tell you if anything we need to know is on it."

Raphael asked Gage, "Where is the garbage bin your brother was found behind?"

Diesel's eyes widened. He answered before Gage could, understanding immediately why Raphael asked. "It's very close to the area where Francine got into that car."

Wyatt said, "I'll go with you to ask Barney about his video feed. Perhaps a law enforcement presence will encourage him to let us look at it."

Lucy looked at Raphael and then back at Axel, as if she weren't sure which direction to go. Axel said something in her ear, but she shook her head. "No. I'll go with you to see Wheeler." She turned to Raphael. "Please find her. Find my sister."

Raphael nodded. He planned to do whatever it took to find Francine. He would not fail.

Lucy was depending on him, but he had his own reasons.

Life without Francine was not a future he wanted to consider.

Chapter 16

Francine was having the strangest dream. She'd been flying through the galaxy with Raphael and all of a sudden she woke up in a car with someone she didn't know. So odd.

The pungent scent of orange peel lingered in the air, but it was fading, as if someone had just sprayed her with a mist of citrus while peeling an orange and then walked away. She was in a bed, but not her bed. Too soft.

Orange peel scent or not, she stretched, trying to wake up and start her day. Her hip bumped something. Was there someone next to her in bed? Oh, right. Raphael.

Was this his bed? She thought he'd have a harder mattress.

Didn't matter. Raphael was awesome. She couldn't wait to marry him. Their trip had been amazing. Whether they stayed on Earth or went off into the galaxy to chase bounties, she would be happy as long as she was with Raphael.

Perhaps she would become a bounty hunter, too. Then they could go everywhere together.

She reached out an arm to wrap it around Raphael, but she wasn't next to a person. Her eyes opened and she saw a large, long pillow. Not Raphael. Huh. *Where did this body pillow come from?* Come to think of it, where was she? This definitely wasn't her house or her bed.

She sat up too fast and fell back on the bed, dizzy from the mere effort it took to rise. What was wrong with her?

Francine rested, eyes closed, scrambling to get her wits about her and remember any current events. She remembered landing at the Big Bang Truck Stop and disembarking. Diesel wanted Raphael's help, so she went home by herself.

She remembered walking toward the parking lot where she'd left her vehicle. What happened next? Francine searched her mind for a clue.

The hazy memory of a car pulling up alongside her made its way into her mind. Oh, right. Someone in a car beeped a horn at her and waved. She smiled and waved back.

The passenger window had lowered. Francine had walked over and leaned in to talk to…one of the Grey brothers. And then there was nothing before waking up here.

Except for the strong scent of popcorn that had wafted nearby, smelling delicious. If there was popcorn nearby, she was too tired to eat it. Maybe she'd just take a little nap before trying to figure anything else out or trying to find any popcorn.

Francine didn't even remember what Wheeler Grey had asked her. Maybe he'd offered her popcorn.

Raphael and Wyatt got to the bank just after noon. He twisted the violet diamond ring on his finger, a nervous tic he thought he'd rid himself of years ago. He was grateful for the gem-studded band, because otherwise he'd be miserable with Earth's solar power beating down on him. His sunglasses were in place, which helped tremendously.

The magic of violet diamonds from Ichor-Delta was their ability to absorb the most harmful Earther colony sun's rays for people of his race and keep from burning a layer of his skin off by the end of the day.

Once inside the bank, he didn't remove his UV-resistant sunglasses. Quite a bit of sunshine streamed through the narrow windows along the walls. Too much indirect solar light gave him a headache unless his eyes were protected. The ring also helped to combat that issue, but the glasses kept his head clear of all pain.

It was very busy inside the Aurora Borealis Bank. Raphael worried the manager would be less likely to help them until customer traffic slowed down. He stared across the room and noticed what looked like a female assistant seated at a desk right outside the manager's office in the back corner of the bank.

Two of the manager's office walls were made of glass. Wide blinds covered the glass walls, hiding the manager from view. Was he even in there?

The assistant got up, walked to the manager's door, tapped lightly, stuck her head in for only a few seconds and promptly exited down the back hallway.

Perhaps it was lunchtime for the assistant. Good.

Wyatt marched over to the door with the plate that read, "Manager—Bert Barney." He knocked so loudly that several people in the bank looked at them. Raphael stood with Wyatt as Bert Barney whipped the door open with what looked like a curse ready to fly from his lips.

One look at Wyatt and he mashed his lips closed before letting loose inappropriate words.

Barney cleared his throat. "Sheriff Campbell, how nice to see you. What can I do for you today?"

Wyatt pushed the door open and walked forward. Barney was forced to back up two steps to keep from colliding with him in the doorway. Raphael followed right behind, closing the door firmly behind them.

"Mr. Barney," Wyatt said in an all-business tone. "I'll come straight to the point. My sister-in-law, Francine, is missing. She was last seen across the street talking to someone in a car."

"I'm sorry to hear that—"

"Thank you. What I really need is to look at the footage from your street ATM facing the truck stop."

He turned to Raphael. "What is the time frame again, Raphael?"

Raphael didn't miss a beat, reciting the ten-minute time frame they wanted to look at from last night. Wyatt knew the answer to his own question, but he clearly wanted Raphael to say it, perhaps to impress upon Barney that he was accompanied by someone who was not going to take no for an answer.

Fine by him.

Barney's brows went from surprise to concern to deeply furrowed in the space of three seconds as he bounced his gaze between them. "Oh, that's too bad...but I'm not certain I can help you with—"

Wyatt didn't let him finish. "I disagree, Mr. Barney. From my perspective, you are the *only* person who can help me find out who took my sister-in-law." He sidestepped him and walked around Barney's desk. "Is this your computer?"

"Yes, but—"

"Great," Wyatt said and pointed at it. "Please bring up the street ATM surveillance video from last night at the time Raphael mentioned."

Barney stood there with indecision practically oozing out of his pores before he moved to the executive chair behind his desk and seated himself to do exactly what Wyatt asked. Amazing.

The next time Raphael had to get information from a reluctant witness, he was bringing Wyatt with him to do the talking.

Raphael did his best arms crossed, angry bounty hunter stance as Barney's fingers danced across his keyboard. Wyatt looked over the man's shoulder, pointing to various things on the screen to help Barney go faster.

"There," he said, indicating the car that pulled into the truck stop lot and inched forward as Francine walked across the empty asphalt toward the parking lot.

The ATM camera was pointed directly at the driver's side of the car.

Wyatt said, "I recognize that car. And it makes complete sense."

"Who is it?" Raphael asked, leaning closer to get a better look at the black-and-white surveillance film.

"Wheeler."

On the video, the car backed up after Francine got inside the passenger side. They all watched as the driver's face was clearly framed in the car window. It *was* Wheeler.

The car stopped briefly, likely to change gears, and Wheeler's features suddenly twisted brutally, becoming grossly unrecognizable before morphing into another familiar face.

"Oh, no," Wyatt said.

"How did he do that?" Barney asked, staring wide eyed at the screen.

Raphael bit back a bad word, managing only barely to keep from saying it out loud. The car moved, turning in a half circle, and headed away from downtown Alienn.

As the car passed the ATM surveillance camera, they all saw Francine, eyes closed, slumped in the seat, one beautiful cheek pressed against the passenger window, clearly unconscious.

Raphael's entire body tightened in merciless fury.

Indigo Smith had Francine.

Francine woke sometime later and wondered why she was so sleepy. Galactic space travel must be exhausting. Maybe it was like having jet lag.

She put a hand on the top of her head, registering that her hair felt damp. How odd. She didn't remember showering. Had she been so tired last night she forgot?

Opening her eyes, she noted she was in what looked like a hotel room. Across from the bed was a mirrored closet door. In it, she could see the bulk of the big, long pillow behind her.

More disturbing was her hair. She sat up. Her hair had been dyed back to blond. Who would do that? Her gaze searched the room for clues as to what was going on.

Was this Raphael's room under the Big Bang Truck Stop? It looked very different from the room she'd stayed in when she and her family had come to Alienn for the arranged marriage. Her parents, especially her mother, had insisted on only the best, so she'd been housed in very nice accommodations at the waystation.

This place looked—well, basically clean, if plain.

Forgoing the issue of her hair color, Francine sniffed the air. The scent of orange peel lingered, but she remembered smelling the distinct scent of popcorn. It had been very strong. Were they next to the movie theater? It didn't matter. The rumble in her belly told her she was hungry. She decided there were three things she needed to accomplish before she looked for Raphael or an explanation for her hair color change.

She needed a bathroom.

She needed a shower.

She needed a giant cup of coffee to function beyond the basics.

The sound of a door opening to her right didn't prepare her for the shaft of sunlight that hit her eyes.

"Gracious! Please! Shut the door!" Francine put a hand to her eyes to block the blinding glare. A thread of piercing pain wound from her eyes to drill straight into her brain. She didn't even see who came in. She didn't care. She wanted the pain to stop.

"You're finally awake," said a familiar voice she couldn't place right away. It was a voice she hadn't heard in a while. *Who is that?*

All Francine knew for certain was it was not Raphael's voice.

The door closed and the light level in the room dimmed substantially. The man lowered his tone to just above a whisper. "I can't wait to talk to you, Francine. We can start making plans for our future."

Our future? Oh no. *I'm in really big trouble.*

Raphael followed the Grey family away from the medical area and Wheeler's room toward the conference room. He did his best not to show it, but on the inside he roiled with the desire to do something, anything. He wanted to leap up and run everywhere Ichor-Delta fast until he found Francine. It was all he could do to remain passive on the outside, his frown likely the only sign he was sick with worry.

Once the group was seated at the conference table—with a clear understanding that Gage would notify them the millisecond Wheeler woke up—Cam told them something surprising. "Wheeler's car is still in Alienn. Indigo may have taken it, but he brought it back, because it's here in the truck stop parking lot."

"When?"

"No idea."

"How is that possible? He drove away from Alienn. Wyatt and Raphael brought back a copy of the bank's street camera view."

"Can we get more bank video?"

Cam shook his head. "Doesn't matter. The bank's camera doesn't include the employee parking lot."

Earlier, Raphael had watched Wyatt pull out a miniature Defender, twist the dial on top and shoot Bert Barney with it before the banker noticed what he was doing. The man slumped back in his chair and they made their escape with the flash drive containing the street footage from the bank's surveillance.

He'd asked, "Isn't this guy Barney an Alpha?"

Wyatt nodded. "Yes, but technically this isn't a completely authorized information grab. I try to stay on the right side of the law, but when it comes to escaped prisoners from another planet along with missing family members, I have to make judgment calls. Today is one of those days I'm calling it for the Grey family."

"I didn't realize there was a Defender for Alphas."

Wyatt smiled. "It's a recent invention. The Defender for Earthers is nicknamed The Big D. This one is called The Little D."

"Interesting. Cam sure is a wizard with stuff like that," Raphael said.

"Actually, I believe Indigo Smith rewired Cam's original Defender device to make one to use on Alphas as a part of his escape plan before he was sent off to the gulag. Cam made a few more adjustments to keep Alphas from suffering splitting headaches if the device is used on them."

Raphael and Wyatt had left Barney to sleep off the Alpha Defender shot while they delivered the security surveillance to the group.

Cam rolled his eyes and stared at the ceiling for several moments, muttering to himself. He then said, "Okay, I understand your confusion, but I'm telling you that after driving for almost an hour, Indigo parked the car for five minutes, turned around and drove Wheeler's car back into Alienn. He put the car back in the employee parking lot. We have no idea when. There's no telling where he is now."

"Why would he do that?" Diesel asked. His exasperation level seemed on par with Raphael's.

"What?"

"Drive out of town, then return to Alienn."

"Find him and ask him yourself, because I don't know." Cam huffed and closed his laptop. All their nerves were a frayed since Wheeler still hadn't woken up.

Aunt Dixie had been called to join them. She promised to bring Miss Penny. Raphael didn't know if that would be helpful, but Diesel seemed okay with the idea.

"Wheeler's car is parked back in the truck stop parking lot, right?" Raphael asked.

"Yes. Right. So I said." Cam popped his laptop open again, typed a few keys on his computer as if to reaffirm his statement.

"I think we need to check it out." Raphael hadn't taken a seat. He looked longingly at the door, ready to bolt through it and do something, anything that would put him closer to finding Francine.

"Well, I think we need to wait until Wheeler wakes up before doing anything else," Cam said.

"What if he doesn't wake up?" Diesel asked quietly.

The room went dead silent.

The mood in the conference room turned so morose after Diesel asked the stupid, foolish question he hadn't meant to speak out loud that they adjourned. They filed slowly out of the room, walking as if Wheeler's condition might have worsened, even though it hadn't been half an hour since they'd left his room.

Diesel noted that Raphael appeared calm, but ready to leap up at a moment's notice to run and rescue Francine if only he knew where to go.

Gage didn't seem surprised to see them back in Wheeler's room. He launched into a slew of medical explanations. Diesel listened to his brother ramble, listing no less than eight causes why Wheeler might still be unconscious. Though there was no clear reason for him to still be out cold, Gage wasn't ready to believe anything horrible was happening to their brother.

Diesel put a hand on his younger brother's arm, saying softly, "Please wake up, Wheeler. Just for a minute." Wheeler didn't move. Diesel had to work even harder to keep his feelings under control. It helped when Juliana took his hand and leaned her head against his shoulder.

The whole family had gathered outside Wheeler's room, waiting either for a sign he was going to wake up or the arrival of any test result or medical person to give them an update on his condition. He wondered if he should summon their parents home from their travels.

Axel motioned him away from the group, taking him aside to add yet one more morsel to his already overfull plate.

"I hate to bring it up now, but I've been meaning to tell you about our cousins."

"What cousins?"

"The Ashcraft cousins."

Diesel nodded. "Oh right, they operate a bauxite refinery on Alpha-Prime, right? Don't we ship bauxite ore to them every month?"

"Yes. And they did run a refinery, but last month they entered into a partnership with some other company who will take over operations there."

"Why do I need to know this?" Diesel asked.

"Well, because the whole family pitched in together and bought a third share in our bauxite mining operation. They are moving here next month."

"To Alienn?"

"Yep. They wanted a change, I guess." Axel shrugged. "I'll be good, Diesel."

"I guess so. But I'll probably forget you told me this later on, be forewarned."

"No worries. And it'll be fine, Diesel. They are all solid and I think they will fit right in."

"No doubt." Diesel looked up in time to see Aunt Dixie headed toward them with her shapeshifter friend in tow.

Axel noticed them and murmured under his breath, "Here comes trouble."

"Double trouble," Diesel said as the two women marched into the center of the assembled family outside Wheeler room.

"Miss Penny might be able to help, Wheeler" Aunt Dixie said and marched into Wheeler's room with Miss Penny on her heels.

She repeated her claim to Gage.

"How?" Gage demanded.

Aunt Dixie frowned. "Just give her a chance."

"Fine." Gage gestured for the elderly women to go in, and the rest of the family followed.

Aunt Dixie whispered encouragingly to her friend, "Go for it." Miss Penny lifted her ginormous purse onto the bed, opened the top, dug around inside and pulled out a small orange bottle. She sprayed a fine mist into Wheeler's face, twice. The strong scent of orange peels wafted through the air.

Wheeler's eyes flew open. He bolted upright, coughing, gasping for breath, waving a hand in front of his nose as runnels of the clear mist traveled down his cheeks. His eyes squeezed shut and he shook his head. Everyone in the room waited, unmoving, unspeaking.

"I hate orange peels," he said angrily, eyes still closed.

Diesel let out a breath he hadn't realized he held. At least his brother was awake and coherent.

"Wheeler?" Gage asked. "Are you okay?"

"I'd be a whole lot better if no one sprayed me with nasty orange peel scent ever again. Ew." He wiped his face, winking one eye open to look at his hand. "Someone sprayed me in the face. Why would they do that?" The single eye gazed around at the faces of nearly his entire family—his brothers, sisters-in-law, Valene and her sheriff, Aunt Dixie— all grateful he was out of his odd coma while he grumped about the smell.

Diesel turned to Miss Penny. "Okay, what was that? How did you know that would work?"

She gave him a cagey look. "Maybe I was just lucky."

"I sincerely doubt that. What *do* you know, Miss Penny?"

"Nothing. I know nothing." She dropped her little orange spray bottle back in the huge purse and slid it from the edge of the bed. It landed on the floor with a *plunk*, like a twenty-pound barbell hitting the mat after a long workout.

Aunt Dixie poked him in the chest with one boney finger, gaining his full attention. He rubbed the spot where she'd bruised him. "Be grateful,

Diesel. Don't start asking questions you don't want the answer to."

"But I do want the answer," he retorted.

She waved her palm in front of his eyes a couple of times, chanting in a low, strange voice, "No, you don't, Diesel. You are happy. You want to go home. You don't have any questions."

"You can't hypnotize me!" Diesel said, incredulous she'd attempt something so ridiculous.

She shrugged. "It was worth a try. I need to work on my suggestive voice skills."

Diesel looked at Wheeler, still wiping orange spray from his face. He finally yanked the hospital sheet up to his face and wiped it with vigor. When Diesel looked back, Miss Penny was no longer at the edge of Wheeler's bed. He turned in time to see her, massive purse hitched up on one bony shoulder, escape from the room. She sure was fast when she wanted to be.

"Hey. Wait," Diesel said, going into the hall after her. Miss Penny kicked it up a notch and walked even faster, but she was tiny and had short legs. Diesel easily caught up before she'd gotten too far. The purse must have slowed her down.

"Wait just a minute." Diesel rounded in front of Miss Penny to stop her forward progress.

She stopped, tilting her head back to look into his face. "I already told both you and Wyatt I can't tell you all my secrets."

"You haven't told us *any* of your secrets."

"Good. That's the way it has to be." Her gaze intense, she added quietly, "I am sorry, Diesel. I can't tell you what you want to know. Please understand."

He was grateful for her help with Wheeler, but after this missing person issue was resolved and Indigo Smith had been recovered—again—he vowed to have a quiet one on one with Miss Penny.

"I just wanted to say thank you for helping Wheeler." Behind him, he heard someone exit the hospital room. He saw Raphael and Wyatt remained by the door, watchful, but not approaching.

Miss Penny noted the two men and nodded in their direction once. She exhaled deeply, as if relieved Diesel didn't plan to interrogate her, nodded once more and skirted him to leave.

Clearly, he needed to gain a better perspective on her brand of rare shifter and what he could expect if more of them showed up on Earth. It would be a struggle, but he put that conversation on a back burner.

First, he needed to find out what had happened to Wheeler.

Diesel, Raphael and Wyatt reentered the room to find Gage finishing a cursory check of Wheeler's vitals.

Gage looked into his eyes, shining a small penlight in each one several times. He grabbed Wheeler's wrist, pressing two fingers against his pulse. "How do you feel? Any pain?"

"No pain, really, just a little achy, like I worked

out too hard. My brain feels a bit fuzzy. Basically, I feel fine except for the gag-worthy scent of orange peels saturating the air."

Diesel moved next to the bed. "I have some questions for you."

Wheeler said, "Shoot."

"What's the last thing you remember before waking up here in the hospital?"

"I was headed home and I went to get my car."

"Which way did you leave the truck stop? By way of the employee's door, leading to the parking lot?"

Wheeler hesitated. "No. I parked in the customer lot because I needed to get gas."

This threw Diesel off. Why had Indigo brought Wheeler's car back to a different place than where he'd retrieved it? "Well, did you get gas?"

"I don't remember. The last thing I remember was walking toward my car. And a weird craving for popcorn."

"Popcorn, huh? Strange. What door did you come out of to get to your car?"

Wheeler paused to think. "I came through the upstairs Earther truck stop area and out the store's front door."

"Do you remember seeing anyone who looked out of place or odd? Anything that struck you as not quite right?"

Again, Wheeler silently pondered his question before responding. "I mean, it's an Earther truck stop. There are sometimes lots of odd people about."

"Like who, for instance?"

Wheeler looked up at the ceiling as if trying to retrieve a difficult to locate memory. Diesel hated to press his brother when he was clearly not a hundred percent, but he needed his help.

He said, slowly, "There was this woman at the furthest pump from the store. She looked like she was either throwing something in the trash can or maybe getting the squeegee to wash her windows. The minute she saw me she stopped and stared.

"In fact, she stared so hard that I waved, thinking I must know her, just couldn't place her."

Diesel asked, "What did *she* do?"

Wheeler lifted one shoulder. "Nothing. She kept staring, so I kept moving."

"What did she look like?"

Wheeler closed his eyes for a few seconds, shook his head and eventually he shrugged again. "I don't know, like an Earther woman."

"Tall, short, old, young, skinny, heavy? Could you give me a hint?"

Wheeler put both his hands to his head. "Let me think. She was very tall for a human, but not skinny or heavy, just average. She was not old or young, but middle-aged."

"What color was her hair?"

"Light brown?"

"Are you asking me or telling me?"

"Don't be a snot, Diesel."

"I'm sorry, I know you aren't feeling well, but this

is important, Wheeler. Lucy's sister Francine is missing and we are looking for information on who took her." Diesel glanced at Raphael. The big bounty hunter looked poised to pounce on any and every word Wheeler uttered. One false move and Diesel expected he would leap onto Wheeler's bed and shake the information out of him.

Wheeler looked instantly contrite. "Sorry. I didn't see anyone truly out of place or odd."

Raphael exhaled, seeming to calm slightly.

"You didn't see Indigo Smith?"

Wheeler's eyes widened. "No way. I would have remembered *that*."

Gage spoke before Diesel could ask any more questions. "I need to run a few tests, Diesel. Are you finished?"

"For now. Thanks, Wheeler. Glad you're back with us, little brother."

Wheeler's head jerked up. "Hey, I remember something! The woman wore expensive clothing and jewelry. I remember thinking she seemed too well-dressed for a truck stop. That was odd. And her height, that's it."

"Thanks, Wheeler. That will help." *I hope.*

A theory as to what might be going on eluded Diesel as he mentally ran through the pertinent facts. A rich, tall woman, a.k.a. Indigo Smith in disguise, might have knocked out Wheeler and taken his car, kidnapped Francine, and returned to the car to a different location.

One way or another, he planned to foil Indigo Smith's plans to retrieve the gold ingots and ensure Francine's safe return. He also hoped his hiding place for Indigo's ill-gotten gains was still a secret.

Chapter 17

Raphael tucked away Wheeler's information to consider later. He needed to find Francine. Nothing Wheeler told them offered clues that would immediately help them locate her. He'd have to wait until Wheeler could see the surveillance video of the pumps at the truck stop. He was barely able to contain his frustration. He wanted to go, run, find Francine. If only he had a hint of where to go.

But he didn't.

He wondered what Diesel and the mysterious Miss Penny had talked about in the hall.

Given the unhappy look on Diesel's face, Miss Penny likely hadn't been very forthcoming about her instant cure. Raphael found Wheeler's sudden consciousness interesting, but it was not his primary concern. Each moment Francine remained missing ratcheted up his stress level. He was becoming antsy and that was never a good look on a bounty hunter. His resolve was to remain strong outwardly. Thankfully, no one could see his insides, where anxiety writhed like a thousand snakes in an angry pit of despair.

They left Gage to continue his tests and reconvened in the hallway outside Wheeler's room to discuss next steps.

Axel had to leave and take care of something so he kissed Lucy and whispered something in her ear. She nodded and watched him leave.

Lucy approached them. Now that Wheeler was awake, her focus had likely shifted back to her sister. "What do we need to do next to find Francine?"

Diesel released a long, silent sigh. "We should locate Wheeler's car to see if there are any clues inside as to where Indigo Smith has taken her."

Lucy nodded. "Great idea."

Indigo Smith was likely too smart to have left any clues, but the bank's video surveillance showed her with the shifter in Wheeler's car. It was the last place Francine had been seen.

It was a place to start.

They found Wheeler's car quickly in the employee parking area. It was unlocked. Diesel and Raphael opened the front doors and scanned every inch of the floorboards and seats. Lucy and Wyatt did the same to the back.

Raphael saw nothing, not a strand of hair, not a crumb. He sat in the front passenger seat, pulled down the visor. He looked in the cup holders of the console. Nothing there. He opened the glovebox, expecting to see more nothing.

His heart nearly stopped.

He reached inside and pulled out the violet diamond ring he'd given Francine. The instant he saw it, he realized he might have been able to track her through a material trace of the violet diamonds. The gemstones from Ichor-Delta were extremely rare on Earth. In fact, he was likely the only other person who wore one.

"This is Francine's engagement ring," Raphael said. The tone of his own voice surprised him. He sounded despondent when instead he was the very definition of determined. He would find her, whatever it took.

Lucy made a soft sound of dismay and touched his shoulder.

Wyatt said, "Pop the trunk latch, Diesel. Let's take a look in there. Maybe we'll get lucky."

Diesel located and pushed a button on the driver's console. A soft *pffmt* sound came from the back of the car.

All four of them stepped out and gathered around the trunk area. Diesel slowly lifted the rear hatch. Raphael held his breath as the trunk lid rose up.

Would she be in there? Would she be alive? She *had* to be alive.

There was nothing in the trunk and, more importantly, no one. Raphael breathed out a sigh of relief. He wasn't the only one.

"Now what?" Lucy asked.

Wyatt asked, "What does Indigo Smith want?"

Diesel narrowed his gaze. "He wants the gold ingots. At least that is what I'm assuming he wants. Why else would he make such an effort to get here after escaping the gulag?"

"Who would know where the gold ingots are stored right now?" Wyatt asked.

"Only a select few. Why?"

Wyatt stared at him. "Is Wheeler one of the select few?"

"Space potatoes!" Diesel straightened. "Yes. He knows." Diesel shifted his gaze all around the area as if a horde of monsters was about to attack.

Wyatt said, "We better check and see if the gold ingots are still where you think they are."

Everyone started to move except Raphael. "Why would Indigo Smith take Francine if Wheeler provided him with the information he needed?"

"Leverage?" Lucy asked.

"But he knocked Wheeler out to steal his car *before* he took Francine and drove an hour away. Then he brought the car to the truck stop, but parked it in a different place? Why?"

"Maybe to ensure the information Wheeler gave him was right?" Lucy shrugged. "I'm not sure what answer you're looking for."

"This scenario seems off to me. My gut is telling me that something is not as it seems, but I can't put a finger on what's wrong."

"Your gut aside, we need to go check on the gold ingot hiding place, don't we?" Wyatt said. "Plus, if he's got that treasure, he'll have to find a way to transport it and that would take some doing. Maybe we can catch him in the act."

"What if he's watching us right now to see if we go to wherever the ingots are?" Raphael asked.

"We can *what if* ourselves until the next century dawns and not find the right answer, but I see your point, Raphael." Diesel stared at the trunk, lost in thought for a few seconds before finally nodding. "I have an idea. Can you all just follow my lead, or do I need to give a lengthy explanation of every detail before we go?"

Wyatt, Lucy and Raphael exchanged amused looks and Raphael spoke for them. "We'll just follow your lead, o Fearless Leader."

"Awesome. We'll take my SUV." He pointed to a large black SUV parked in a slot with a sign that read, "parking space reserved for our Fearless Leader."

Diesel slammed Wheeler's trunk lid closed and they all followed him to his vehicle. They selected the same doors they had when searching Wheeler's car. Diesel driving, Raphael riding shotgun, with Lucy and Wyatt in the back.

Raphael typically appreciated Earth's beautiful landscape. Today, not so much. His usual low-key temper was riled to the point of imminent explosion with the least provocation. Diesel better have a good plan or Raphael might lose it altogether.

Diesel drove slowly and carefully out of Alienn,

Arkansas, and into a neighboring township, Skeeter Bite, Arkansas.

"Are you driving slow so that anyone following us won't lose us?" Raphael asked after Diesel came to a full stop at a stop sign and waited a good thirty seconds before taking a left toward a sign along the road announcing Skeeter Bite, pop. 5,703.

"Maybe."

"Are you really driving to the hiding place to see if the gold ingots are still there?"

"Probably not."

"Wow, you're just a fount of information."

Diesel smiled. "If I'm wrong, then I don't have to admit it."

"Where are we going?"

"Daphne Charlene's restaurant, Critters Café."

Raphael frowned. "Isn't that sort of an obvious place for Indigo to have searched?"

"Yep. But in case Wheeler was forced to give up the real location, this will throw off the scent for anyone checking to see if his information is accurate."

"Will I ever be one of the privileged few who know where the gold ingots are hidden?"

"Why do you need to know?"

"I don't. I'm just rabidly curious."

"Sorry, rabid curiosity isn't the secret password. But I'll take your feelings into consideration and think about it."

Raphael said, "All I can ask."

They made their way to Skeeter Bite and Critters Café without mishap. If anyone was following, Raphael didn't see them.

The blue sky filled with puffy white clouds was beautiful, but that was another thing Raphael barely noticed as they all disembarked from Diesel's SUV.

In a few hours, it would be a whole day since he'd been with Francine. It was intolerable. The moment he found her, he might sling her over one shoulder and take her to the nearest place that they could get married, running Ichor-Delta fast the whole way.

His belly roiled with worry for his love.

Wyatt led the way into Critters Café. He didn't seem happy about it, but knew that Daphne Charlene would likely talk to him because it was no secret she wanted Skeeter Bite's sheriff for her own. It didn't matter to her that he was married to Valene, the youngest Grey and only girl, or that Valene was pregnant with their first child.

Daphne Charlene told anyone and everyone within earshot that when the time came—as it naturally would—that Wyatt and Valene's foolish union was over, she was ready, willing and able to step in and make Wyatt happy.

Raphael followed Wyatt, with Diesel and Lucy behind him.

Daphne Charlene didn't see them enter, but when she spotted Wyatt standing in her café, she squealed like she'd just won the lottery.

"Wyatt! What are you doing here?"

He opened his mouth, but she didn't let him speak before answering herself. "Oh, that doesn't matter. How can I help you?" She walked the short distance to the foursome and moved directly into Wyatt's personal space, pressing her body into his.

Raphael saw him stiffen and quickly form a smile. Daphne Charlene was likely the only one in the room who didn't see that his smile was an uncomfortable one.

Wyatt said, "We were wondering if you'd seen Francine Duvall lately."

Daphne Charlene took half a step back and acted like Wyatt had just slapped her. "Francine Duvall?" Her sudden frown made Raphael uneasy. "Why are you asking about another woman?"

"She's missing and her fiancé," he pointed to Raphael, "is looking for her. I'm helping him."

Her posture relaxed. "Oh, that's nice of you, Wyatt. You are such a good man and a truly great sheriff." She eased closer to Wyatt as she stared at Raphael. "I haven't seen Francine lately. I heard a rumor going around at the Supernova Supermarket in Alienn that she left town with some guy."

"That was me, but we came back last night," Raphael said. "Have you seen her today?"

Daphne Charlene looked around the room, her expression confused. "Francine Duvall? Today?" She crossed her arms, hugging herself as though chilled. "Nope. I don't know anything about her."

Raphael didn't believe her. She was acting odd. "I don't believe you."

Daphne Charlene stiffened and gave him a menacing stare. "I don't know where she is. I don't know her very well. I don't have any information about her. Just like I told that other man."

"Other man? What other man?" Raphael moved into her personal space, the tips of his boots a whisper from the pointy toes of her stiletto-heeled shoes. His gaze drilled into her eyes as he willed her to spill her guts. "Tell me everything you said to him."

She sucked in a breath. "There was a man here asking about her a couple of weeks ago or so."

"What did he look like?"

She shrugged. "Um, I don't know."

"Make an effort."

Her eyes widened slightly. "Okay. Well, he was tall and sort of attractive, I guess."

"Sort of? You guess? Be more specific."

Daphne Charlene tilted her head. "Well, he was handsome, in a rough around the edges sort of way, but he had a beer belly he tried to hide by sucking in his breath when he wasn't talking. It didn't work." Her scoffing tone was quickly replaced by more description once she caught Raphael's impatient gaze.

"He said he was a bounty hunter and was looking for a woman. He kept going on and on about her. That he had been watching her and he wanted to make a good first impression when he introduced himself and that he wanted to take her away from here forever. That woman's name was Francine." *Is it…? Could it be? Edgar? Randel Edgar?*

Raphael reassessed that night at the Supernova Supermarket. Edgar had shown up so soon after he and Francine started talking and truly out of nowhere.

Without further prompting, Daphne Charlene added, "He even asked me what I thought he should do to impress this woman. I gave him an idea and that's all I know."

Raphael lowered his face. "What did you tell him?"

Daphne Charlene gulped once. "I told him to bring her a special present."

"Such as?"

"I should have told him jewelry, but I thought I could kill two birds with one stone, so to speak."

"What does that mean?" Raphael said in his, *I'm losing patience with you* tone. He leaned forward, his breath ruffling a strand of hair alongside her face.

"Okay. Fine. A stray cat made a home in my storeroom a few months back and gave birth to a litter of five kittens before I could shoo it outside. My staff gave me grief about getting rid of them. I've been trying to give away kittens for quite a while. I gave this man a black kitten—the last one in the litter—to give her."

Raphael's memory zoomed to the night he'd rescued Francine from falling onto the black kitten. The one she'd named Angel, for him. He hadn't been outside the Supernova Supermarket very long before noticing the little black kitten on the sidewalk. But then Francine had exited the building and his focus went immediately to her. He'd been running through scenarios of what he could say to impress her, while watching as she walked toward the kitten.

She'd lost her balance and he hadn't thought, just moved to keep her from hitting the ground, and the kitten, too.

"Was this man's name Randel Edgar?"

"He didn't tell me his name."

Raphael fished out his communication device and selected the photo library. He found an older, and much more flattering, picture of Edgar and showed it to her.

Daphne Charlene nodded. "That's him, only he didn't look that good."

Raphael took a deep breath. Edgar was a bounty hunter. It wasn't a stretch to imagine that he would have information and insight as to the whereabouts of Indigo Smith. Perhaps he'd been in the cadre of outside help Indigo had used to escape the gulag.

Diesel said, "Is there anything else you can tell us about him?"

She looked to the ceiling as she thought and her face lit up. "Oh, one other thing. When we went into the storage room to get the kitten, he noticed a fifty-pound bag of rice I didn't even remember ordering. He asked how much it was, so I threw that in for free if he agreed to take the kitten. He did."

Raphael's brain stilled to consider the new information. Edgar being a shifter was so shocking he had difficulty coming to terms with the contradiction of this new knowledge combined with his years' long, but distant association with the brash, unkempt bounty hunter.

Edgar was obnoxiously boastful on a good day. On a bad day, he was impossible to be around. If he could shift into the countenance of other beings, he'd hidden that exceptional talent very well, presenting a wholly different personality in public.

A café employee called out that Daphne Charlene was needed in the kitchen, breaking Raphael's solemn realization.

Daphne Charlene looked annoyed, but seemed to sense the conversation was over. She gave Wyatt a bold head-to-toe stare as she backed away as if reluctant to remove herself from his presence, finally scuttling out of the café's dining room and through a door marked "employees only."

That wouldn't stop him from going after her if he needed to, but Raphael was thinking through a whole different set of facts. Was Edgar a rare shifter? He couldn't imagine that, given what he knew about the man.

And more disturbing, how could Raphael have been blind to Edgar's infatuation with Francine?

✳

Francine tried to keep calm. The familiar man seated himself on the edge of the bed beside her. She quickly stood, fighting not to wobble. She didn't want him to help her stand, but also didn't want to share such an intimate space with anyone but Raphael. She moved to flatten herself against the wall beside the bathroom door.

She kept her eyes averted from his as he continued to stare at her with a manic zeal she found disconcerting.

"Where are we?" she asked.

He glanced around the small space and clearly found it substandard, because a small frown surfaced. "Oh, don't worry. This place is just temporary. It was the best I could find until I acquire a hidden treasure and capture a very special bounty. Then I'll have enough credits so we can travel the galaxy forever in grand style."

Ah, yes. He's a bounty hunter, too. She remembered that much. She also remembered she didn't like this man. Hadn't liked him from the second she laid eyes on him.

He turned his zealous focus back on Francine. She looked away, not wanting to encourage him.

"Are you hungry?" he asked. "I've made us some food." He lifted his arm, gesturing to the door he'd just come through. He'd left it ajar.

Francine wasn't about to eat anything prepared, even if she starved herself. But she nodded, keeping her eyes lowered to the floor. *Just go along until you can escape.* She moved to the open door, keeping track of where he was behind her.

"Your hair came out very nice. I love the blond. That's the way you should keep it," he said.

She put a hand to her damp hair. "Why did you change my hair back to this color?"

"Because your blond hair is beautiful. The red was a hideous mistake." He came alongside her, staring at her head with satisfaction. He reached up to touch her hair, but she dodged him and moved toward the door.

Raphael liked her red hair, but she didn't voice that. She kept moving.

They exited the small bedroom and entered a larger room. It looked like a cabin. Beyond the two windows she saw forest thick with trees. If she ran out the door next to one of the windows, she likely wouldn't make it very far before the man caught her.

She'd save that move for later, when she could be assured the door was unlocked and unbarred. Two metal brackets bolted to the door held a wide plank of sturdy wood nestled securely in place. If the door was the only way out, she wasn't certain she could lift the wood plank without help.

The window closest to the door was a simple, single-paned plate glass window, perhaps four feet tall by two or three feet wide. However, the glass looked like it was hand poured. It was wavy in places, obscured in patches and slightly yellowed. Was it really old? Or perhaps someone had tried to apply tinting to curb the sunlight streaming inside. She didn't see that it was needed, as the room was dank and dim.

To the left was a small wooden table set with two plates and utensils along with two chairs across from each other. It was next to the small kitchen. On the right was a small living room with a sofa and recliner in front of a stone fireplace that stretched high to the A-frame ceiling.

The man closed the door to the bedroom, brushing her sleeve as he passed by to pull out a chair for her. It took all she had not to flinch when they came into contact. Perhaps he was simply being gentlemanly, but she remained wary. She'd been drugged and brought to a strange place by someone who was as good as a stranger to be cautious of, as far as she was concerned.

"Have a seat." He gestured for her to take the chair.

Francine weighed her options and decided to play along, for now. She'd be looking for the best time to escape.

He moved into the tiny kitchen area, grabbing the metal handles of an industrial-sized soup pot from the three-burner stove. It looked like he needed all three burners to accommodate the pan.

On the closest kitchen counter was an odd rectangular device. Black with silver bolts and various dials on one side, it looked sort of like the home version of a fancy espresso machine. Beyond the fact that a cup of coffee sounded really good, the machine looked wildly out of place in this rustic cabin with its mid-twentieth century decor.

"I hope you like rice. I made a big batch for us."

Francine narrowed her gaze as he plopped the enormous pot of rice on the small table between the two place settings. She could have sworn all four table legs groaned trying to hold the weight.

Big batch? It's enough for a battalion of Royal Guardsmen.

Raphael once again rode shotgun in Diesel's truck as they headed to the Big Bang Truck Stop basement. They had to figure out their next move, but Raphael was at a loss for what it might be. He was all revved up with nowhere to go.

He mulled over all his memories of Edgar. He tried to view them in a new light, but didn't remember anything that would have hinted at the other bounty hunter's amazing powers of shifting.

They were in sight of the truck stop when Diesel asked, "Are you okay?"

"No. Francine is missing. I won't be okay until I find her."

"Fair enough," Diesel said quietly.

"Why do you ask? Is my inner scowl showing?"

"No. You've just been quiet for quite a while."

"I'm worried about her. I won't relax until she's safely in my sight again."

"Understandable. We'll do everything within our power to help."

"I appreciate that."

The rest of the three-minute ride was silent. They all got out of the SUV and used the secret aliens-only door into the basement. They made their way to the conference room, filing in one by one to take seats around the oval table.

Axel walked in with an electronic clipboard in one hand. "I have a message package for you, Boudreaux."

"When did this come in?"

"Not long ago. I was on my way to your quarters when I saw you four heading here."

Raphael signed for the package, noting it was from Zendorr. He pushed out a sigh. He wasn't looking for a bounty right now, but he'd have to take time to respond and turn it down.

He almost pushed it aside for later, but decided to suck it up and deal with it.

Everyone else had seated themselves around the conference table. He looked around for a quiet place, then decided he didn't care if any of the Grey brothers, Lucy or Wyatt knew what was inside the package.

He opened it. It wasn't a dossier for a bounty. It was a private note from Zendorr.

Greetings, my friend,

I do not have a bounty for you, but I saw a surprising news account recently from Paludion-Epsilon that I thought you might want to know. I believe you were acquainted with Randel Edgar.

Raphael stopped reading. Zendorr must have discovered Edgar was a rare shifter. *How many others know?* He shook his head and continued reading.

I don't know if you two were close, but I'm sorry to tell you that he's been found dead.

His vision blurred with shock. The message crumpled in his fingers. His immediate thought was of Francine. If Edgar was dead, where was she? *No! She can't be dead!* He flattened the paper on the table and finished reading

The most surprising news was that he's been dead for almost a year.

Can you believe it?

Strange, because recently I sent him a dossier for Victor Campion.

I was delighted to distribute the reversal on that bounty, by the way. I know you and Victor are closely acquainted.

Hopefully, this unfortunately sad message finds you in good health.

Very respectfully, Zendorr

What? A year! That was not possible. He shifted his thought to an even more devastating one. If Edgar was dead for the last year, who was running around shifted into his body for the past several months? Certainly not Indigo Smith.

Raphael stood up without realizing he'd done so.

"What's up?" Diesel asked, looking more concerned than he let show during the drive back from Critters Cafe.

Raphael looked at the crumpled message. "A friend just told me Randel Edgar is dead."

There were gasps in the room. "When? Was Francine with him?" Lucy asked.

Raphael shook his head. "His body was found on Paludion-Epsilon. He's been dead for a year."

Diesel also stood up. "Then who got a black kitten and monster bag of rice from Daphne Charlene?"

No one said a word.

A song started playing in the room. *Bad boys, bad boys.*

Wyatt quickly pulled his phone from his pocket and answered, "Hey, Hunter. I'm kind of busy right now. Can I call you back later on?" He listened for a few seconds. His eyes widened and he stood up, pushing his chair back from the table. He started moving to the door. "Thank you, Hunter. I owe you big-time."

Diesel said, "Wait a minute! First of all, how does your cell phone work through the transmission blockers down here?"

Wyatt grinned. "Valene told me about a recently enacted secret fix. If I keep my phone on a special frequency, it works. So, I do."

"I won't ask how you got my sister to talk."

"Good idea. You probably don't want to know anyway." Wyatt winked once and grinned. Anyone looking could tell he probably kissed the secret information out of his wife.

"You got that right. Second, what did Hunter tell you and where are you going?"

"I had him keeping an eye on something for me. He just called to let me know that something had changed. I'll explain on the way."

"Where are we going?"

"Skeeter Bite. Outskirts of town. A cabin passed down to Daphne Charlene's father from his parents. It was on a list of properties we looked at back when Valene was kidnapped by Indigo Smith. Hunter spotted some activity there."

Chapter 18

Francine pushed sticky grains of rice around on her plate with her fork, not daring to actually put any in her mouth. Her "host" worked his way through a second heaping plate with the gusto of a man consuming his food in order to win the grand prize in a rice-eating contest.

He didn't seem to notice she wasn't eating. She reconsidered asking for a cup of coffee, then rejected that idea. She didn't want anything from him. She didn't trust it not to be drugged.

Across the room she noticed another box positioned low to the ground in front of the only door. The box was wooden, slatted on each side and looked sort of like an old-fashioned chest filled with dynamite. Hopefully not.

"Are you done eating?" he asked abruptly, not finishing the mouthful he was chewing. She did her best not to make a distasteful face, only nodding and placing her fork down next to the plate of uneaten rice.

"You need to fill up. We won't be able to eat for quite a while."

"I'm not hungry, thank you," she said. "What happens next?"

He finished chewing his mouthful and took a drink of whatever was in his glass. His expression said he was pleased with himself. "Well, the next agenda item will be rather explosive."

Francine glanced at the wooden box. He saw her, and a slow, frightening grin shaped his mouth.

"We're about to have our own big bang. Get it?" He laughed uproariously.

The only thing I get is that you are crazy, Francine thought grimly.

The time it took to reach the cabin strained every fiber of Raphael's fragile nerves. Diesel sped the whole way to the cabin deep in the woods on a barely passable dirt road through the trees, but it wasn't fast enough for Raphael.

Who had taken Francine if not Edgar? How many more rare shifters were out there wandering about? For a race that supposedly died out a century ago, he now knew of four: Miss Penny, Indigo Smith, a man discovered in Nocturne Falls who caused some trouble a year ago before being caught and now a mystery shifter who snatched Francine and, as it turned out, wasn't Randel Edgar.

Diesel hit a pothole going too fast and everyone in the vehicle briefly launched into the air, yanked back by their seat belts to land hard in their seats like a choreographed routine. Raphael didn't care if bruises covered his entire body. He certainly wasn't going to tell Diesel to slow down.

No one complained. Diesel kept his SUV flying through the woods. Raphael was grateful.

At long last, Raphael caught a glimpse of a cabin through the trees.

"Is that it?" he asked.

From the back seat, Wyatt answered, "Yes. That's it."

Raphael was ready to leap out of his seat, leg muscles tensed, hand on the inner door handle as Diesel somehow pulled more speed from the SUV, slewing wildly on the windy dirt road. They saw more of the cabin during each curve in the road. He wanted to run Ichor-Delta fast, but calmed himself. His friends wanted to help, and Lucy had an equally strong stake in this race.

Diesel slowed through the last curve and stopped inside the tree line just shy of the clearing where the cabin stood. He drove onto the grassy area to one side of the road, facing his truck grill toward the centered front door as if he might drive straight into the cabin.

Raphael silently voted for ramming through the door, but logic changed his mind. He wanted to know exactly where Francine was before taking any aggressive tactical moves.

A narrow window to the right of the door didn't offer much of a view inside.

"I'm going in," Lucy said. Raphael heard her seat belt click and she opened her door.

"Wait!" Diesel said.

"For what?" she shot back.

"What's our plan? What are we doing? Beating the door down with guns blazing or taking the softer, more sensible approach?"

Lucy sighed. Raphael did, too. Diesel was right.

Wyatt suggested, "Why don't I slip around back inside the edge of the forest here and see what I can see?"

"Great!" Lucy nodded. "I'll get out, too."

Raphael unclicked his seat belt and opened his door a crack. "I'm not waiting in the vehicle."

Diesel leaned forward over the steering wheel and took a good look all around the area. It was quiet.

Raphael heard a gust of wind ripple through the trees and the leaves rustled, making a noise he usually found calming. Not today.

"Fine," Diesel said, unclicking his own seat belt. "Let's all go. Wyatt, head around through the woods to the rear of the cabin. Try to keep out of sight. Maybe we can surprise whoever is inside."

"Got it," Wyatt said. "I'll whistle if I see anyone."

Wyatt was out of the truck and quickly into the thick line of brush and pine trees at the edge of the clearing. Hopefully his exit had been hidden from anyone inside the cabin.

The three of them left the SUV together, fanned out and walked toward the front of the cabin, Lucy on Raphael's right, Diesel on his left.

Lucy squealed. "I see her! She's sitting inside!"

Raphael changed direction, heading toward Lucy, who practically jumped up and down as she pointed at the window. "Francine!" she called.

He came alongside Lucy, looked through the narrow window into the cabin...and there she was. Francine. At long last.

The breath slowly left him as he watched her beautiful profile. She was seated at a table. The window was obscured by what looked like decades of grime, but it was Francine. Raphael's muscles tensed. He readied himself for whatever fight loomed within the walls of the dilapidated cabin.

Lucy waved one arm high above her head, shouting, "Francine!" and moved toward the door.

A blast of heat, debris and force lifted them up and flattened them on the ground.

Lucy landed half on top of Raphael, the back of her head striking his shoulder hard enough for him to notice. It would bruise, no doubt, but Raphael couldn't quite process why it had happened. His hearing was gone, his head filled only with the sound of blood pulsing through his eardrums as debris rained down on them.

He turned his head and saw Diesel flat on his back, a burning board resting across one thigh. He should get that off before it burned a hole in his pants.

That was as much rational thought as Raphael possessed.

Raphael lifted his head to look at the cabin, but it was no longer there. Every wall was obliterated, raining down on them or gone. Part of the stone fireplace remained, but it was blackened, the upper portion gone, likely having been blasted apart and deposited in the surrounding forest.

They were lucky not to have been beaned in the head with a flying fireplace stone. He stared at where the cabin should have been and a very important thought finally registered.

Francine. No. Just no.

Raphael sat up as Lucy stirred against him. She shook her head, sitting as he did. He rose unsteadily to his feet and Lucy did the same. He stared at the near complete ruin of the cabin and fell to his knees as his legs gave out. *No. No!*

He heard screaming. Was that Lucy? Or was it him? Maybe it was both of them.

Francine gave her captor a death stare as he opened the trunk, clearly expecting her to climb inside and be happy about it. She wanted him to understand just how deeply *unhappy* she was.

"What if I don't want to get in there?" She stood on wobbly legs, having just woken to discover her captor had tied her wrists together.

"Too bad." He reached out to touch her shoulder. She flinched, dodging his touch.

He didn't seem fazed by her sour attitude. He pointed at the trunk again, making her furious.

She didn't move.

He angrily pulled out the tranquilizer gun and waved it at her. She frowned, but didn't get in the trunk. She wasn't fond of tight spaces on a good day.

With a menacing grimace, he shot her in the belly again.

You skanky little crust fish.

That was the last thing she remembered before waking up inside the trunk. Her hands were tied in front of her and her ankles were also bound. The car was moving. She could hear the engine noise and feel the jostling of the moving vehicle. Where were they going? She didn't know. She didn't want to know where he planned to take her, she wanted to be free. Frustration at this whole kidnap situation rose inside her like a volcano waiting to erupt.

Francine screamed and kicked her bound feet against the trunk lid until her legs grew weary. The car jostled her for a few minutes, but stopped soon enough.

She tried to focus on what happened before she was stuffed in the trunk. She'd been pushing jasmine rice around on her plate, trying to make it look like she might have consumed a grain or two.

A loud klaxon sounded throughout the cabin as her captor finished his third heaping plate of rice.

He'd eaten nearly half of the soup pot of rice.

"Hmm," he said, sounding surprised as he chewed his last bite of rice. "They are early." He pushed his chair from the table, dropped his fork on the table and stood up.

Francine asked, "Who is early?"

Her captor grinned that maniacal smile she'd quickly grown to hate. "Never you mind that for now." He walked past her and rummaged in a large box next to the strange-looking espresso machine thing on the kitchen counter.

She stood from the table, carefully pushing her chair out and stepping away from her uneaten plate of food. She turned to see what he was doing as he pulled a big handgun out of the box and pointed it at her forehead in one smooth move. "Are you gonna be difficult?" he asked.

Francine looked cross-eyed at the gun barrel that was only six inches from her face and shook her head, quietly adding, "No," to ensure he understood she didn't want to die.

"Good answer." Then he lowered the gun and shot her in the belly.

Francine felt the shot and looked down to see how big of a hole he'd made. Dang it, she'd said, "No," out loud so he'd understand. But there wasn't a bullet hole. A dart-like thing protruded from her shirt. A wave of dizziness rolled through her. She swayed to one side, caught herself and tried to straighten, but couldn't seem to tell which way was up.

She pulled the barb out and said, "That was so mean." She heard loud buzzing in her ears. The floor rushed up. She slammed her eyes shut, expecting to feel the pain of smacking the cabin's hard, dirty wood floor. Instead, she only saw stars in a field of obsidian.

When she woke, her hands were tied at the wrists and he was trying to get her inside the trunk. When she refused, expecting another dart in the gut, he sprayed something that smelled like popcorn in her face.

She glared, wishing looks could smoke him to cinders in his boots as she crumpled onto the dirt road next to the car. Whatever he'd sprayed her with knocked her unconscious—again.

Awake once more—and very annoyed at being knocked unconscious every other minute—Francine did a mental review. Her aching body was in a dark space, bouncing around like whatever she rode in was rolling down a hill.

What in the world?

The vehicle's brakes squealed as she slammed backward, grasping that she was in the trunk. How rude! Tranquilized—twice—tied up and stuffed in a trunk was the trifecta it took to put her in panic mode. She tried to break her restraints, to no avail. Something covered her mouth, but she could at least breath through her nose.

The vehicle stopped moving.

Struggling only made things worse, and the

prospect of freedom seemed more distant than ever. She strained against the ties at her ankles, but felt no give. She took a deep breath, relaxed all her limbs and tried to calm herself. She took a deep breath and released it slowly. Then she did that again.

Francine heard the muffled sound of a car door opening and closing. When the trunk lid opened and light flooded in, she squinted, then glared at the man responsible for her predicament.

He ripped the tape from her mouth, sending burning pain across her face.

Francine gave him another silent withering gaze, unable to speak without shouting a stream of vulgar expletives. She was not going to stoop to that coarse level. No matter what he did.

"Don't look at me like that. It couldn't be helped."

"Whatever," she managed. "Get me out of here."

He reached in, grabbed her arm and half wrestled, half lifted her out of the trunk. They were still in the woods, parked on a narrow dirt road. They could be anywhere.

Francine was barely on her unstable, bound feet when the sound of a loud explosion filled the air. Her captor grinned wider as he turned toward the sound.

"What was that?"

"Our freedom."

"What?" Francine had a really bad feeling. "What does that mean?"

He turned back, his expression gleeful, eyes filled

with maniacal delight. Nodding in the direction of the plume of smoke she could see rising into the sky, he said, "That was the cabin we were just in."

"You blew it up? Why? Why would you do that?"

"Now they think we are dead, at least for now. Once I get my payoff, we can go anywhere."

Francine's bad feeling grew tenfold. "Who thinks we're dead?"

"Anyone chasing us."

"Like Raphael?" Francine's eyes filled with tears. She couldn't look away from the plume of smoke above the trees in the distance. Her captor slammed the car trunk closed.

"Are you going to cooperate?" he asked.

His surly tone shoved her despair aside and made anger well up inside her.

"I wouldn't count on it."

"Do you want to ride to our next destination inside the car or in the trunk?"

Francine watched the plume of smoke spread, drift and dissipate in the sky above the treetops. It did not serve her possible escape to be trapped in the trunk.

"I'd like to ride in the car." She added a quiet, "Please."

"Are you going to be nice and get along?"

"Yes." Thinking hard in her mind, *I will for now, you despicable crust fish.*

He bent down and cut the zip tie binding her ankles with a small knife he pulled out of his front pants pocket. She scanned her surroundings. She saw only thick, dense woods in every direction, with the exception of the dirt road they were parked on. If anyone else came along, both vehicles would scrape the tree bark on either side of the road and still might not be able to pass each other.

Perhaps this was a private road to the blown-up cabin. She didn't know where she was. She hadn't recognized the rustic cabin.

The height of the trees and the canopy above blocked her ability to even tell what time of day it was. Morning? Late afternoon? She didn't know.

"There's nowhere for you to run. Besides, I'd find you."

She nodded, knowing no matter what he said she'd bolt at the first opportunity to do so. Then another thought occurred. "Why?"

"What?" He seemed startled.

"Why would you chase me and find me? We've never even spoken before today. You don't know me. So why?"

His expression of shock grew until he flashed a smile. "You don't recognize me!" He laughed. "Do you remember seeing me on the flight from Alpha-Prime to the Ossuary Valerian Space Station?"

"No. Were you there?"

He nodded, smiling in satisfaction. She had no memory of him there.

Francine studied his features. He was a bounty hunter. Someone Raphael knew. As she stared, his features shifted and changed, morphing and moving into those of someone else. Her mouth fell open.

Oh my. It was the scruffy, grubby woman from their flight leaving Alpha-Prime. The one with dusty, cut-up clothing that got angry when she wasn't identified immediately as a first-class passenger. The woman's face shifted into one of satisfaction as if she wanted to ensure Francine how clever she was, or rather how clever the shifter bounty hunter was.

Before Francine could comment on the shocking revelation, his face melted and changed yet again. It was another man. A different man. A familiar man.

Francine's mouth parted in disbelief. It was the *other* bounty hunter. The one she'd seen at Wyatt and Valene's house, pushing Raphael out the door. The man she'd labeled a nameless enemy she would never forgive. She had been right about him from first glance.

"Do you recognize me now?" he asked. He held his arms out, inviting her to look. "I'm Charlie Adler. This is the real me."

"You're a shifter. How rare." Stunned, Francine tried to process the possibilities.

The maniacal grin returned. It looked the same no matter what face he wore. "Yes. I've hidden that fact my whole life. You're the first person I've ever told." A look of renewed zeal appeared on his expression.

"Why me?"

"Because I want you. I have since you were one of the Duvall Five. The first time I saw you was at your home in the protected sphere on Alpha-Prime."

"When was this?" Francine asked.

"Oh, years ago. You and your sisters were having your pictures taken. I was on the hunt for the photographer, but I waited until my prey had completed his task before claiming him for my bounty. I got to keep the pictures he took that day. That's when I knew."

"Knew what?" she asked, not sure she wanted to know the answer.

"That we clearly belong together. It's taken me years and a lot of effort to realize my dream to make you mine."

Francine's mind raced. It wasn't clear to *her* that they belonged together.

"But I don't even know you." She tried logic, not expecting it to work, but found the need within her soul to give it a try anyway.

"You have the rest of your life to get to know me." The look on his face was one of satisfaction. It occurred to her that her parents had used this very line when trying to convince her that an arranged marriage was best. *You have the rest of your life to get to know the stranger we are forcing you to marry.*

Reason and logic were obviously not going to work on him.

"What if I don't want to get to know you?" The words were out of her mouth before she could stop them. She shook her head, as if that would help suck them back inside. It didn't.

His maniacal smile of joy turned dark and menacing. He shifted back into the bounty hunter who'd interrupted her and Raphael when they spoke to each other over a sweet little black kitten. Poor Angel. Francine missed her little troublemaker ball of fluff.

"I've gone to a lot of trouble to get us to this point. You should be grateful." The gun appeared. He shot the dart into her arm this time. "I've changed my mind. You will ride in the trunk."

Francine stumbled as the woozy effects of the drug hit her system. She sent a mental wish out into the universe before surrendering to the power of the drugs rushing through her system.

Falling to her knees, her last vision was of the dirt road and the towering trees on either side of the narrow lane. Her last thought was repeated until she was out.

Raphael, I love only you.

Chapter 19

Raphael, still on his knees, palms pressed to each side of his head as if he could squeeze away the excruciating vision before him, braced himself for the intrusion of the facts. Francine could not have survived the blast. No one could have, human or Alpha.

That hard truth aside, he couldn't seem to wrap his mind around the horrid idea of her being gone forever.

Lucy had seen Francine inside, too. She was distraught, couldn't stop screaming, crying or babbling nonsense, pointing at the blackened and flaming remnants of the cabin.

From somewhere in his head came the screaming phrase. *No! Stop!*

What if Raphael refused to believe she was dead? How could she be gone? Answer: She couldn't be. She had to be alive somewhere.

A tiny particle of his soul sparked to life. He would not give up. Not now. Not ever.

Francine is alive. He continued to repeat the phrase in his head. *Francine is alive.*

Raphael grasped that notion hard, wrapping his optimism around it and squeezing with all his mental might. He stood up and turned to Lucy.

"I don't believe it," he told her calmly, much more serenely than he truly felt.

Her wail of anguish subsided. She looked confused and pointed at the ruin again. "But…I saw her in there. You did, too. Her hair was blond, but it was her. I know it was." Tears streamed through the dust, ash and fine debris on her cheeks.

Wyatt sprinted from the tree line opposite where he'd entered before the cabin blew to smithereens. He went straight to Diesel, pulled the burning board off him and knelt to ensure he was still breathing.

Raphael and Lucy walked over to join them as Diesel coughed and sat up.

"You okay?" Wyatt asked him.

Diesel stared at the space where the cabin used to be. "It blew up." He lifted his gaze to Raphael and Lucy, pain in his eyes. "I'm so sorry."

"She wasn't in there," Raphael said, his voice unwavering. "She's alive."

"Are you sure? I thought you saw her," Diesel said.

"It's a trick. We are being led to believe something that isn't true."

Lucy, voice trembling, said, "What makes you think that? I need to know it's not just wishful thinking."

Raphael wasn't sure he could explain his gut feeling. His brain worked furiously on an outlandish explanation he wasn't certain should be shared just yet. He looked into Lucy's eyes, full of misery, but showing signs of hope. Hope he'd placed there, waiting for him to clarify his wild assumption.

"Maybe it's a feeling or simply slim speculation—"

"I'll take it." Lucy wiped her face quickly. "Tell us what you think is happening. Where is Francine?"

"I don't know. But she's alive. Somewhere."

Wyatt spoke up. "I need to show you something."

They followed him wordlessly around the mess in the center the clearing, stepping over burning boards and piles of debris. Wyatt led them into the woods, twenty feet or so behind remains of the cabin. They all stopped walking when they saw it.

"What *is* that?" Lucy asked.

Raphael took in what appeared to be a thirty-foot trench cut through the forest. The last several feet of the hallway-wide hole curved to the north, toward Skeeter Bite.

Diesel said, "Is that a tunnel?"

Wyatt nodded. "That is my guess. The force of the blast probably caused it to cave in. Not many tunnels in the area because of the water table, but there are a few here and there in higher elevations across the state. Back in the day, moonshiners were creative beyond just driving their cars faster on back roads."

"Where do you think it goes?" Lucy asked.

Wyatt pointed a thumb over one shoulder. "If I had to guess, I'd say Daphne Charlene's place."

"House or café?"

"Café. Her restaurant is built on a knoll and I know she has a basement there. It wouldn't be a stretch to imagine that's where it connects or maybe somewhere in the forest nearby along the same trajectory. There are rumors of just such a tunnel, though I've never personally been in it or seen it."

"How far? Do you think it goes all the way there? That's got to be ten miles, right?"

Wyatt shrugged. "Maybe not all the way, but close. Plus, there are a couple of access roads cut through the forest in that direction. Could be the tunnel comes out near one of those dirt roads, leading to the café, or it's an easier path between the café and the cabin."

A piercing squeal made all four of them look at the remains of the cabin.

"Good heavens, what is that?" Lucy asked, putting her hands over her ears to block the sound.

Wyatt moved toward the rubble and the three of them followed.

After some digging, they found a mangled metal box with silver bolts that was the cause of the nails on a chalkboard screech. Wyatt stomped the box several times with his booted foot until the sound stopped.

"Is that what I think it is?" Diesel asked.

Wyatt shook his head. "I have no idea. I'm just

glad I could smash away the shrieking ugly noise it made."

Raphael nodded. "It's a holographic projector from Alpha-Prime."

"Get out of town," Wyatt said, then added, "Wait, what's that?"

Lucy started to smile. "A holograph. Someone tried to fool us into believing that Francine was dead." She turned her gaze to him. "How did you know?"

Raphael shrugged. "I didn't exactly. Just a gut feeling." He couldn't explain that feeling was the certain knowledge he couldn't go on without Francine in his future.

Diesel looked at his vehicle. "Let's get out of here. Wyatt, you can call Hunter and report the explosion."

Wyatt pulled his phone from his pocket.

Raphael usually kept his unique Ichor-Delta skills under the radar. Not today. "I'm going to head toward Skeeter Bite through the woods in that direction." He pointed at the trench.

"On foot?" Wyatt asked.

Diesel's expression said he understood Raphael's abilities. "Call if you need any help."

Raphael nodded. "If I don't find her, where will you be so I can catch up with you?"

Wyatt shrugged. "We can meet you at Critters. Do you think that's where they are headed through that tunnel?"

Diesel said, "I'm not certain, but it's my best guess. Raphael?"

Raphael pondered the question before answering. "Indigo Smith is the one with the connection to Daphne Charlene Dumont. He's most likely on the hunt for his gold ingots. However, this mystery shifter is more likely the one behind Francine's abduction. He changed her hair color, which makes me believe he's not looking for a payoff from anyone for her return. He took her to keep her." Saying the words out loud made acid boil in his belly.

"That makes sense. Why would the mystery shifter and Indigo Smith be working together?" Diesel asked.

"My best guess is the mystery shifter wants a portion of the gold ingots in payment for helping Indigo Smith escape the gulag and secure transport to Earth. They likely arrived on the transport last night together and enacted their plans. They knocked out Wheeler, possibly got him to give up the location of the gold ingots and used Wheeler's face to lure Francine. Their next goal must be attaining the gold."

A smile slid over Diesel's features.

"What?" Raphael asked.

"The truth is, I'm one of only two people with the exact knowledge of where the gold ingots are. Cam's the other one, and you can bet he'll never tell what he knows."

"I thought you said Wheeler knows," Wyatt said.

"Well, he knows what Cam and I told everyone. But you know Cam and his security protocols. At the time, he said, 'Two can keep a secret if one is dead' or something equally disturbing. The end result is the two of us changed the location at the last minute, but didn't tell anyone."

Raphael nodded. The Grey brothers were a smart bunch. "Good. They will make arrangements to get the gold ingots from the wrong place. So where did Wheeler tell them the gold ingots are?"

"Cam would probably kill me for revealing it, but what the heck." He told them the initial secret location in a voice so quiet it was as if he expected Cam to leap out of the forest and catch him tattling.

Wyatt said, "I smell a stakeout."

"I'm still going to follow the tunnel toward the café and see if I can find Francine," Raphael said. "If I don't find her, I'll meet you at the stakeout."

Diesel, Wyatt and Lucy turned toward Diesel's vehicle. Raphael was gone before they took their first steps.

He ran as fast as possible, dodging thick stands of trees as he raced toward Skeeter Bite and Daphne Charlene's café. The first intersecting road was a narrow cut through the woods. Dust floated in the air above the dirt track, indicating someone had just driven by. He followed the road with his gaze, seeing more dust clouds further down the road. After a straight quarter-mile run, the road curved northwest and out of sight.

He raced in that direction, keeping hidden in the woods. No need to let the kidnapper know they hadn't been fooled by the explosion.

Raphael traveled about a mile before he saw a vehicle parked by the side of the road. Abandoned. No one was inside that he could see from this distance, unless they were huddled in the footwell—or in the trunk. He approached cautiously, slowing his Ichor-Delta speed.

He went to the driver's side door, pulled the handle and opened the door. Unlocked. Interesting. No one crouched on the floor. Raphael checked the back seat. He popped the trunk using the button by the steering wheel.

Raphael held his breath as he walked to the rear bumper, wanting desperately to find her alive inside, but almost afraid to look.

He counted to three silently before lifting the trunk lid.

Francine opened her eyes as the trunk popped open. Now what?

She slammed her eyes shut and pretended to be asleep. No sense in making her fate come faster, whatever her fate was.

"Francine? Is it really you?" Raphael's voice eased past her fear. "Are you okay?" She felt a hand on her waist and cracked her eyes open. Raphael. She opened her eyes wide.

Raphael looked around the area as he spoke. "I can't believe I found you."

"Me either."

He scooped her out of the trunk and set her on her feet while searching the road both ways as if he expected marauders to appear and slay them where they stood.

She looked, too, but didn't see anyone or anything. She waited for him to encompass her in his warm, tight embrace and kiss her senseless.

He turned toward her, but didn't display the expected passion. Hadn't he missed her? Wasn't he desperately grateful he'd found her? She expected him to be more physical. More loving. Happier to see her.

He looked more distracted than anything else. Maybe there was something dangerous in the area, like her hidden captor. She looked around. Nothing.

When she turned her focus back on Raphael, he wore an odd smile. He eyed her leisurely from head to toe, but didn't make any move to hug or kiss her. What was up with him? He said, "We should get out of here, Francine. Never know who's lurking around."

She narrowed her eyes in surprise over his odd perusal and lack of physicality, but shook it off. Perhaps there were things she didn't know and he needed to get her to safety quickly.

"Do you have a car?" she asked, watching him carefully.

"No. I walked." He pointed in the direction of where the car had been headed. "Come on. Let's go."

Francine didn't move. "What if I can't keep up?"

He was teasing. He knew she couldn't walk Ichor-Delta fast. A timid smile shaped her lips.

Raphael looked bewildered. "Don't worry. I'll walk slowly enough for you to keep up. Come on," he repeated, adding a quick hand gesture to ensure she understood. "Let's go."

She tried again, wanting him to act normal. "Oh? You aren't going to walk Ichor-Delta fast and leave me in the dust?" She waited for him to crack a smile. He didn't. He remained confused. Or at least the expression on his face was mystified. Something was wrong. Something was truly off.

"What do you mean? I would never leave you in the dirt." Raphael was good at looking like a bad boy bounty hunter when he was serious, but he did it without frowning.

Francine stared at Raphael for a few seconds, at the dour expression she'd never seen shape his mouth before. An awkward smile appeared on his lips. Another oddity she'd never seen before. Raphael never did anything awkwardly. Dread rose within Francine. She was not relieved to see this man try to smile.

Why?

Francine tilted her head as growing alarm filled her. This man was acting strangely and didn't seem to understand the notion that walking Ichor-Delta fast was an inside joke between them. He didn't act happy to see her after being apart. With all the tranquilizers and popcorn sleep spray, Francine wasn't certain how much time had passed since her capture.

They hadn't seen each other since parting in the basement of the Big Bang Truck Stop, after being together almost every moment for ten days. They'd been practically joined at the hip for the duration of their trip. And each time he'd seen her—whether they'd been separated for a minute or an hour—he hugged her, kissed her and let her know she was the most important thing in his life.

This Raphael didn't act right, he didn't look right, he didn't treat her like he had before.

She dropped her head to hide her expression and keep her doubts to herself. Her newly colored hair slid across her sight line. This Raphael hadn't commented on the color change back to blond. When they met over a cute black kitten, he said he liked the red. Why hadn't he commented on her blond hair?

"What do you think of my hair?"

A genuine smile shaped this Raphael's mouth. "I love it. I hated the red color. Now you look like part of the Duvall Five again."

That sealed it. This man was not *her* Raphael. He was an imposter.

Francine lifted her head and frowned.

"What's the problem now?" the imposter asked.

Her shoulders lifted and fell without comment. Her displeasure remained. She couldn't help it.

He reached out to put his hand on her face. She dodged him.

"Don't touch me."

"Francine? What's wrong with you?"

"Change back. I know you aren't Raphael. You don't know the first thing about him or how he treats me. He would have noticed and commented on my hair color and walking fast, because it's a private joke between us."

"What are you talking about, Francine?" It looked like Raphael and sounded like him, but it was most assuredly *not* him.

"He told me he liked both, but preferred the red."

Her captor changed back into Edgar's form. "Of course he did. But he still doesn't love you the way I do."

"What? Like a crazy zealot?"

"I've loved you for years, Francine. Five long years."

She shouldn't speak, since this man was obviously out of his mind, but part of her felt she had nothing to lose.

"Well, just so you understand, I love Raphael and only Raphael. When he looks at me, I see that he loves me from his soul. When you look at me, regardless of what form you take, I only see your fervor in attaining a long-sought prize."

He grimaced. "You're wrong. We belong together. I know we were meant for each other."

"I'm not wrong. You don't care about me. You merely want to revel in your attainment of me. I'm not some prize you can put on a pedestal and gloat to the world about. Hear me when I tell you that I will not be treated like an object deposited on a shelf so that others can praise your powers of acquisition."

Edgar frowned. "That is not true," he said, but she saw the accuracy of her claim in his gaze.

"Yes, it is. Raphael knows the definition of what a priceless treasure is and treats me accordingly. You do not."

He put a hand on his gun, as if to threaten her to behave or else.

"Raphael would never shoot me with a tranquilizer gun, or change my hair color against my will, or knock me out and shove me in a trunk."

Edgar took his hand from the dart gun and looked down the road. "Well, as you've established, I'm not Raphael."

Francine closed her eyes. He'd spoken the truth. She suspected that didn't bode well for her. Perhaps she should have played along.

He drew the gun quickly and ended the conversation and any retort she might have made with another dart to her midsection.

Raphael was both alarmed and relieved to find the trunk empty. He searched the cargo space carefully, finding only a couple of blond hairs stuck on the mat, but no other trace anyone had been inside. In the fake hologram of Francine, her hair had been blond. He didn't care what color it was, he just wanted to find her.

He noticed a set of footprints on the passenger side of the vehicle. One, not two, which worried him. He followed the trail away from the parked car and around a bend about a quarter of a mile to where another vehicle had obviously been parked. The footprints ended and a different set of tire tracks continued. Another half mile down the dusty dirt road was a main street and it was blacktop. Not as easy to follow or discover what direction the unidentifiable vehicle had gone.

Raphael tamped down the roiling worry in his gut. Every moment without Francine was agony, but he would not stop until he found her. Scanning the area, he noted the darkening sky.

The only thing he could do was head in the direction of the stakeout, where Indigo and the mystery shifter thought the gold ingots were located. He was intrigued to discover how they planned to extract their treasure. It wouldn't be easy.

Raphael ran Ichor-Delta fast toward the Alienn, Arkansas, water tower, where Maxwell the Martian dangled one handed from the edge of the spaceship shape. The Greys initially planned to hide the gold ingots inside the water tower, right in plain sight, just like the Grey brothers and their family did everything else.

He found Diesel's vehicle hidden in a grove of trees a hundred feet from the water tower, but with a good view. Lucy sat in the front passenger seat, so he opened the back door and jumped in next to Wyatt.

"Anything thrilling to report?" he asked once he'd softly closed the door. They didn't seem startled by his appearance.

"Nope. Nothing yet," Wyatt replied.

"How will they attempt to get the ingots out of there?"

"No telling," Diesel remarked, sounding intrigued.

Raphael scanned the base of the water tower supported by four metal legs, each with a ladder built in to climb to the top if need. It was surrounded by a chain-link fence on three sides, with the fourth side sporting a chained gate secured by a big lock.

He couldn't think of an easy way to get heavy gold ingots out of the water tower.

Raphael asked, "Is that why you decided not to hide the ingots in there? Too difficult to haul them all up the ladder? I mean, ingots aren't lightweight."

"That is exactly why we didn't put them there. It was a good hiding place in theory, but not in practice. As we discussed the plan, it became clear we'd have had to call in all manner of heavy equipment and establish some sort of steep conveyer belt system to accomplish the task.

"Not to mention, dropping them one by one into a metal water tower, one clanking into another, would have been loud enough to wake the dead in another galaxy. It would have taken forever to get the whole treasure up there. Would have been a big pain in the patootie, as my aunt Dixie is fond of saying."

"So where is the treasure?" Wyatt asked.

"Not telling."

"Killjoy."

"Now *you* sound like Aunt Dixie. That woman rubs off on everyone."

"It's part of her charm," Lucy said. "I like her."

"I like her, too. I only wish she'd settle down sometimes."

Raphael pointed. "Something's happening under the water tower."

A large box truck with an orange stripe on the side panel pulled alongside the water tower's base and came to a stop.

Diesel lifted a set of binoculars to his eyes. "I see two men and a large U-Haul vehicle, looks like a twenty-five footer. One is Indigo Smith, clearly not shapeshifted. I don't recognize the other guy. I also don't see Francine."

He handed the binoculars to Raphael. "Do you know who that is?"

Raphael focused on the two moving figures exiting the truck's cab. Indigo was in the driver's seat. Was Francine inside?

Raphael scanned the cab for further movement, but didn't see her.

Indigo moved to the back of truck, looking over his shoulder and at the surrounding area. He unlocked the rear door and shoved the rolling gate over his head, then climbed inside. The other man was out of sight, but he came into view a few seconds later at the back of the truck.

They pulled out two narrow metal ramps and attached them to the inside bed of the truck.

"What is that?" Raphael asked.

"Looks like car hauler ramps to me. Maybe they are going to drive away in whatever vehicle is in that U-Haul. I don't think that's legal."

"I recognize the other guy. He's wearing the shape of Randel Edgar."

"The guy you just found out has been dead for a year?"

"Yes."

"Crazy," Wyatt said.

Who could the mystery shifter be? Raphael had a few thoughts rolling around in his head. Not many people could have killed Edgar, hidden his body well enough for a year and then assumed his life. Raphael could only think of a couple of names.

The distant sound of a mechanical rotor grew louder. "What *is* that noise?" Raphael asked.

Wyatt and Diesel both looked up, even though they couldn't see through the truck's roof. "Helicopter," they both said as the sound of propeller blades grew even louder.

Raphael had never heard an Earther helicopter and he'd only seen one pictured in a book.

Diesel opened his door, reached for the binoculars

and eased out of the truck, leaving his door open. He lifted them to his eyes and searched the skies until he found what he was looking for. "It's coming from the north and heading in this direction fast."

The noise of chains rattling sent Diesel's binocular focus to the fence around the water tower. "And they just cut the lock on the gate. Someone's about to climb the ladder up there."

Raphael looked at the water tower. "Can the helicopter lift the water tower?"

Wyatt said, "No way. The heaviest helicopter payload capacity on Earth couldn't lift that thing."

Diesel got back in the truck. "They could maybe peel the top off, though." He started the engine. "Wyatt, call in reinforcements. We're grabbing them now."

"Got it." Wyatt dialed a quick number and talked to Hunter.

Raphael saw Indigo climbing one of the water tower ladders with a large backpack slung over one shoulder as Diesel's truck approached the U-Haul.

The moment fake Edgar saw Diesel's truck, he glanced once at Indigo, then scrambled into the back of the U-Haul. Before Diesel even parked, a subcompact car emerged from the back, rolled down the car hauler ramps and sped away back in the direction the U-Haul had come from.

Raphael wanted to chase the car, but it was out of sight by the time Diesel's truck stopped. He jumped from the vehicle and raced Ichor-Delta fast after it, but didn't see so much as dust hanging in the air. Where had the tiny car gone? He made his way back to the water tower, searching each little road and path he passed, but saw nothing.

At the water tower, Diesel and Wyatt had guns drawn on Indigo Smith, now stuck at the top of the structure. He looked shocked and enraged.

Raphael called up to him, "Come down here, you coward! I have questions." He would shake the information about Francine's whereabouts out of the man if he was forced. And likely even if he wasn't forced.

"I'm not going back to the gulag. You might as well kill me now," Indigo shouted down at them.

Raphael put a hand on Wyatt's shoulder. "Please don't shoot him until we find out where Francine is."

"Don't worry. I wouldn't shoot to kill in this instance—probably."

Chapter 20

Francine woke up in yet another new place. At least she wasn't crammed in the trunk of a car this time. There wasn't any tape over her mouth and she wasn't bound. A veritable hat trick of good news.

Woozy, she stood up slowly and looked for a way out. Where was she?

The room looked like a small airship compartment on the Royal Caldera Forte cruise liner.

Exploration showed she was in a small spaceship, like one of the gulag ships deployed to transfer small numbers of prisoners. She'd been sent back on a similar ship when she was kicked out of Drucilla's reception. However, this ship smelled like a new car. Nothing like "new" smell in a brand-new vehicle, whether auto or spaceship.

It didn't take long to discover she was locked in. No amount of tugging on the door hatch lever would allow her to open it. Space potatoes.

Francine anxiously opened doors, panels, and drawers, looking for anything that might hold the key to her escape. Next to the pilot's console, she pulled open a magnetized drawer and saw something helpful. "Operator's manual," she read out loud.

She thumbed through it, looking for a way out, but finding other useful information as well, like tracking and cloaking and weapons, oh my.

Francine flipped more pages. "Ah-ha," she said triumphantly. She pushed a few buttons on the console panel and, voila, something clicked on the outer door hatch. When she tried it, the lever moved up, the door pushed out and a three-step ladder descended to the grass below. She stepped down, only then realizing the ship was cloaked, which made the open door into the ship look strange, hanging in the air as it was.

She breathed in the scent of pine needles and flowers. It was nearly dark and she had no idea where she was. Another dirt road led from the clearing into the woods.

Francine kept an eye out for her captor and scanned the manual to see if there were any other useful items. Three quarters of the way through she saw exactly what she needed—a fully fueled land rover.

Hurrying to the compartment that held the rover, she got it ready to use, lowered the back hatch and rolled it to the grass. She climbed back inside the ship, raised the back hatch and made a few adjustments. She checked the manual for each button she pushed, including decloaking the ship. She dropped the operator's manual back into the magnetized drawer and exited through the main hatch door, locking it on her way out.

Now if anyone was looking for her, they'd see the ship. Francine didn't plan on being here when her captor came back. She straddled the land rover's seat. It was wider than a motorcycle seat, but a little narrower than a four-wheeler.

Lucy had given her a ride on Axel's four-wheeler. This was a different setup. There was a helmet and goggles in a basket behind the seat, so she put them both on. She'd probably be straining bugs through her teeth, but hopefully she wouldn't have to go far to get help.

She turned the rover on. The low hum of the liquid bauxite fuel didn't make much noise. She pressed the foot pedal on the right side of the little vehicle and it moved forward. She took her foot off and it stopped. Getting a feel for how the rover operated, she drove it through the grassy clearing next to the spaceship and onto the dirt road. Her choices were left or right. A coin toss.

Suddenly, she heard a loud engine approaching. Oh no. Where was it coming from? Her heart pounded in her chest.

The noise got louder, but she couldn't tell which direction it was coming from. She looked up just as a helicopter flew by overhead. Maybe it's going to town.

Left it is, Francine thought, and hoped she was headed west to Alienn. Anywhere was better than here.

She took off on the bumpy dirt road, pressing the pedal as far down as she dared. She didn't know how fast she was going, not flooring it. The dial on the display was pegged at half. Any faster and she'd risk being thrown from the rover. She hadn't gone far before the dirt lane led to blacktop.

Relief flooded her system as she carefully steered the rover onto the main road. She'd only gone a few miles when she came to a four-way stop. Arrows on a sign pointed to Alienn, Old Coot and Skeeter Bite.

Alienn was to the left, the other two towns to the right. *Left it is again.*

She pushed the accelerator until the dial read three quarters of maximum. The smoother highway allowed her to go faster. She wanted to find someone to help her get to Raphael as fast as possible.

A few miles later, the double glow of twin headlights appeared on the horizon. She gunned the engine, pressing the pedal as far down as it would go, and considered how she'd flag down the occupant of the car.

The best she could think of was to slow down and wave one arm in the air. As it passed her, she got a look at the face in the driver's window. Mentally, she cursed her luck. Her captor's face was the picture of shocked.

Francine lowered her arm and floored the

accelerator pedal. The whine of the engine increased as the dial inched toward maximum. In the sideview mirror, she saw the car do a U-turn and come after her. The twin headlights lit up the road around her. Space potatoes.

Her top speed didn't seem fast enough to beat the car bearing down on her. It didn't take long for her captor's car to gain on her, moving ever closer. The lights got brighter and brighter.

She was forced to slow for a curve in the road to keep all four tires on the pavement, but sped as soon as it straightened out.

Her captor continued to gain on her. Pretty soon he'd be close enough to ram her off the road. Was that his goal? Or was he going to try and get her back on that spaceship? Not happening.

Francine lowered her head and body as if hugging the frame of the rover would make her more aerodynamic. It didn't.

The car started to pass her. She tried to accelerate, but was already going the maximum. She wove across the road, making him fall back and try to pass her on the right. Nope.

Francine steered to the right to keep him behind her. If he got past her it was all over.

Another curve in the road slowed them both momentarily, but he started gaining on her as soon as they were through.

Ahead on the right side of the road was a sign she couldn't read yet. What was that?

Joy burst inside her at the sight of the Alienn city limits sign and plummeted in the next second when her captor came alongside her in a burst of speed her rover couldn't match.

The passenger window lowered. "Francine!" he screamed. "Turn around or else!"

Or else what? Francine thought.

Hard no.

She stomped the accelerator and moved ahead of him, but he matched her easily and shouted out the passenger window again. "No one else can have you if I can't!" His face was a scary mask of determination.

Francine thought about making a vulgar Earther finger gesture, but didn't want to have to explain that it was an insult. She kept going forward as fast as the rover would go, her body hugging the frame. She heard a helicopter, wondered if it was the same one and wished it was friendly and looking for her.

Her captor moved ahead of her and started to pull in front of the rover as they climbed a small incline. At the crest, looking down the hill that was steep and long, she saw salvation.

The chopper came into view overhead and a spotlight from the undercarriage shone down on both of them as they sped toward a police barricade at the bottom of the hill.

Francine eased her foot off the accelerator. Her captor must have slammed on his brakes, because his vehicle began to fishtail, tires squealing, as she passed him.

Wyatt Campbell stood behind the barricade, bullhorn in one hand. Or was it a Defender? Hard to tell.

Her captor stopped his car, did a sloppy, off-road U-turn and disappeared back over the hill. Francine drove her rover into the space between two law enforcement cruisers with just enough room to get through.

The first person she saw was Raphael approaching at a blurringly fast clip. He grabbed her off the rover before she came to a complete stop, squeezing her in his sturdy embrace, kissing her cheeks, face and lips, repeating, "I love you, Francine," in between each kiss.

Francine held tight and breathed his luscious scent deeply into her lungs, joyful for the first time since they'd been parted.

"It's you," Francine managed. Not a fake Raphael.

He stopped kissing her to stare adoringly into her eyes. The love in his gaze reached her soul. "I've been looking for you, Francine."

He pulled her violet diamond engagement ring from his pocket and slid it on the appropriate finger. Francine teared up. "I thought I lost it. Thank you so much."

"Edgar left it in the glovebox."

"It's not Edgar," she said.

He nodded. "I know. Apparently Edgar's been dead for almost a year."

"The shifter is Charlie Adler."

Raphael's eyes widened in surprise. "Charlie? Are you sure?"

"He showed me his true self. He said he's been tracking me for five years."

"Unbelievable. We've worked together several times in the past half a decade. I never knew he was interested in you. Never knew his true colors or his secret shifting abilities. Not even a hint of it."

He was interrupted by a distant, explosive sound. She looked in the general direction of where she'd escaped from the spaceship. A search of the skies yielded no visible craft.

"He must have re-engaged the cloaking device."

Diesel was talking on the phone, a stern look on his face. He hurried to join them. "Did I hear you say cloaking device?"

"Yes. I also enabled the ship's tracking module while I was inside," she said. "Maybe he didn't notice that."

Diesel talked into the phone again, "Check to see if you can track it." And then, "You can? Excellent." He gave Francine a thumbs-up.

"I didn't know you were a spacecraft engineer," Raphael said.

"I'm not, but I can read. He left the operational manual unsecured. That's how I got the rover."

"Great job, Francine," Raphael said. "I see you didn't need me to rescue you. But I did try."

"I've not a single doubt. After he blew up the cabin, I was afraid you all thought I was dead and would stop looking."

Lucy raced through the crowd and almost bowled Francine over in her exuberance to hug her. "I thought you were gone, but Raphael insisted you couldn't be dead. He refused to go down that path."

Francine gave her sister a strong hug, then plastered herself to Raphael's side.

"Next time," he said, "I take you home."

"Next time I will be attached to your side and let you."

"Are you tired?"

"A little."

"Too tired to get married?"

"What?"

"I swore that if I got you back, I'd insist we get married as soon as possible. So I'm insisting. What do you think?"

"I think I'd like to change clothes first, but my answer is yes. Let's go."

He grinned. "We'll face your mother's wrath together or pretend to get married again for her benefit."

"I'll marry you as many times as you want."

"I love you, Francine. I never want to be without you ever again."

"Awesome. I love you, too. And I've been considering a career change from grocery clerk to bounty hunter so we can travel the galaxy joined at the hip. What do you think?"

Raphael kissed her hard, and she decided he must love the idea.

Epilogue

Charlie Adler strolled into the bar on the backwater planet of Carnos in the Tri-Spiral galaxy. No one would ever think to look for him here.

He was disappointed to have lost Francine and any share of the gold ingots Indigo Smith stashed away, not to mention the healthy bounty he could have gotten for Smith if he'd been able to stay behind and turn him in. However, escaping punishment and a possible trip to a gulag for the rest of his life was a win. Of a sort.

The bartender came out through a swinging door and walked toward him. Instead of a grizzled old guy, it was a beautiful, buxom brunette. His luck was already changing for the better.

"What's your name, sweet thing?" he asked.

"Barbie," she said with a shy smile. "What can I get for you?"

Barbie had long dark hair, engaging eyes and a smile that made him glad he wasn't tied down anymore.

"Got anything to eat?" He wasn't so much thirsty as he was starving.

"I can make you a blue plate special smoothie." She pointed to the menu board above her head. "It's the only real food item I offer, but it's my own special blend of nutrients. It will fill you up and keep you strong."

"I'll take it, thanks."

She nodded and disappeared through the swinging door. He noted that her backside was as attractive as her front side. Maybe he'd stay a few days here on Carnos.

He hadn't changed into his Charlie Adler persona, certain that Francine would have told Raphael about his true form. He'd heard Randel Edgar's dead body had been discovered, so that cover was out, too.

Wearing Raphael's appearance would deliver justifiable payback when he robbed the XkR-9 gulag payroll ship tomorrow.

Raphael could explain he was on Earth at the time of the robbery, but not before he was questioned by the authorities from the United Galactic Gulag.

The reflection of Raphael's handsome face in the mirror behind the bar grinned cockily, but Charlie didn't care what he looked like. He hoped they arrested Raphael first and asked questions later. Raphael had it coming for stealing his woman, to his way of thinking.

"Here you go," the buxom brunette said. She placed a clear glass, filled to the top with a purple concoction, on a small napkin in front of him.

"Thanks." Charlie picked it up and took a sip. It was delicious. He downed half the glass with his next drink. "Good stuff," he said to her. She smiled again.

He sucked down the rest of the glass with another gulp.

"Can I get another?" he asked, placing the empty glass on the napkin.

"Sure." She picked up his empty glass and headed through the swinging door to presumably a kitchen area. She soon returned with another filled-to-the-top blue plate special smoothie and placed it in front of him on a fresh napkin.

He drank half the glass in one swallow. "What are you doing later after your shift?"

A satisfied smile appeared on her lovely face. "Oh, I expect I'll be on my way back to Earth with you parked in the brig."

"What?"

The brunette beauty shifted before his eyes into the form of a wizened old woman. She cackled and shock rolled through him.

A shifter? One of his own kind?

"Who are you?"

In the mirror, he saw his face begin to morph from Raphael's to his own. Charlie closed his eyes and concentrated on keeping Raphael's face. He opened them to see the other bounty hunter's features melt away from his own like an iceberg on Lava Rock World.

"What did you do to me?" He stared at the half-finished drink. "What was in that?"

"Oh, that was my special kale smoothie."

There were certain green plants on Earth he'd learned to avoid, but this drink wasn't green. "Purple kale?"

"Oh no. The blueberries cover the green. I knew you'd be smart enough to evade any green drinks, like I always do."

"You tricked me."

"Well, you've been a bad boy, and you needed to be stopped."

"I'm one of your kind. How could you?"

"It was easy. I don't kidnap, kill or clone myself into others to get what I want, do I?"

"I didn't kill anyone."

"How did Randel Edgar end up dead then?" asked a familiar voice from behind him.

Charlie spun on the stool to face the real Raphael. "The stupid fool did it to himself. I just hid his body and took his persona."

"Can't wait to see how you prove that, but Francine is pressing charges and Indigo is blaming you for everything, including breaking him out of the gulag because you wanted the gold ingots he stole."

"That ingrate."

"Guess there is no honor among thieves, after all."

Two months later —
Ossuary Valerian Space Station asteroid

Francine held Raphael's hand tightly, her heart pounding with bliss and delight. Together, they walked down the petal-strewn aisle toward a platform decorated on each corner with a large Earther arrangement of red and black roses framed by greenery and baby's breath.

Lucy had brought the flowers and a few other artful accompanying displays with her from the Earth colony the night before as a precious gift for today's event. Francine was elated to see *any* flowers at her more "important" wedding, let alone roses in the unusual color scheme. The only other decoration was the candles that lined the walls along either side of the center aisle.

As per Raphael's single stipulation, the color peach was absolutely forbidden. Francine had no trouble agreeing to that. Besides, she preferred the dramatic red-and-black theme. That color combo seemed to better accentuate their surroundings.

The quaint, historic justice building on the Ossuary Valerian Space Station asteroid served as the unusual, but magnificent, location of their tiny wedding. Well, their first wedding.

Her mother was planning the kind of grand affair only she could—or would want to—manage, to be held next month on Alpha-Prime. She'd promised to restrain the celebration to a small to medium wedding, but after only a couple of months of planning, the guest list topped one thousand essential invitees.

Francine bent to her mother's will, grateful to be back in her parents' good graces.

Today, Francine and Raphael were getting married the way *they* wanted to, with only the attendance of a very few loved ones able to transport to this odd venue for a "destination" wedding, as it was called on Earth.

The magistrate waited at the walkway's end, Lucy and Axel on the left, Elda and Victor on the right.

Francine and Raphael took the last few steps toward the platform, stepping up together to be officially married.

The magistrate opened a large book and began. "We are gathered here today to join together these two souls in blessed matrimony."

Suddenly, all the candles in the room glowed a little brighter, as if the spirits in the old justice building wanted more light for a better view. Francine glanced askance at them, then focused her attention back on the magistrate.

She'd asked her parents if they wanted to come to this smaller ceremony, but her mother preferred to wait to see the fifth and final Duvall wedding celebrated with all the pomp and circumstance that only an Alpha-Prime upper-class wedding venue could provide.

Raphael agreed—very surprisingly—to the grand

Alpha-Prime nuptials without much prodding. He told her he viewed it as a small price to pay for future harmony in each of their respective families.

Lucius Boudreaux, Raphael's obstinate father, had been no match for the will of Adeline Duvall in the matter of the pretentious wedding and agreed to not only participate, but to pay for half of it, including the couple's two-week honeymoon on the Gothic Ice Floe Planet.

Raphael told Francine he suspected Will and Alex had more to do with the financial offer and any of the "getting along with the bride's family" than his father, but Lucius hadn't growled or tried to halt any of the preparations.

A major victory, according to Raphael.

"If there is anyone who has just cause to keep these two apart, let them speak now or forever hold their peace."

The candles dimmed noticeably.

Lucy sucked in a shocked breath. Elda whispered a swear word. Francine held her breath. None of the men said a word. As everyone turned to stare, the candles resumed their regular flame. Odd. But what else could she expect from an old justice building on the Ossuary Valerian Space Station asteroid? There were probably more ghosts here than anywhere else on this terraformed asteroid.

Unmoved by the candle display, the magistrate continued. "The couple will now exchange tokens to pledge their vows to each other."

Francine and Raphael exchanged the violet diamond rings they usually wore, their ceremony nearly complete. Simple. Meaningful. Flawless. Just the way they wanted.

"I now pronounce you joined together in blessed matrimony. You may kiss your bride," the magistrate said, smiling as he closed his book, seemingly unfazed by Francine's request to close the ceremony with the traditional Earther kiss.

Raphael stared deeply into Francine's eyes and kissed her tenderly for their first kiss as man and wife. Francine reveled in the sweet, yet sensuous caress of his lips.

When they parted, Raphael whispered, "I love you, Francine."

"I love you, too," she whispered back.

"By the power vested in me by the laws of this galaxy, I now introduce everyone to Mr. and Mrs. Boudreaux, Raphael and Francine."

The assembled witnesses clapped as the newly minted couple turned to walk back down the aisle. The candles brightened and dimmed back to normal flame, one after the other as they walked from the platform to the doors.

Behind her, she heard Lucy say, "Ooh. Nice."

Elda said, "Let's hope they're all friendly ghosts here."

Francine looked forward to not only her honeymoon, but their return to Alienn, Arkansas, to begin their lives together.

A huge shakeup at the Supernova Supermarket meant she could return to her job there, too, head held high. Roberta the Gossip had quit rather stridently when the store was sold to a branch of the Grey family and noises were made about sending her to work in the office away from the customers. The oddball assistant manager, Mr. Petey, failed three leadership tests required by the new management, even one regarding Earther laws in Arkansas, and promptly refused the offer of a cashier job.

Diesel Grey and the rest of the clan in Alienn were surprised the day their cousins arrived en masse to take over the Supernova Supermarket. They were even more surprised to learn the Ashcraft family had bought a one-third share in the bauxite mine and planned to take a hands-on approach to both businesses. The Ashcrafts, their three sons and two daughters settled into Alienn and seemed ready to work hard.

After only the first day, Francine adored the new Ashcraft management team and agreed to continue her duties as night stocker. It didn't hurt that they gave her a raise and a back-pay bonus she apparently should have had all along for working nights.

Raphael would be busy, too, with full-time contract employment with the Grey brothers in the Big Bang Truck Stop. He planned to do the occasional bounty-hunting gig when lucrative opportunities presented themselves. Cam and Diesel agreed wholeheartedly to his terms.

Francine and Raphael were staying at the small house they'd rented during their previous visit. At the small dinner after their nuptials, Raphael cautioned Elda not to break the door in or he'd have to bill her for the destruction. Elda only laughed and gave Raphael her wedding present—a gift certificate from an Earther hardware store in case repairs were required.

As they climbed into bed for the first time as man and wife, the candles Francine lit for ambience dimmed noticeably as they embraced and kissed.

"I see the ghosts followed us here," Raphael said, sounding amused.

Francine shrugged. "I don't care. Let them dim the lights as much as they want. I'm only interested in you."

She kissed him. He kissed her back and neither of them noticed any illumination changes for the rest of the night.

*

Coming next:
Crazy Rich Aliens, Alienn, Arkansas 6

Elise Midori ran a galaxy away to escape the man she loved, but could never have. But it wasn't far enough, thanks to a crash in Nocturne Falls, and a crazy Druid high priestess intent on claiming him as her own.

THE ALIEN WHO FELL TO EARTH

Pilot, Holden Grigori is lost on an alien world, with no memory. A pretty woman claims she's his wife and loves him. He'd do anything for her.

Victoria Greene is sent to find the pilot and keep him safe as he recovers. Pretending to be his wife is not a hardship. Falling in love is even easier. But what happens when he gets his memories back and realizes that to him she is…no one.

HAVE YOURSELF A MERRY LITTLE ALIEN
MERRY & BRIGHT: A CHRISTMAS ANTHOLOGY
(NOCTURNE FALLS)

Draeken and Stella Phoenix are celebrating Christmas in Nocturne Falls with a festive holiday party in their new vacation home. Each has a big surprise for the other, but all's fair in love and secret Christmas presents. Right?

THE DRAGON'S SPELLBOUND ALIEN

Mind-reading Alpha-Prime alien Bianca Forrester leaps at the chance to work as a psychic in Nocturne Falls and rub shoulders with werewolves, gargoyles and fae in the Halloween-themed Georgia town. Not only will it be an adventure, it's the perfect place to dodge her mother's matrimony mania.

Half-human, half-dragon shifter Warrick Hart has never forgotten the fear and loathing he faced as a child in Europe when superstitious humans and human-hating supernaturals chased his family from town to town. It taught him to rely on no one but his mother and brother.

Bianca doesn't believe in love at first sight.

Warrick would never trust a woman with his heart.

But Nocturne Falls is a place where never becomes now and beliefs can change on a spell.

THE VAMPIRE'S UNINTENDED ALIEN

Isabel Winstead has found acceptance and excitement in the hidden alien community growing in Nocturne Falls, where werewolves and gargoyles and witches live in plain sight. She loves her life in the Halloween-themed Georgia town, loves her job and her friends and—sigh—loves an absolutely delicious and unattainable vampire who doesn't know she exists.

Half-vampire, half-sorcerer Viktor Hart revels in his bachelorhood. He adores his family, is a respected craftsman, drives a fast car and hangs out every night at Insomnia with his buddies. He's never met a woman he'd be willing to sacrifice his independence for. Until Isabel and one mind-blowing birthday kiss.

Naturally, it must be a love spell.

The honorable thing would be to break the spell and let Isabel make up her own mind—even if she doesn't choose him.

THE WITCH'S ENCHANTED ALIEN

Paranormal private investigator and witch Ruby Hart needs a man—specifically, a man with a unique tattoo. Finding him for her anonymous client will put her fledgling business in the supernatural haven town of

Nocturne Falls, Georgia in the black for months.

Maximilian Cornelius Vandervere the Fourth was a privileged and respected member of one of Alpha-Prime's most elite families before the Incident made him a social pariah. An uncomplicated life as Max Vander in the secret alien colony on Earth is the perfect solution.

The double whammy of a love spell and a truth spell is definitely a complication he doesn't need.

Ruby can't help but notice the tall, gorgeous blond alien. It's hard to ignore a man who keeps declaring his love and proposing marriage to a woman he's just met. And it's clear he needs help.

Sweet, sexy Max is a puzzle she can't resist.

YOU'VE GOT ALIENS
ALIENN, ARKANSAS 1

Librarian and aspiring journalist Juliana Masters has a mystery to solve: Who am I? Armed with the truth about her past, she can leave her humdrum present behind and get on with her future. She just needs to complete one lucrative investigative writing assignment and she'll be on her way. All she has to do is prove aliens live and work out of a secret facility based under the Big Bang Truck Stop. No problem. Getting her socks knocked off by the Fearless Leader isn't part of the plan.

Diesel Grey worked for years to achieve his goal of heading up the family business in Alienn, Arkansas. Mission accomplished, but being Fearless Leader of a galactic way station comes with a lot more headaches than anticipated. It's hard to consider the shockingly well-informed writer a headache, though, especially when she makes him ache in all the right places.

If he's not careful, he'll give her everything she needs to blow his family's cover and expose to the human world that aliens do walk among them.

All he really wants to do is sweep her up in his arms and never let her go.

HOW TO LOSE AN ALIEN IN 10 DAYS
ALIENN, ARKANSAS 2

Alexandria Latham Borne is supposed to marry into one of Alpha-Prime's most prestigious families. Her unwanted future fiancé has wealth, breeding, social status...and that's about it. She is less than wowed during their luxury get-to-know-you journey to Earth. Once the spaceship docks in Alienn, Arkansas, Ria jumps at the chance to jump ship and explore the colony of extraterrestrials hiding in plain sight.

Cam Grey takes his job as chief of security at the galactic way station and the Big Bang Truck Stop operated by his family very seriously, but even he needs a break. No one suspects the by-the-book enforcer's secret refuge is the karaoke bar just over the county line from Alienn, Arkansas. It starts out as just another night of uncomplicated amusement. But no one is more surprised than the jaded Alpha when the gorgeous woman with blue-streaked hair sings her way into his bed—and his heart.

When he learns his sexy karaoke singer has defied colony rules, putting them all at risk of discovery by the unsuspecting earthlings, he knows his duty. What he should do is lock her in the brig. What he does do is ignore all the rules he's spent his career upholding.

Cam's also been burned by love before, but his mischievous Ria is a rule-breaker he can't resist.

Is she a heartbreaker, too?

AVAILABLE NOW

MY BIG FAT ALIEN WEDDING
ALIENN, ARKANSAS 3

Lucinda Hayward Duvall, of the Designer-class Duvalls on Alpha-Prime, has never quite fit the mold in her noble family. Her four sisters are more beautiful, their behavior more acceptable and their bearing far more regal than she could ever pull off. Even so, she's happy enough with her books and her routines and to fall in line with the marriage arranged by her demanding parents. Until a chance encounter with a handsome stranger at a galactic way station on a wild and wonderful colony planet makes her question everything she's ever known.

Easygoing Axel Grey, second son and head of communications for the family business at the Big Bang Truck Stop in Alienn, Arkansas, doesn't care a lick of spit for protocol or pompous off-world VIPs. On the other hand, he has all the time in the world for a captivating young woman with red-streaked hair, a mesmerizing smile and a contagious sense of wonder. One stolen dance in a convenience store doorway later and he's ready to give Lucy anything…including his heart.

Lucy basks in Axel's admiration, blossoming under his regard like a flower starved of sunlight. In their too-short time together, he makes her feel amazing instead of awkward, a treasure instead of an obligation.

Of course, a future together is impossible. Her mother has seen to that.

10 THINGS ALIENS HATE ABOUT YOU
ALIENN, ARKANSAS 4

Valvoline Ethyl Grey, the youngest sibling and only daughter in the Grey clan, knows the rules when it comes to Alpha-human relationships—it's fine to have a little fun, just don't get too attached, unless you want a one-way ticket back to a homeworld that's never been home.

Skeeter Bite Sheriff Wyatt Campbell is as easygoing as they come, but even he has his limits. At first he thought Vee wanted to keep their romance under wraps to protect him from a butt-kicking from one—or all—of her six brawny older brothers. Since they seem to like him well enough, that can hardly be the case. Now he just has to convince his commitment-shy girlfriend to take a chance. She already has his heart. Why not his ring?

A woman raised among oblivious humans in a super-secret alien colony in Alienn, Arkansas should know better than to have a super-secret love affair with a human, let alone a sheriff. But strong-willed Valene is all too weak when it comes to a certain tall, blond and utterly scrumptious lawman.

Although he comes to her family's aid when they need him most and vows to keep the secret from other humans that aliens live among them, Valene is determined to sacrifice her love for Wyatt's greater good.

Wyatt has other plans.

AVAILABLE NOW

BIKER
BAD BOYS IN BIG TROUBLE 1

Despite the danger, there are some definite pluses to undercover agent Zak Langston's current alias as a mechanic slash low-life criminal. He doesn't have to shave regularly or keep his hair military short. He gets to ride a damn fine Harley. And then there's the sweet, sexy lady next door who likes to sneak peeks at his butt. Yeah, that was a major plus.

Kaitlin Price has had the worst luck with men. As if her unearned reputation as a frigid tease isn't enough, she also has to deal with her stepsister's casual cruelty and taunting tales of sexual conquests she can only dream of. So Kaitlin has never been with a man. So what? So what...

So maybe the sexy bad boy next door would be willing to help her with that.

Gunfire, gangsters and a kidnapping weren't part of her Deflower Kaitlin plan. Good thing for her bad boy Zak is very, very good. At everything.

BOUNCER
BAD BOYS IN BIG TROUBLE 2

DEA Agent Reece Langston has spent a year at the city's hottest club, working his way closer to the core of a money laundering operation. Women throw themselves at him all the time, but there's only one he's interested in catching. And she won't even tell him her name.

FBI Agent Jessica Hayes doesn't know much about the sexy stranger except that he's tall, dark and gorgeous. Best of all, he seems just as drawn to her as she is to him—in other words, he's the perfect man to show one kick-ass virgin what sex is all about. No names, no strings and no regrets.

Their one-night stand turns into two. Then a date. Then…maybe more.

Everything is going deliciously well until Jessica's boss orders her to use her lover to further an FBI operation.

Everything is going deliciously well until Reece's handler orders him to use his lover to get closer to his target.

Is their desire enough to match the danger and deception?

BODYGUARD
BAD BOYS IN BIG TROUBLE 3

The baseball stadium is torture for Chloe Wakefield, from the noisy stands to the slimy man her colleague set her up with.

Too bad she isn't with the sexy stud seated on her other side. He shares his popcorn. Shields her from the crowd. And, when the kiss cam swings their way, gives her a lip-lock that knocks her socks into the next county.

Goodbye, vile blind date. Hello, gorgeous stranger.

Staying under the radar is pretty much a job requisite for bodyguard Deke Langston, but he can't resist tasting Chloe's sweet lips. Nor her sweet invitation into her bed, where the sensuous little virgin proceeds to blow his mind.

But someone doesn't like how close they are getting. The thought that scares Deke the most is that another woman in his care might be hurt because of his past.

All of Deke's skills are put to the test as he and Chloe race to solve the puzzle of who is plotting against them.

Chloe's in danger and Deke has never had a more precious body to guard.

AVAILABLE NOW

BOMB TECH
BAD BOYS IN BIG TROUBLE 4

Bomb tech and firefighter Alex Langston has a reputation around the station as a bad-boy, love 'em and leave 'em type, but that couldn't be further from the truth. He wants nothing more than a quiet life after a military tour that saw him in some very hot situations overseas. He garners more than his fair share of feminine attention, but hasn't felt so much as a spark of interest for any woman since landing in Ironwood, Arizona...until now.

Schoolteacher Veronica Quentin was warned to keep her guard up around Alex. The last thing she wants is to be a notch on some sexy stud's bedpost. She's been used before, and knows well the heartache that can bring. But that was before she saw him. And before he rescued her from a mysterious kidnapping that saw her chained half-naked in the town square with a bomb strapped to her chest.

But is Veronica the real target? Or has someone set their sights on Alex?

Until they find out, they can't trust anyone but each other. And the sensual flames that ignite whenever they're together.

AVAILABLE NOW

BOUNTY HUNTER
BAD BOYS IN BIG TROUBLE 5

Dalton Langston has a sixth sense when it comes to tracking his quarry. He has a talent for getting in his prey's mind. Now, the only thing he's interested in hunting is some rest and relaxation in Las Vegas. The last thing he wants is to get dragged into chasing after some runaway rich girl.

Lina Dragovic has eluded everyone her parents have sent after her in their efforts to force her into an arranged marriage. She's served her time as the Dragovic crime family's cloistered daughter. Now all she wants is her freedom. What better place to hide than Sin City, where the bright lights offer the deepest shadows?

But there's no outrunning the dangerously sexy bounty hunter...especially when getting caught by him is so tempting. And so deliciously rewarding.

Falling in love was never part of the plan.

AVAILABLE NOW

BANDIT
BAD BOYS IN BIG TROUBLE 6

Miles Turner, a handler and operative with The Organization, a private security firm, is used to always being the man with the plan, the guy in control of everything around him. He can't imagine any situation that would get the better of him—until he meets Sophie.

Travelling sales rep Sophie Rayburn has been burned by love before, but she's determined not to spend Christmas Eve alone. When she spots sexy Miles at a run-down bar in a Podunk New Mexico bar, she decides he'd make the perfect gift to herself. Why shouldn't she indulge them both with a little holiday cheer between the sheets?

Sensual sparks fly as soon as they come together, like they were made for each other, in bed and out. A kidnapping, a drug scam and a dangerous mole don't stand a chance.

Sweet, sexy Sophie is enough to make even a good man lose total control. And Miles is not good. He's all bad boy.

BILLIONAIRE
BAD BOYS IN BIG TROUBLE 7

Sexy, single hunk and secret billionaire JD Macalister never expected to fall so hard or so fast. He's been burned by love—and a long-distance relationship—before and swore he'd never get hurt again. But the blond beauty in the jade-green dress he meets at a friend's wedding isn't going anywhere. Especially not out of his arms.

Samantha Duke can't take her eyes off the tall, dark and dangerous-looking man she spots the moment she walks down the aisle. Their instant connection dazzles her. And once he reels her into his grasp, she knows one night will never be enough. But that's before she leaves JD behind, choosing career over love in another city.

Still nursing a broken heart, JD discovers that Samantha is in big trouble and being pursued by a nefarious entity. He'll stop at nothing to protect her, even if it means carving his own heart right out of his chest.

About the Author

FIONA ROARKE is a multi-published author who lives a quiet life with the exception of the characters and stories roaming around in her head. She started writing about sexy alpha heroes, using them to launch her very first series, Bad Boys in Big Trouble. Her latest series is light, funny Sci-Fi contemporary romance set in Arkansas. When she's not curled on the sofa reading a great book or at the movie theater watching the latest action film, Fiona spends her time writing about the next bad boy (or bad boy alien) who needs his story told. Laughter is essential each and every day along with lots of coffee first thing in the morning.

Want to know when Fiona's next book will be available? Sign up for her Newsletter:

http://eepurl.com/bONukX

www.FionaRoarke.com
facebook.com/FionaRoarke
twitter.com/fiona_roarke